THEN HE SMILED DOWN AT HER

Wow.

It was the first time she'd ever seen a man smile with just his eyes. The line of his mouth never changed. But the corners of his eyes crinkled in a very sexy way and there was a glitter of light in the stone grayness of them.

"Thank you, Mr. Masters," she said, feeling the warm strength of his hand as he took the one she extended to him.

"Lije will do."

"Okay, then Lije it is," she said. "You're my hero." She blushed again, not sure why she'd said that.

"Am I?" Mockery glinted in his eyes and he touched his hat and turned the horse away. "Happy to help a lady."

Lije Masters. All the way back to the trailer the sound of it rolled silently on her tongue. It was an unusual name and she was sure there was an interesting story behind it. And she was even more sure that his last name fit him perfectly. Sitting tall in the saddle the way he did, he looked like the master of all he surveyed, just like an eagle did in the skies.

She wanted to see Lije Masters again. Diana had never been so certain of anything in her life.

Santa in a Stetson

JANET DAILEY

ZEBRA BOOKS
Kensington Publishing Corp.
http://www.kensingtonbooks.com

ZEBRA BOOKS are published by

Kensington Publishing Corp.
119 West 40th Street
New York, NY 10018

All Kensington titles, imprints, and distributed lines are available at special quantity discounts for bulk purchases for sales promotion, premiums, fund-raising, educational, or institutional use.

Special book excerpts or customized printings can also be created to fit specific needs. For details, write or phone the office of the Kensington Special Sales Manager: Attn. Special Sales Department. Kensington Publishing Corp., 119 West 40th Street, New York, NY 10018. Phone: 1-800-221-2647.

Zebra and the Z logo Reg. U.S. Pat. & TM Off.

ISBN-13: 978-1-4201-0664-0
ISBN-10: 1-4201-0664-3

First Printing: October 2009

10 9 8 7 6 5 4

Printed in the United States of America

Chapter One

"I'm out of hairspray, Diana. Can I borrow yours?" Stella hovered behind her, taking care not to move her head for fear a lock or two might slip out of place.

"Right there." Diana pointed with the end of her eyebrow pencil to a tall aerosol can on the table before concentrating again on her reflection in her makeup mirror.

She assessed her features in a professional way, figuring it didn't count as vanity if you got paid to make pretty faces for the camera. She absent-mindedly took inventory. Large, luminous blue eyes, framed by curling eyelashes that took twenty minutes to do. Nose exactly right—not too short, not too straight, not too large. Her lips were her best feature—the top one was a cupid's bow and the lower one was sensually full. She was fooling around a little, putting layers of gloss over pink-tinted lipstick to boost the shine.

Humming, she took in the whole picture. Oval face. Creamy, clear complexion for which she was very grateful. She just didn't get breakouts, and most of the models she knew did. The heavy makeup was irritating to the skin. Even so, she needed base and foundation—digital cameras picked up the tiniest flaw, though pictures were always retouched to perfection on a computer later on.

From long experience, Diana added light, feathery strokes of eyebrow pencil to fill in and accent her finely arched brows. Removing the blue band that had held her pale blond hair, she began brushing it briskly away from her face.

"Ooh, just look at those silken tresses," Stella kidded her.

"They're a lot of work," Diana said.

"Really? The wind doesn't style your hair?"

Diana had to smile. Her hair had a naturally windblown look and it looked even better when it actually was tossed around by the wind.

The door of the trailer swung open and a swirl of cold air admitted in a willowy girl, who shivered as she quickly closed the door behind her.

"They're ready for you, Stella," she said through chattering teeth.

"Tell them I'll be there in a minute." Stella inspected her reflection to see if she needed any last-minute adjustments.

"You tell them. I'm not going out in that cold again until I have to," the other girl retorted. "I don't think I'll ever get used to wearing summer clothes in winter! You could die of pneumonia on some of these shoots."

"It's not usually this chilly in February, Vanessa," Diana reminded her.

Vanessa shrugged indifferently, not saying anything to her but calling after Stella, who was just leaving the trailer. "Watch where you step or you'll get manure all over your shoes!"

Diana hid a smile at that warning, but not in time for the disgruntled Vanessa to miss it. Whatever. Diana let the other model's glowering look pass without comment.

"Wait until you get into that white outfit and have to wander around all those horses and cows with Connie shouting at you all the time not to get it dirty." Vanessa slipped out of her brilliant, flame-hued halter dress and into a long smock. "I don't understand how Connie comes up with these crazy concepts. Whoever heard of clothes being photographed at a rodeo? It's kinda ridiculous."

"I don't think so. The clothes mix Western traditional with Native American designs. It's a very cool look."

"Don't say that word," Vanessa muttered.

"What?"

"Cool. Chilly. Cold. Any of those are against a law I made up just now."

"Got it." Diana laughed as Vanessa wrapped her arms around herself. "I bet you wouldn't like it if it was scorching out, either. San Antonio summers are hot."

"So what else is new in Texas? I'll just suffer," Vanessa grumbled.

"Don't. I'll ask the mayor to move the date of the annual rodeo," Diana said.

"Do you know him?" Vanessa didn't wait for an answer to that silly question. "Hey, there is a positive side to my abject misery, though. I've never seen so many good-looking, rugged men in one place before, ever."

"I was wondering when you were going to get around to that."

"Seriously, Diana, they are, like, so sexy," Vanessa went on. "And so not shy." She bent over a little to look at herself in the mirror. "I don't know when I've had so many whistles, winks, and invitations to come on over and—"

"And look at manly belt buckles?" Diana finished for her.

"Shut up," Vanessa said, laughing. "No, no one said that, but, you know, those buckles are eye-catching. All that engraving and stuff. And some of them are *huge*."

"Don't get carried away," Diana warned her lightly. "Rodeo riders don't stick around."

"That's not always a bad thing."

Diana shook her head. "Vanessa, you're terrible."

"Am not." She watched Diana brush her blond hair until it glistened and crackled. "Not every guy you go out with has to be the one you marry. Cowboys look like fun."

"I hear they are. But do you know the definition of cowboy sex?"

Vanessa groaned. "No. Tell me."

"You get half a bottle of bourbon and ten seconds of foreplay before he knocks the ashtray all over the bed. Then it's 'thank yew and good naht.'" She tipped an imaginary cowboy hat at Vanessa. "And he never even takes off his jeans."

"I don't smoke and he'd better duck when that ashtray comes flying at him. But gee, you sound so experienced." Vanessa laughed.

"I'm not. A friend told me that joke. A sadder but wiser friend."

"Okay. All the more cowboys for me, I'm not complaining."

"They're not my type. Just point me to a nine-to-five guy with a little home in the suburbs and I'll be happy."

"You're so domestic," Vanessa sighed. "How come you were born that beautiful? You're a disgrace to the modeling profession!"

"Well, it doesn't rule my life, if that's what you mean." Diana smiled. "And I bet you sit alone at night as often as I do. You have to or you wouldn't get enough sleep to keep away those circles under your eyes and those extra inches from party food and booze."

"Being a model does have its limitations," Vanessa admitted reluctantly. "And so does too much attention, but maybe that's just because we're here in Texas where the all-American look is idolized. In New York you don't get a second look sometimes. Every model in the world ends up there sooner or later. I'm going too. Someday."

Diana nodded her head. "Good luck. The work is demanding wherever you are and not very glamorous once you get behind the scenes."

Vanessa smiled ruefully. "And some people seem to think we look that perfect in real life. Hello, digital retouching. We don't!"

"Well, people believe what they want to believe. We could be doing a runway show at Neiman Marcus or shooting nine thousand studio photos for a catalog, but it's no day at the beach, wherever you are."

The other woman went to the rack of clothes for the next set of shots and looked through them, pulling out an ensemble and looking it over. "Wow, this is nice. I think this is a Kathy Katchurian original." She inspected the label. "Yes, it is. And just my size if I don't eat for a week. There are some advantages to slaving for Connie, right?"

"Sure. But wouldn't it be nice to not starve?

To be able to come home to a meal and your happy little family sitting down together?"

"Ding-dong. Do I hear wedding bells?" Vanessa asked absently. "When's the big day? Who's the lucky guy?"

"I don't have one at the moment." Like Vanessa didn't know that, Diana thought. "I just meant that I wouldn't mind being a wife and mother." She walked over to the rack, selected a white jumpsuit and took it off its hanger.

"Not me. I don't want a baby spitting up on me and pulling my hair. And pregnancy— forget it. You can kiss your fabulous figure good-bye."

Diana winced at the unfeeling comments, which hit a wound that had never healed, though they weren't meant to. But that part of her past was something she'd never talked about with anyone, mostly because there had never been anyone who'd ever been close enough for her to confide in. She'd always hid her loneliness behind a serene mask of beautiful composure and no one guessed it was there.

"Di, what you need to do is go out a little more. It's about time you had a bigger goal than marriage and kids."

Vanessa couldn't help being a know-it-all, Diana figured. She only laughed. "You say that as if all I have to do is snap my fingers to get a line of men standing at my door. Do you know why I sat at home by myself on New Year's Eve?"

"I know you're about to tell me why, and that's all I know."

"Because nobody asked me out, Vanessa. Everyone assumed that I was invited somewhere fabulous. The nice guys in this world figure that a model has all kinds of men ready and willing to date her, so they don't want to join the throng. So we end up attracting rich jerks." She lowered her voice and pretended to be one. "Hello, my name is Mr. Gigantic Big Deal and you must be Miss Arm Candy. Nice to meet you, I think I love you, but I have to ask my lawyer if that's okay. Hey, somebody take our picture. Right now. And post it online, please."

"Okay, I get the point," Vanessa said, eying her curiously. "So when did you get burnt?"

"A long time ago," Diana answered grimly, remembering the shock she'd suffered when she'd discovered that she'd been just a beautiful possession to a man she had liked very much.

It had hurt at the time, but now she could barely remember what he looked like. She wasn't bitter about it, although she might have sounded that way. But thinking about him only reaffirmed her desire to marry and settle down, but not with anybody, only Mr. Right.

Hey. At the tender age of twenty-four, she told herself, you shouldn't be wondering if and when he would ever come along. But like everything else, Diana bottled up her mixed feelings on the subject. Projecting an air of confident poise was a model's stock in trade, anyway.

She wasn't going to tell Vanessa about her not-great Christmas, though. No childhood home to go back to, no one to welcome her with open arms. She'd just stayed in her apartment, contemplating a little artificial tree from a discount store, with plastic ornaments that kept falling off and minilights that flickered once and went out. The thing had been about as decorative as a stack of old newspapers. It was ironic that she'd bought it at the last minute to keep herself from getting too depressed. It'd had the opposite effect and she'd been happy to toss it after the holidays were over.

"Oh, wow, you look fantastic in that!" Vanessa exclaimed as Diana zipped up the white jumpsuit and turned to inspect herself in the mirror.

It clung to her body like it loved it a lot. Narrow legs. Fitted waist. Attached halter that bared her back—all fabulous. The most striking element was an embroidered thunderbird in bold turquoise down the side, designed to look like a tribal-type tattoo. It was a powerful motif in that standout color, which accentuated the blueness of Diana's eyes. The white material complemented the pale color of her hair.

"You don't think it shows too much, do you?"

She pulled the plunging V front together in an attempt to hide the cleavage that the jumpsuit was meant to reveal.

"Of course it does," Vanessa said, smiling, "but it's supposed to."

At that moment the trailer door opened again and an older, auburn-haired woman walked in. She was dressed in practical black underneath a heavy-looking walking jacket in a rusty color that accented the red in her hair. Glasses hung from a chain around her neck and there was a no-nonsense look on her face.

"Okay," she said briskly, looking Diana over. "You look good to go. Here's the jewelry that goes with that."

Diana slipped the heavy turquoise and silver bracelet she was handed over her wrist and began putting on the matching earrings, aware of the scrutiny she was getting from Connie Deveronne. After six years of modeling, being stared at impersonally, as if she were a department store mannequin, still made Diana uncomfortable, but she never let it show.

"Are you gaining weight?" Connie demanded in an accusing voice.

"No." Diana was unruffled, knowing the number on her scales hadn't changed for over three years, thanks to a closely watched diet.

"Your measurements look a little different." Her manager focused on the rounded curves that the low neckline revealed. "We're actually trying to sell the jumpsuit and not you, if you really want to know. Are you wearing a bra?"

"Yes." She kept her eyes averted and concentrated on securely fastening the second earring. Only Diana knew that the light pink on her cheeks wasn't blusher from a compact.

"Take it off. It might flatten you a little if you do." With that order given, Connie turned and walked to the door, going out without looking behind her. "Rick will be ready for you in about ten minutes."

"She's just nuts!" Vanessa made a face at the door. "Doesn't she realize that you're only going to look more sexy without a bra?" She blew out a disgusted breath. "Sheesh."

"We can't look more fabulous than the clothes," Diana reminded her.

She couldn't admit how uncomfortably naked she felt without all her underpinnings. Not to Vanessa, for sure, who would only laugh at her for being ridiculously modest and old-fashioned. Still, a few minutes later when Diana stepped out the door of the trailer, she couldn't help thinking that all the eyes turned her way were looking at only one thing. Or two things.

She forced herself to act unconcerned, but her fluid movements were hurried as she tried to avoid being noticed.

The weather was cool. A sweater would have been great to cover her bare arms, which broke out in goose bumps. The nippy weather made the animals frisky. Horses were prancing and pulling at their bits, snorting and sending puffy clouds of frosty breath into the air. Halfway to where she was supposed to meet the photographer, Diana ran into Stella, who was on her way back to the trailer.

"How's it going?" Diana asked as Stella paused in front of her and turned to smile at a cowboy who gave her an admiring whistle.

"Pretty good." Stella glanced around. "Connie's a little uptight because we're beginning to draw a crowd, but believe me, some of the looks will keep you warm."

"Hey, babe! Got any plans for tonight?" A cowboy pulled his horse to a stop beside them and eyed Diana boldly.

"I'm staying home with my sick mother," she answered easily. "Better luck next time."

The lean cowboy was not at all put off by her obviously fake excuse, but he tipped his hat and rode on. Diana watched him for a moment before turning back to Stella to see a knowing twinkle in her eyes.

"See what I mean?" Stella winked.

Diana smiled in agreement before catching sight of Connie.

"I'd better get going. Here comes the boss." Diana nodded toward the older woman.

Connie Deveronne hustled Diana to where Rick, the photographer, waited. After only a few shots, he lowered his camera, shaking his head. Connie went over at once to see what was wrong.

"The white outfit needs a better background." He looked around searchingly. "Something with a bolder color. More defined."

Diana hovered to one side, shivering in the skimpy jumpsuit. Patience was the byword of a model, with endurance coming in a strong second. The sun was brilliant and steady, although it didn't warm her. She didn't have to wonder why Connie had decided to do without an assistant for Rick, so he had no one to help him with jobs like handling the fill lights—Connie liked to cut corners and had told him he could make do with the strong flash on his camera.

Rick wasn't giving up on going somewhere else, though. Diana kept her attention focused on her colleagues, ignoring the cowboys seated on a nearby fence rail. She knew she was the object of their muffled, good-natured laughter and whispered remarks. Dressed as she was, she felt really vulnerable.

"Come on, Diana," Rick finally said. "We're going to try the arena instead of these livestock pens."

Dutifully she joined them, seeing the cowboys out of the corner of her eye as they hopped down from their perch and joined the procession. If she hadn't been so ill at ease, she would've thought it was funny, especially considering the wrathful mama-hen expression on Connie's face.

It wasn't a long walk to the rodeo arena but it wasn't made any shorter by the chill in the air. Diana hugged her arms around her shoulders to take advantage of her body heat. The gesture brought an instant offer from one of the cowboys to take his jacket.

"Don't you dare say yes! That grubby thing doesn't touch that white jumpsuit, do you hear me?"

"I wasn't going to." But Diana gave the cowboy a smile of appreciation when Connie wasn't looking.

Then they were all walking into the arena over red-brown dirt. There were only a few horses and riders inside, but their entourage of cowboys quickly positioned themselves on the heavy wooden rails. Diana stood quietly as Rick and Connie discussed the situation, not paying close attention until Rick gave a low whistle.

"Look at that guy," he said to Connie. "Straight out of a classic ad, isn't he? I never saw a horse like the one he's on, but they're both freakin' perfect. Exactly what I had in mind."

Even as Rick started walking forward, his hand raised in the air, Diana was trying to follow his direction. It took her only a second to see what had caught the photographer's eye. On the far side of the arena a horse and rider were cantering through a series of figure eights. The horse was bloodred with flashy black stockings to above his knees and a black mane and tail. The rider in the saddle was the personification of male in every way, a dream of a cowboy. He sat tall and erect, matching every fluid movement of the horse as if the two of them were one. He was lean and muscular, dressed in faded blue jeans and a very broken-in denim jacket lined with sheepskin. On his head was a weathered brown Stetson, pulled low over his face.

As the cowboy caught sight of Rick waving to him, he slowed his horse to a stop and walked it in their direction. Diana watched as he sat immobile in the saddle and listened to Rick. Something in the man's bearing made her think he would refuse to have himself and his horse used as a backdrop for fashion photographs. There was the slightest hesitation before he looked to where Diana was standing beside Connie, and then he nodded in agreement.

Rick motioned her forward and Diana quickly complied. Precious time had been spent finding a suitable background and Rick didn't waste any more of it making introductions between his model and his cowboy. Diana didn't even get a chance to study the man up close as Rick hurriedly moved her into position on the right side of the horse and began giving instructions. She was intrigued by the man atop the horse, and in between shots she sneaked quick looks at him.

Rugged guy. He was clean-shaven, with deep grooves around his mouth and a hardworking type of tan. The shadows cast by the brim of his Stetson made it hard to figure out the color of his hair, but she was pretty sure it was brown. His eyes were a different matter. At first glance they'd seemed blue, the next, gray. Yet one thing about him was very clear, and that was his remoteness, as if what he was doing was beneath his dignity. For some reason, Diana wasn't put off by that. If it came right down to it, she'd have to say he fascinated her.

"Put your left foot in the stirrup," Rick ordered Diana, his face mostly concealed behind the bulky professional camera. "Stand in it, suspended beside the horse."

Diana did as she was told, finding she had to hold on to the rider's shoulder to keep her balance. His sheepskin-lined jacket gave until it pressed against the solid muscle of his shoulder and arm. It was a strange sensation to be so near him. On the ground, she'd thought he was no taller than average, but she realized she hadn't factored in the horse. The man was tall, easily over six foot.

"Now turn and look at him, Diana," Rick instructed.

The man in the saddle had gray eyes. She wondered how she had ever thought they were blue. They were slate gray—no, she reconsidered quickly. They were the color of granite, and as hard and unyielding as granite. Even the contours of his face were angular and uncompromising, too rugged, actually, to be handsome. But too compelling not to be attractive.

There was an obvious virility in the sensual line of his mouth. *Down, girl,* Diana thought to herself.

And she liked the pride she saw in him. The slight bump in his nose gave him the look of an eagle, commanding and free. She pushed away the thought that the eagle was a predatory bird.

His study of her had been just as thorough, only less obvious. Then Diana noticed his gaze lingering on the low V of the jumpsuit's front and immediately her cheeks flamed with color. It didn't take an expert eye to figure out that she was braless. Diana doubted a man like him would be shocked by the discovery but it still embarrassed her. When his gaze lifted to her eyes, she saw the gleam of amusement in it.

Maybe that was just because she was blushing so hard. Maybe.

Rick was shouting more instructions to her and Diana was thankful she had to turn away. In seconds, she had her cool, poised expression back, or at least a pretty good imitation of it. But she was intensely aware of the man in the saddle. The thought kept running through her mind that she had never been so self-conscious in the presence of a man. What was so different about this one? He was only a rodeo cowboy. Not an investment banker or a corporate lawyer, as Vanessa would be bound to point out, those being the types of men who usually interested her.

Why should it matter to her what he did for a living? She silently asked herself the question, already knowing the answer: because he clearly wasn't husband material.

So what? asked a wicked little voice in her head.

Just as Diana was striking another pose, one of the chute gates swung shut with a loud bang. The blood bay horse that had stood with such restless restraint jumped forward and Diana let out a startled gasp as she felt herself falling backward to the turf. But the man's reflexes were instantaneous. His right arm shot around her waist as his left hand drew on the reins to check his mount.

In a span of seconds, Diana was clutched tightly against his chest, held by the iron band of his arm. Her own arms circled his shoulders with her head buried beneath his chin. The closeness and warmth heightened his masculine scent, and she breathed it in. She could feel the flexing of his muscles as he controlled the horse and maintained his grip on her. The horse had stopped, his head tossing in agitation and his hooves beating an in-place cadence.

The danger was over, but the blood still pounded in Diana's temples and her heartbeat had accelerated. She moved her head away from beneath the man's chin to stare wide-eyed into his calm face. Her waist was pinioned tightly against him, making her arch her back more than a little.

Only inches separated their faces. They were bonded by the look they exchanged, a look that held a message without words. Diana felt transformed by the wonder of it. His face stayed hard and remote but something about it had changed. Whatever had been transmitted between them was still tingling through her body, she knew that much.

"Are you all right?" His quiet, deep voice seemed to come from a long way off.

She suddenly realized he was still waiting for an answer. "Yes," she said softly.

Then they were no longer alone. Rick and Connie came rushing up to them, the older woman's concern divided between Diana and the white jumpsuit. Effortlessly the cowboy lowered her to the ground using one strong arm. Deprived of the warmth of his body, Diana shivered again as Connie squawked about the smudge mark on the knee of the jumpsuit. The mark was too noticeable and would show up in photographs, so she would have to change.

Rick consoled Connie with the fact that he'd gotten in plenty of shots with an action vibe, telling her that they needed to get going while they still had the strong natural light. The older woman waved Diana back to the trailer.

The man was just reining his horse to leave when Diana stepped toward him. She had to tilt her head way back to look up into his still-impassive face. The serene expression she'd put on was in no way connected to the tumult she was experiencing inside.

"Thanks for saving me." She was amazed at how composed her voice sounded. "I'm Diana Mills, by the way. And you are—?"

"Name's Masters. Lije Masters."

She'd never heard a first name like that—he'd pronounced it "Lyzh"—and wondered what it was short for. Then he smiled down at her.

Wow.

It was the first time she'd ever seen a man smile with just his eyes. The line of his mouth never changed. But the corners of his eyes crinkled in a very sexy way and there was a glitter of light in the stone grayness of them.

"Thank you, Mr. Masters," she said, feeling the warm strength of his hand as he took the one she extended to him.

"Lije will do."

"Okay, then Lije it is," she said. "You're my hero." She blushed again, not sure why she'd said that.

"Am I?" Mockery glinted in his eyes and he touched his hat and turned the horse away. "Happy to help a lady."

Lije Masters. All the way back to the trailer the sound of it rolled silently on her tongue. It was an unusual name and she was sure there was an interesting story behind it. And she was even more sure that his last name fit him perfectly. Sitting tall in the saddle the way he did, he looked like the master of all he surveyed, just like an eagle did in the skies.

She wanted to see Lije Masters again. Diana had never been so certain of anything in her life.

Chapter Two

The photo shoot lasted the rest of the afternoon. Diana dressed and undressed so many times that her shoulders and arms ached. The muscles around her mouth quivered from smiling so much. At every opportunity she looked over at the cowboys that roamed about, hoping to see the man on the blood bay horse.

Only once had she been that lucky.

It had been outside of the arena shortly after their first meeting. He'd been walking his horse to the stable area.

Diana had believed that he would come to watch her work. By the end of the day, she realized Lije Masters wasn't the type to join the crowd of ogling cowboys. That brought up another question. How was she going to see him again? Connie Deveronne had brought her trio of models to San Antonio for a two-day session.

Thursday and Friday. Tomorrow the shoot would be all wrapped up and on Saturday they would be traveling back to Dallas.

"Di, honey, you were terrific today!"

Lost in thought, Diana jumped as Rick threw an arm around her shoulders and hugged her close to him. That was Rick, totally professional behind a camera, only to turn into a wolf after they were done. He wasn't really a wolf, Diana amended, since they were dangerous. He was probably only a wolf cub. Rick liked to come on strong because he thought it was part of his image as a photographer. It was vitally important to him to have a gorgeous girl at his side, which was probably the reason Diana steered clear of him. She disliked the fact that it was only her beauty that got so much attention.

"Thanks for the compliment." She smiled coolly at him as she removed his arm from around her shoulders.

Rick ignored Diana's attempt to put him off. "Vanessa, me and Connie are going out to tonight for dinner and all. I didn't get a chance to ask Stella what she's doing. Why don't the two of you join us?"

"It would be tough to split your attention between the four of us, wouldn't it?" Diana asked pointedly.

"You'd be surprised at what I can do." His blue eyes roamed over her figure.

"Ooo. You animal."

"So true. I am."

He didn't even notice her sarcastic tone. But she had made the mistake of going out with him once and—back to the creature-feature comparisons—discovered that Rick could turn into an octopus after a couple of drinks.

"Whatever. But no thanks. I have other plans for tonight." Her refusal was brisk and firm.

"Don't tell me you're going to use those tickets the manager gave Connie for the rodeo?" He stared at her incredulously.

"The free tickets, you mean," Diana guessed astutely, although it didn't take a genius to figure that one out. A gleam of an idea was already forming in her mind.

"What else? Come on, Di honey, you don't want to go to a cornball rodeo tonight," Rick wheedled.

"That's where you're wrong." Diana smiled firmly, moving away from him to scurry to the trailer.

Once inside, it took her searching gaze only seconds to find the tickets carelessly tossed on the counter. Diana knew Connie wouldn't give them another thought and quickly extracted two from the stack. Stella wouldn't want to spend her evening with Rick, Vanessa and Connie, either. With luck, Diana could persuade her to go see the rodeo rather than spend the evening in their hotel room.

At first Stella said that Diana had gone off her

rocker, but then she warmed to the idea. Her one-track mind hadn't forgotten the admiration of all those lusty cowboys. And neither of them had ever been to a rodeo, despite being born and raised in Texas. They were city girls, and city girls were the same all over the world. Planning a night at the rodeo brought out a spirit of adventure in both of them. Of course, Diana's reasons had nothing to do with Lije Masters.

Their seats in the grandstand were strategically located near both the chutes and the gates where the riders entered. Diana couldn't believe her luck. Her eyes searched the parade of riders during the presentation of the colors and the national anthem. There was no sign of the blood bay horse and Lije Masters.

He had to be here, she told herself, switching her attention to the ever-changing group of cowboys perched on the chutes and rails. She checked the program and noted that saddle bronc riding was first. Although Diana listened closely, she never heard his name called by the announcer. She applauded after each successful or unsuccessful ride, but not as loudly as Stella did.

The next event was calf roping. Lije Masters was in the arena before Diana saw him. This time he was riding a sedate buckskin horse. Just watching him she felt an odd breathlessness take hold of her chest. Her hands clapped for the roper completing his tie on a calf, but the only man that existed for her was Lije Masters.

"Lad-eees and gennelmen," the announcer was saying, "our next contestant hails from the state of New Mexico—Elijah Masters!"

As soon as his name was announced, the rider set the now-alert buckskin well back in the enclosure next to the tunnel chute. He gave a quick nod to a cowboy atop that chute and the door was pulled up. A hefty black calf came charging out. With a bounding leap, the buckskin was after it. Diana saw the rope snake out from Lije's hand and settle over the calf's neck in a perfect throw. With the precision of a trained athlete, the buckskin sat back on its haunches, the slack in the rope taken up in a few quick dallies around the saddle horn. The calf was yanked off its feet as Lije vaulted out of the saddle in one fluid movement. He reached the calf just as it got back on its feet. He threw it to the ground, catching a front leg with his piggin string and making the tie with the two back legs before throwing his hands in the air to signal to the official timer that he was done.

There was a brief wait by the officials to make sure the calf couldn't free itself while Lije mounted his buckskin and rode it forward so the taut rope went slack. Diana joined with the thunderous applause when it was announced that Lije Masters had the fastest time so far in that event. In response to the applause, Lije took off his Stetson, revealing nut-brown hair as he rode out of the arena.

Diana's heart was in her throat as he neared the place by the entrance where she was sitting. Would he see her? Should she call to him? No, she couldn't do that. The last thing she wanted was to have Lije think that she was chasing him. The brown hat was on his head again when he did ride by Diana. The brim shadowed his eyes so that she had no way of telling whether or not he had seen her.

His calf roping time didn't stand, as another contestant, riding the same buckskin horse that Lije had ridden, beat him out of first place in the event by a full second. Bareback bronc riding was next, but Lije didn't compete.

Diana didn't see him again until the steer wrestling event, which, the announcer explained for the benefit of out-of-town tourists, was also known as bulldogging. This time Lije was astride the blood bay from the afternoon.

Lije Masters was one of the last contestants in the event, although he also acted as a hazer to keep the steer running straight so his competitor could vault from his horse and wrestle the steer to the ground. His big bay horse was used just as often.

When the moment came for Lije's attempt, Diana didn't know whether to cheer him on or hold her breath. The idea of him diving from his horse at a full gallop to grab the horns of a big, burly steer that was also galloping sent shivers of icy-cold fear down her spine. She didn't have much time to dwell on it, though, because it was over almost before it began. Four strides out of the gate, Lije was off his horse, had the steer by the horns, brought him to a halt and wrestled him to the ground. What was more important to Diana was that Lije was standing, completely unharmed.

It frightened her how a man she hardly knew could be so important to her all of a sudden. It just felt natural that he was. Her concern and interest for Lije Masters seemed like just about the most natural thing that had ever happened to her.

The rodeo might've been her first, but she couldn't shake the strange sensation that she had done this many times. And she couldn't explain why she felt that way.

This time when Lije rode out of the arena gate he didn't continue on out of the stands as he'd done before. He stopped his horse next to another cowboy who was leaning against the stands not too far from where Diana was sitting.

"With that big red horse of yours, you can't never lose," the other cowboy said, laughing as he looked up at Lije, who stroked the glistening neck of his horse.

"That's the idea, Les. How's the ribs?"

"I'll tell you after the bull riding tonight. I drew that spinning devil," he answered grimly. "How about you?"

"I've got the gray," Lije replied.

"Watch him. He hooks to the left on a downed rider," the cowboy warned before he lifted his hand in good-bye and walked to the back of the chutes.

Diana didn't understand what the conversation meant exactly. It sounded like serious advice. Her clouded blue eyes were studying Lije as he looked up and met her gaze. Again he touched his hat in that courteous Western way that Diana liked so much. He inched his horse closer to where she sat.

"Enjoying the rodeo?" His drawl was not as pronounced as most that Diana had heard and there was a compelling quietness in his voice that matched its authority. Lije Masters was a man who would be heard no matter how softly he spoke.

"Very much," Diana answered as, out of the corner of her eye, she saw Stella glance at her curiously. "I've seen rodeos on TV before, but this is the first time I've been at one."

"I hope it won't be your last."

"I don't understand all the slang yet, but it doesn't matter. It's just really fascinating." Diana smiled. Her nerves were jumping as she waited anxiously for him to say something a little more personal.

"There are a lot of things that happen behind the scenes that the spectators don't get to see. Later on when you're free, I'll show you around."

His expression was neutral, neither this nor that. It was hard for Diana to tell how sincere the invitation had been.

"I'd like that," she answered.

"If you'll excuse me, I have to get ready for the next event." Touching his hat, he reined the horse around and left.

Stella waited—barely—until Lije was out of earshot. "Do you know him?"

"I met him today." Diana watched his retreating back until it disappeared.

"Lucky you! He's not really handsome, I mean, not in the usual sense of the word. But who cares? He's hot. Kinda takes my breath away. No wonder you wanted to come to the rodeo tonight."

Diana really wanted to change the subject. "What's the next event?"

"Bull riding," Stella answered after consulting her printed program.

That was what Diana had been afraid it would be. And Lije Masters was entered in it. Her stomach twisted itself in knots. The apprehension she'd felt during the steer wrestling seemed minor compared with the agony she knew she would go through in this, the most dangerous event.

"Are you going to do it?" Stella asked, her

dark head cocked inquiringly at her blond companion.

"Do what?"

"Take him up on his offer to show you around." Stella gave a mock frown when she saw Diana's blank expression. "Tonight after the rodeo would be a perfect time."

"Do you think so?" Diana asked earnestly before seeing the teasing look on her friend's face. Then she tried to seem nonchalant. "I haven't made up my mind yet."

"We're only going to be here for another day." Stella had a point to make, and she was going to make it, judging by the look on her face. "This isn't the time to play hard to get, Di."

"I just don't want it to look as if I'm chasing him," she sighed.

"He invited you. Just say *yes*. I wish he had a friend for me." A resigned smile played across Stella's face.

"Okay. If you come along," Diana said quickly.

"I would make it a crowd. No thanks." Stella shook her head emphatically. "And if you decide not to go with him, then you're a fool."

Diana knew that Stella was right. She also knew that she was going to accept Lije Master's invitation, but that didn't ease her tension. She hadn't been this much on edge since her first kiss as a teenager. Some inner voice told her that this was the most important evening

in her life, and she couldn't be as blasé about
it as Stella was.

Bull riding was an event that Diana watched
with fascinated horror. The cowboys who were
able to stay on the vicious bulls for the requisite
eight seconds still had to get off. In this event
there were no pickup men on horses in the
arena. The only protection the riders had were
the rodeo clowns. Diana's fear was so strong that
she couldn't even join in with the rest of the audience as they gasped, then laughed, at the
daring antics of the brave clowns with their
baggy pants and painted faces, who, by one
means or another, diverted the bulls' angry attention from the defenseless riders.

It was worse when Lije was announced. The
fear of watching the spectacle was not as over-
powering as the fear of not watching. He went
the full time on the twisting, bucking, spinning, infuriated bull, a giant of a beast with a
big hump on its neck and an evil face. As the
buzzer sounded, Lije slipped from the bull's
back. It spun around, hooking its huge horns
to the left as Lije dodged out of danger to the
right. Diana's heart didn't start beating again
until he was safely astride the fence.

There were only two riders left after him,
and for Diana they were an anticlimax. The
man she'd met only that afternoon had completed his ride safely. Although all the cowboys

who participated were strangers to her, he was the only one that mattered.

The rodeo was over and the grand exodus of the audience began. This was the moment Diana had both been looking forward to and dreading. She smoothed her clothes and moistened her lips with her tongue, then looked over at the girl standing beside her.

"Do I look all right?" she asked anxiously.

"Are you angling for a compliment?" Stella laughed. "That cowboy really got to you, didn't he?"

Twin spots of pink appeared on Diana's cheeks as she tried to ignore the teasing statement and endured Stella's once-over.

"How come you brought that gigundo shoulder bag?" the other woman asked critically. "As an accessory, it really doesn't do it."

Diana threw her an exasperated glare. She wanted to know how her outfit looked. "I just grabbed it on the way out without thinking," she said, "because I didn't have time to find a smaller one. Besides, an evening clutch would look pretty damn silly at a rodeo."

"Tell me about it." Stella peeked inside the bulging bag. "But why lug makeup, magazines and your new headshot sheets? Too much to carry and it ruins the lines of—"

"Stop it!" Diana wailed, attracting a few curious glances. "I just want to know how I look," she said much more softly.

"You look fine," Stella assured her, laughing. "You'll knock him out and you know it. Now run along. I'll see you later at the hotel and you can give me all the juicy details."

Diana reluctantly left her and walked in the opposite direction to the parking lot. The street-lights had come on in the darkness but even with them it was difficult to distinguish the features of anyone who was more than a few feet away. Diana had only a general idea of where to look for Lije and that was the stables. She was hesitant to ask any of the numerous cowboys lurking around about where to find him, not wanting to be flirted with.

For several minutes she searched, hoping to get a glimpse of Lije. But after ignoring another guy asking what she was doing that night and whether she wanted to join him, Diana realized that her silence was getting her nowhere. The only way she was going to find Lije was to ask for him.

"Excuse me." She chose a mature-looking cowboy with bowlegs and a kind face. "I was wondering if you could help me."

"Be glad to." He smiled, stopping a few feet in front of her. He was lean and wizened, not much taller than Diana herself, who was five foot seven.

"I'm looking for Lije Masters. Do you know where I could find him?"

"Shore thing, ma'am. You go to the second

row of stables and turn right. He'll be some-where in the middle."

"Thanks so much." Diana headed off in the direction he gave. The unhappy thought kept running through her mind that Lije might've already left the rodeo grounds. A lot of people were doing just that. When she rounded a corner, she felt both relief and nervousness at the sight of groups of cowboys standing near the stalls.

As she walked toward them, their loud voices fell to whispers, and then there was silence when she went by. She glanced at them on the sly, but only to see if the tall, lean man she was looking for was there. She dodged the bold gazes, but she could feel them.

Act like you know where you're going, she told herself.

It worked with them. But not for the next group.

"Hey, Blondie!" one of the men called to her. "You gotta be lookin' for me, baby, because I'm the only one around here who's got day money in his pockets." He planted himself in her path and moved to block her when she would have gone around him. "Hi, sexy. Talk to me." He looked her up and down.

"Excuse me," she said angrily, but he still wouldn't let her by.

"Say, I've seen you. You're one of them models that was strutting around here this afternoon.

Listen, dollface, why don't you and me go have a drink somewhere, huh?"

This time Diana met his stare with a cool and contemptuous one of her own. The cowboy was young and much too good-looking, obviously the cause of his swelled head.

"I'm meeting someone."

"Baby, there ain't no one around here that could possibly be better than me," he assured her.

His friends behind him sniggered at that statement.

Diana said something really rude.

"You've cornered yourself a fiery little filly, Jack," one of the other men hooted.

The situation was tricky. She couldn't go forward because he wouldn't let her, and she couldn't go back because he'd just follow her. Diana could see the brazen cowboy thinking over his chances. She couldn't just kick him where it counted and run for it. He hadn't touched her. Yet.

"I might've known you'd be the one to waylay my girl, Evans."

Diana gave a sigh of relief. Lije Masters was walking toward them. His arrival shut the cowboy up, fast. There was a hint of a smile around Lije's mouth as he met the grateful look she gave him. The cowboy named Jack Evans was already stepping aside.

"The lady never said she was meeting you, Masters."

Diana was glad to see him humbled and without a punch being thrown. Her heart was still singing with the words "my girl." But she did sort of realize they'd been said to keep the guys in line.

"I was wondering what kept you, Diana." Lije Masters smiled and Diana felt bathed in a golden glow of warmth. He guided her away from the group of cowboys, who soon dispersed. He looked down at her. "It is Diana, right?"

"Yes, Diana Mills." Her breathless embarrassment made talking a little difficult. "I have to thank you again for rescuing me."

"Not a problem," he said. "I was settling my horses for the night. It'll take a few more minutes. Okay with you?"

"Sure."

The buckskin and the bay were in adjoining stalls not far from where Lije had found her. The stalls were large and roomy, but Diana stayed by the door. She had never been too comfortable around horses, mostly because she hadn't had too much to do with them. She was content to watch Lije as he picked up a curry comb and began to brush the broad back of the dappled buckskin.

"What are their names?" Diana asked, noting the ease with which he moved around them.

"This fellow"—he slapped the buckskin on

the side to get him to move over—"is just plain Buck. Red, my other horse, is registered with the American Quarter Horse Association as Firebrand."

Diana watched while Lije picked up the horse's hoof and began cleaning it. It made her wonder if she could ever behave that naturally with an animal that size. The thought made her laugh inwardly, because where would she ever have the chance to find out?

"Okay, why do you have two horses? Am I annoying you yet?"

The gray eyes smiled at her last question, as Lije lifted the last hoof and cradled it on his knee.

"No. Buck is the best all-around horse a man could have. He ropes calves, does a good job of hazing, serves as a pickup horse if he's needed, can cut and rein as well as any, and in a pinch you can bulldog off him. For steer wrestling, nothing can touch Red." He set the hoof back on the floor. "There, all done."

Brushing the straw from his jeans, Lije walked over to the stable door where Diana was standing. His shadow loomed over her momentarily before he stepped into the outside light.

"There's not really a lot I can show you this late." It wasn't an apology but a statement of a fact they were both aware of. "There's a little café down the street. Would you like some coffee?"

Diana agreed. But later when they walked into the brightly lit restaurant, she wished he had chosen somewhere a little less public. Looking across the table at him, it was hard for her to believe that she had ever been crushed against that broad chest. In fact, it was hard to believe any of this was happening to her. She couldn't think of anything to say and she never remembered being this tongue-tied on any date.

"Are you from San Antonio?" Lije was leaning back in his chair, his long legs stretching beneath the table. If Diana seemed uneasy, Lije appeared totally relaxed and in command—which he was.

"No, I'm from Dallas. I grew up there and except for a few weekend trips I really haven't been anywhere. That probably sounds pretty boring to someone like you. You travel all over the country, don't you?" Diana nervously clasped her hands around the heavy mug of coffee.

"Not quite what you would expect a model's life to be," he said dryly.

"Oh, modeling is just like any other job or profession. It may sound glamorous, but it's really a lot of hard work and self-discipline."

"Don't you enjoy it?" One eyebrow raised briefly.

"I . . . I like it well enough."

"What made you decide to become a model?"

She crossed her arms on the table and looked at him for a few seconds before replying.

"In high school I was tall and really skinny and I thought I was ugly."

"Really?" She nodded at his dubious look. "Okay, then. If you say so. Go on."

She took a deep breath. "Anyway, I went along with a friend to a look-see in Dallas. That's where reps from the big modeling agencies look at new girls and sometimes guys, and interview you. It's really quick. It's either thanks-for-coming-in-but-you're-not-what-we're-looking-for, or, for one in a hundred, a *yes*."

"I would say you're one in a million."

"Oh—well, thanks." She could feel herself blush like an idiot.

"So why didn't you ever go to New York or Europe and try for the big time?"

She shook her head. "I'm not that adventurous, mostly. Anyway, that international supermodel stuff is kind of a myth. Only a few girls ever hit that level. Most of us work for a few years, do tons of catalog work and local ads, then get told we're too old at twenty-two."

"That's crap," he said firmly. "Women don't even start to get beautiful until they're at least twenty-five."

"Which puts me on the wrong side of your line. I'm twenty-four."

He gave her a big smile. "Then you have something to look forward to."

"I don't know," she said more seriously. "Even though I'm making an okay living, I still can't keep on doing this forever. But it's all I've ever done."

"What about college?"

"You sound like a guidance counselor," she huffed.

Lije laughed at that. "That would be a nice, restful change from chasing bulls and steers around, let me tell you."

"Hmm."

"Anyway, you didn't answer my question. And if you want to know, I didn't go to college, either, for the same reason as you. Never had the time. But I read a lot about everything under the sun. And I would say I know a lot."

His confidence in himself didn't seem misplaced. It encouraged her to continue. "Well, I did answer you but not directly. As I said, you have to start young. Some models are as young as fourteen these days. And that means, if you want to be available for lots of bookings, going to college full time isn't easy. Plus, I never made enough money to pay for it."

"What about your parents? Couldn't they help?"

"I have no parents." Camouflaged defiance made her look at him boldly. "I was your typical baby on the doorstep."

His gaze made a slow study of her face. There was authority in his expression but Diana couldn't detect any other emotion. "That's not a typical situation at all. You were never adopted?"

"I was very sickly as a baby and a child," Diana replied. "My earliest memories are of hospitals and doctors and nurses. By the time I got over all the illnesses, I was too old to be considered cute. Like I said, tall and skinny. Basically, people want to adopt babies or children under five. So I had a succession of foster parents, who seemed to be in it for the monthly payments. Sometimes I had a room of my own, but I never had a home of my own, put it that way."

"Got it."

"Want to hear more? Fair warning, it's not exactly heartwarming."

"If you want to talk about it, I'm here. Listening."

She sighed, remembering. "Often I got placed in families where there were children about the same age as me. So I was dealing with a lot of envy and jealousy that I just didn't understand. I mean, I felt like an outsider. How could anyone be jealous of me?" All the little long-ago hurts brought a haunting wistfulness to her expression. "The last family I stayed with had a daughter who was a few months younger than me. When I first came there, she had a steady boyfriend, but—I thought it was coincidence—then they broke up. I never did anything to make him think I was interested in him. It was really awful. He kept calling me and calling me, trying to get me to go out with him. She was really a nice girl and I would've liked her to be my friend, but nothing doing. So it wasn't long after that when I went to the modeling agency."

"Ever think of doing something else?"

"Sometimes," she admitted, "when I get a second to breathe. My career as a model is going to end soon enough—that's just how it is. Here today, gone tomorrow."

"Oh, do I know where's that's at," he said with feeling.

"My longest gig was at a super-upscale department store in Dallas. I did showroom modeling for them—you know, rich chicks sitting in rows, talking a mile a minute on cell phones while they try and figure out how they're going to get their husbands to pay for the clothes I have on."

"Actually, I wouldn't know. But it's a funny description."

She smiled at him. "It's true. Connie Deveronne saw me on the catwalk. She books most of my assignments now, breathes down Rick's neck, makes sure I don't gain an ounce."

He nodded, taking all that in. "So what would you do if you were able to choose?" he asked at last. "Say for instance, you had money saved from modeling and you could go to college without having to take out loans—what would your dream job be?"

"You really want to know?"

"Yeah."

"I've thought about a lot of things. Like

writing for magazines and newspapers, for one. But it's tough to break in and that business is hurting right now. Ad pages and circulation are down."

"Sounds like you looked into it."

"Well, it is kind of related to what I do." She thought about what she had in the shoulder bag Stella had teased her about taking, and reached into it, pulling out some copies of fashion and lifestyle magazines. She set out one that was all men's fashion, figuring he wouldn't want to look at *Vogue*.

Lije glanced at the cover, then flipped it open. The photo spread had been shot against a distant backdrop of snowy mountains, and a hunky model in layers of designer outerwear was dragging a Christmas tree home, waving and grinning in a phony way at nobody.

"That looks a little like my land in winter," he said.

Diana peered at the caption. "It was shot in Colorado."

"One state over. Not too far from my ranch. But are they kidding?" Lije asked with amusement. "His boots don't have a speck of dirt or snow on them and his jeans are ironed. And that Christmas tree is fake." He turned the magazine around so it was upside down to him, facing toward her. "See what I mean? The stump is made of brown plastic. Guess he went into a plastic forest and pushed it over."

Diana looked closer and giggled. "You're right. Well, everything has to be perfect in a magazine."

"But real Christmas trees never are. You know, there's that hole in the side that you have to hide with tinsel or extra lights. And the scraggly branches at the bottom that look like some critter was gnawing at them that you have to cut off. And it smells great, like deep woods at night."

She thought of her little discount-store tree that didn't smell like pine or anything at all. Then she returned her attention to Lije, who had definitely warmed to the subject.

"That tree he's dragging doesn't have one thing wrong with it. And that's not right."

She laughed at his statement, finding it funny that he would defend imperfection with so much sincerity.

He tapped a finger on the photo. "Besides, you shouldn't drag a tree unless you want to drag a whole lot of mud and ice and snow into the house with it."

"I wouldn't know. I bought mine at a store last year and it was only a foot high. How do you do it?"

"I put the damn tree over my shoulder. The needles scratch the hell out of my ear, but a man's gotta do what a man's gotta do." He winked at her and she laughed again at his silly-on-purpose speech.

"Now there's one more thing and then I'll shut up. Look at how he's got ahold of that trunk. Like he hates getting his hands dirty."

Diana thought back to Connie's dismay over the smudged white jumpsuit and felt like she had to explain.

"He can't get dirty. The clothes have to look flawless or the client has a fit."

He nodded, but reluctantly. "Okay, I can understand that. But I wouldn't wear one stitch of those fancy togs. Wouldn't want to worry about them all the time."

"Clothes like that are for neocowboys, not real ones," she said lightly.

His brow furrowed. "And what the hell is a neocowboy?"

"You know," she said, "what they used to call a 'dude,' but with a whole lot of money."

Lije nodded, looking more serious. "Okay, I know what you mean. The ones driving up land prices around Taos and Santa Fe, buying second homes and whatnot. Jim told me he saw an old adobe house on the market for two million dollars. Nothing anybody can do about it, but it's a shame that folks who've lived around here for generations can't afford to buy a shack nowadays."

She nodded in agreement. "That's true almost everywhere, unfortunately. Just saving up for a down payment gets tougher and tougher."

Lije gave her a considering look. "You looking to buy or do you live in an apartment?"

"An apartment. It's convenient. I fixed it up a little, but I'm not there much. I'd like to buy, yeah. But to do that, I'll have to get a job with more of a future than modeling. Something with stability."

He leaned forward a little and crossed his arms so that they rested on the table. "And what would that be?"

She realized that he was really interested in the answer, not just making conversation, and it sort of surprised her.

"Um, I was thinking of getting a teacher's certificate when I finally do go to college, become an elementary school teacher. Or I could teach kindergarten. I like little kids. They have incredible enthusiasm." She looked at him wistfully, not sure why she felt so emotional. "The world is still new to them, I guess."

The remark came out of nowhere and it seemed to genuinely touch him. Diana blushed faintly. He looked at her for a long moment.

"Seems to me you're pretty new to the world yourself."

"I don't feel like it."

"Now, girl—"

She reached into her shoulder bag again and pulled out the proof sheets for her new headshot. "Connie says she's going to send me out for the older-woman stuff. I just don't have that dewy look anymore, according to her."

"You mean the old boss cow in the dark pant-suit and reading glasses? The one who was bellowing at everyone?"

His description made her laugh again. "That's Connie."

"Shoot, she doesn't know what she's talking about."

Diana sighed. "But she books my assignments, sends me out, handles my checks—"

"Mind if I ask if she gets a cut?"

"Well, yeah. That's how it is in the modeling business. I couldn't pose for hours and do all that too."

He sat back, studying her. "Well, sounds to me like you got plans for your life and maybe it is time for a change. But you're always going to be beautiful." He pointed a finger at her in a friendly way. "And you oughta know that."

Diana swallowed hard.

Chapter Three

"Well." Diana breathed in deeply. "I've managed to give you my life history. Now tell me about yourself. I know you're a rodeo rider and you come from New Mexico. There must be more."

She liked the amused glint that came into his eyes. Did he guess that she had changed the subject so she wouldn't reveal how really empty and lonely her life had been?

"That about sums me up, though," Lije said with annoying calmness.

"Nobody's life is that simple. Are you married? Single? Divorced? What about your parents? How long have you been riding in rodeos? What's your shoe size?" Diana lightheartedly rattled off a list of questions, hoping she wouldn't betray her intense interest in his answers.

He gave her an indulgent smile. "I'm

thirty-one. Never married. It'd be tough to succeed on the rodeo circuit if I was—that's just how it is."

She nodded without saying anything.

"My mother died when I was seven and my father passed on a few years ago. I've been competing in PRCA-sanctioned rodeos off and on for the last twelve years. I wear a 13½ shoe, when I wear shoes. Mostly it's boots. Custom-made, if you need to know that."

"Oh—I guess I shouldn't be so nosy."

"I don't mind." He was smiling a little.

"What does PRCA stand for?"

"Not that old record company, and Nipper the Dog has nothing to do with it."

"Okay. Just tell me."

"It's the Professional Rodeo Cowboys Association. Do you want any more coffee?"

At his swift change of subject, Diana realized that he was as reluctant to discuss his past as she had always been about hers.

She declined the coffee and rose to leave when he did. They strolled leisurely back to the stable area, ignoring the cold bite of the night breeze. Lije shortened his long stride to match hers.

"Why do you ride in rodeos?" Diana glanced up at him curiously.

"When I started, it was for the rush. There's nothing like it. Pure adrenaline. It's a battle but not a life-or-death one like a bullfight. It's a pitting of skills with animals and against a clock."

"Isn't it cruel, though, to the animals?"

"Hardly," Lije answered. "In the first place, I don't recall ever seeing a horse treated for anything more severe than a strained muscle unless he accidentally got tangled in the chutes, but I wouldn't even want to count the number of riders with broken bones and/or internal injuries. Anyway, every rodeo has people from the ASPCA to make sure the rules get followed. But some horses are born to buck, just like some are born to run."

"Tonight I heard one of the cowboys tell you something about the bull you were going to ride."

"Riders always share tips about the character of an animal. You'll always see a cowboy helping another in the chutes or acting as a hazer in the bulldogging or calf roping. As I said, you compete with the animal and against the clock, not against the animal, exactly."

"Sounds like a fine line there," she said dryly.

"Well, I grant that the bull or the calf or the steer would rather be someplace else. But it's not a blood sport like bullfighting," he said. "Or ice hockey." He winked at her.

"You still haven't told me why you ride," Diana said, aware that he had dodged any specific answer before.

"For the same reason you model, and I have

the same problems with what I do. The money's not bad, but hitting it big is harder than it seems when you were starting out. That's why I'm here in San Antonio."

"Don't you ever want to settle down? I mean, you can't rodeo forever." She tried hard to see his expression in the dim light.

They went on for several more steps before he answered her. When he did, Diana had the thought that he'd weighed each word carefully before answering.

"Another two years on the circuit and I'll be able to quit—as long as nothing changes," Lije said firmly, too firmly for it to have been for her benefit.

"What would change?" She glanced up at his face as they passed beneath a streetlight. The harsh expression in his eyes startled her before he turned his face away.

"Nothing will," he stated.

"After two years, what then?"

"I'll go back to my ranch in New Mexico."

"If you own a ranch, then why are you here? Somebody has to run it." They were walking past the stables to some parked vehicles and SUVs.

"I can't afford it," Lije answered grimly. "Eleven years ago, when my father was alive, we had a drought that just about wiped us out. It took a couple of years with me riding in rodeos and him working on the ranch to get it together again. I kept riding so we could make improvements to the place. Then three years ago he died and I got hit with all the inheritance taxes. I had to go back on the circuit to make ends meet."

He'd stopped walking and so had Diana. His last statement explained a whole lot of things. Lije Masters was a man with roots, with a heritage and pride that made him stand out from the other rodeo cowboys she'd heard, who seemed to live only in the moment with no thought of tomorrow.

"It's not much," Lije said, lifting a hand toward a battered pickup truck parked in front of them. "But I think it'll make it to your hotel. Where are you staying?"

"At the Hilton," Diana replied, accepting his helping hand into the cab, smiling her thanks as he made sure the door was shut tight. After he'd started the engine and pulled onto the street, she said softly, "You must miss your ranch very much."

"I do."

"Would you tell me about it?"

The gray eyes swept over her face, as if he were trying to figure if she was really interested in it or just making conversation.

"It's in the mountains up from Socorro, New Mexico. The Continental Divide bisects one corner of the ranch and the lava beds are to the north. It's miles from the nearest neighbor or town. We run mostly sheep right now, although we're making the switch to cattle. It'll be a while before the herd builds up, which is just as well since it would be hard for one man to handle both. My buddy Jim—the two of us were raised like brothers—is taking care of it for me. It's beautiful country." He glanced at her. "Wild, rugged mountains covered with pines and lush green valleys. Sometimes I get hungry just for the sight of it."

The warmth in that brief look made Diana swallow hard. Lije seemed more remote than he'd been before. As he had been describing the ranch to her, she could tell he was picturing it in his mind. She realized that there was probably no sacrifice that he wouldn't make to keep that land. Born and raised in the city or right near it, Diana knew nothing about ranches, cattle, horses or most anything else that was a part of Lije Masters's life. It was scary to think of how little they had in common. She was thankful Lije didn't seem to expect her to make a comment about his favorite place on earth, because it obviously was that and more to him. Diana just nodded and smiled.

Her hotel was directly ahead of them. Lije parked the truck along the curb and Diana studied his carved profile as he turned off the engine. She admired the sense of purpose that was etched there because she knew the cost he paid. When he turned toward her, she wanted to reach out and touch him, give him some of the softness he'd been denied, but it was impossible to do.

"How long will you be staying here?" Lije propped his elbow on the top of the steering wheel as he leaned against his door.

"The shoot's supposed to wrap up tomorrow," Diana said reluctantly. "We'll probably go back to Dallas on Saturday. What about you?"

"After the Sunday show, I'll be heading on to Houston."

Diana shivered—not from the cool air. The thought that in less than two days they would be in separate parts of the state and maybe never see each other again made her feel cold inside. Their paths hadn't crossed for very long.

"I suppose I'd better go in," she sighed, not able to think of anything else to say that would prolong their conversation.

"You going to the rodeo tomorrow night?" Lije made no move to follow up on her suggestion.

His question caught Diana off guard. "Yes, I thought I would." Actually she hadn't thought that far ahead.

"I'll probably see you then." This time his hand did reach down for the door handle. He opened the door and stepped out of the truck.

Diana shook her head. She'd honestly expected him to make a date to see her, but he'd left it at "probably." With that impassive expression on his face, it was impossible to tell what he might want. There was a constriction in her throat as she took the hand he offered her and clambered out of the truck. No matter how many catwalks she'd gone down, there were some things it just wasn't possible to do elegantly, and getting out of a vintage pickup with a high cab was one.

"Good night, Diana," he said, touching his Stetson, his gray eyes smiling.

"Good night, Lije."

The area was well lit. People were walking along the pavement behind them. A more personal farewell, such as a more-than-friendly smooch, wouldn't be comfortable, and Diana sensed that Lije had arranged it this way. Before she turned to walk toward the hotel, he was already heading back to the driver's side of the truck.

Stella was awake when Diana entered their hotel room. She was sitting up flicking through channels on the TV, remote in hand. When Diana came in, she switched off the set and turned expectantly to her.

"So how'd it go?" Stella asked eagerly.

"Fine." Diana slipped off her jacket and hung it up before sitting down in front of the little vanity to begin brushing her long hair.

"Fine? I want details, please. What did you do? Where did you go?"

"We went to a restaurant, had some coffee, talked, and he drove me home." Diana shrugged, knowing how unbelievably dull that sounded.

"Are you serious?" Stella squeaked, sitting upright in the bed and hooking her dark brown hair behind her ears. "There had to be more to it than that. He did kiss you, didn't he?"

"No, he didn't," Diana replied sharply, setting the brush back on the vanity table.

"Oh, Di, I know you told me once you like to be romanced, but we're only going to be here for another day." Her friend shook her head sadly. "You just don't have time for three dates before a guy kisses you."

"I'm doing the best I can!" Diana took a deep breath to control her rising temper. "I'm going to see him tomorrow."

"Then did he ask you out?"

"Not exactly," Diana sighed, turning her bewildered gaze on her friend. "Stella, I just don't understand him. It's infuriating. He makes a point of asking if I'm going to the rodeo tomorrow night. When I say that I am, he says that he'll probably see me. And that big cowboy doesn't even sound as if he cares!"

"It's obvious that you do." Stella leaned back against the pillow and studied Diana thoughtfully.

"I've just met him." Diana tried to sound off-hand and she failed. "I don't know. I don't understand why he's so important to me."

"I wouldn't let it bother you," said Stella, punching her pillow and slipping under the covers. "That man has cowboy magnetism. It's what makes them stay in the saddle, did you know that?"

"Stella, I'm going to tell your mother you say things like that."

"Go ahead." Stella yawned. "She says worse things. You should hear her."

Sighing as she got undressed and got ready for bed, Diana didn't think the answer she was looking for was all that simple, even though Stella had been joking.

But if Diana was honest with herself, she didn't want it to be that simple.

The shoot on the following day seemed to last forever. Diana had never known the hours to drag so slowly. Her attention wasn't on her work because she kept searching the crowd for some sign of Lije Masters. More than once Rick barked at her while Connie did her part by nagging more than ever. Diana was so depressed by the end of the day that after she scrubbed her face clean of all its heavy makeup, she didn't even have the energy or the desire to apply a touch of mascara or light lipstick.

Wearing a nondescript jacket over a pair of beat-up jeans, she followed Stella from the trailer, feeling dejected. From habit, her gaze moved over groups of cowboys along the route to the parking lot. She was so busy trying to identify the faraway figures that she wasn't conscious of the approaching horse and rider, not until the man was abreast of them and Stella poked her sharply in the ribs.

"Hello, Diana."

She stared in disbelief at the man reining in his horse beside her. His gray eyes looked calmly back. She had to swallow several times to get her voice to work.

"Hello, Lije," she replied in a small, tight voice.

"I'll see you at the car," Stella said, walking away quickly to leave them alone.

"Are you through for the day?" he asked.

"Yes." Her hand went nervously to her hair as Diana realized she probably looked pale and colorless without any makeup, not realizing a sparkle lit her eyes or that there was a glow of pleasure on her face at seeing him. "We . . . we were just heading back to the hotel."

"I almost didn't recognize you without the war paint." His gaze swept over her face with a certain coolness, the light in his eyes indicating that he saw the spreading pink in her cheeks. "I think you're a lot more beautiful without it."

"Thank you." Diana lowered her gaze. That was a compliment she couldn't brush off like most of the others she tended to get in her line of work. This one was totally sincere and it was from Lije.

"Would you like to have dinner with me tonight after the rodeo?" he asked suddenly.

"That would be nice." Yes, indeed. It most certainly would. She smiled up at him.

He nodded and started to turn his horse away to leave, then stopped to look down at her again. "Meet me at the stables about seven and I'll show you around."

Diana was too happy to take offense at the way he had put it as an order and not a request.

"I'll be there," she assured him as he touched his Stetson and nudged his horse into a canter.

She nearly floated to the parking lot where Stella was waiting. Her companion didn't need to ask the reason for the blissed-out expression on her friend's face. It was just as well, because Diana was too wrapped up in her own happiness to talk.

At seven, she was still walking on air as she rushed to meet Lije at the stables. It wasn't the hurrying that had caused her breathlessness. Diana had chosen her clothes with care and then settled for something chic but made of denim. She had been just as careful applying her light makeup because Lije had made such a point of saying she was beautiful just the way she was.

The way she looked tonight must have pleased him, because upon arrival she was rewarded with one of his rare smiles that so completely transformed his face.

Lije kept his word, taking her all around the adjoining rodeo grounds, pointing out everything he thought would be of interest to her. Diana was too dazzled by him to take more than a cursory interest in most of it, though she did manage to pay enough attention to ask intelligent questions now and then.

Much too soon for Diana, the time came for the grand entrance. He led his buckskin to the arena gates with Diana walking beside him. There was a thrill of belonging when an official started to stop her and Lije spoke up right away, saying that she was with him and she was allowed in. Handing the reins of his horse to another cowboy, he took her by the arm and led her to the side toward an old, battered-looking cowboy on crutches.

"I want you to stay here with Lefty," Lije commanded gently. "He'll keep you out of trouble and tell you the finer points of rodeoing."

"All right," Diana agreed, liking the protective and possessive way those gray eyes were looking at her. Lije turned to the cowboy named Lefty.

"Take care of her," he told him.

"You bet. If anyone comes near her, I'll whack 'em with this here crutch," the cowboy assured him with fake ferocity.

Lije's hand touched her shoulder lightly before he walked back to his horse. In one lithe movement he was astride, his boots automatically finding the stirrups. Diana would have been content to watch him, but the older man was already claiming her attention.

"Lije didn't introduce us right and proper," he was saying. "I guess you heard my name but not the whole thing. I'm Lefty Robbins."

Diana shook the callused brown hand he held out to her. "I'm Diana Mills." She was aware that now Lije was elsewhere she was undergoing a close scrutiny.

"Well, Diana," said Lefty. "Let's wander over to the stands behind the chutes. You can get a good look at the action from there."

There was no choice but to follow him, although once they had reached their vantage point, she had to admit he had chosen well. They had an unobstructed view of the chutes and the arena.

"What happened to your leg?" Diana asked as she watched him gingerly lower himself to his seat, making sure his leg was stretched out comfortably.

"Ah, a fool horse kicked me in the stables and fractured an old break," he replied gruffly. "I was doin' pretty good until then."

"That's hard luck," she commented sympathetically.

"Heck! If it weren't for bad luck, I wouldn't

have no luck at all." His weathered face creased into an engaging smile. "That's how I got my name, you know."

"Lefty? I don't understand."

"My left arm has been broken over a dozen times. The boys were going to chip in and buy me a permanent cast," he chortled.

Diana tilted her head back as she joined in his laughter.

Just as on the night before, after the parade and national anthem, the first event was bronc riding. The winning ride was by the cowboy who'd stopped Diana in the stables, Jack Evans. His swagger was even more pronounced than it had been when she'd met him.

"Why doesn't Lije ride bucking horses?" she asked, turning to Lefty as the arena was cleared for the calf roping.

"He's too big. A good bronc rider is usually lean and only average height. Ya gotta be small and wiry like me to stay on those sun-fishin' horses," Lefty said proudly. "Not that Lije couldn't stay on, he just couldn't rack up them points you need with any consistency. Now bull ridin' is something different. It's still better to be smaller, but he can use his strength to make the ride. Lije may not make day money in the event, but he'll end up somewhere in the placings."

"What's day money?"

"A cowboy rides in a particular event every night. The one with the highest score, like in bronc or bull ridin', or the fastest time for calf ropin' or steer wrestlin' wins that day's prize money. But the scores accumulate each day so at the end of the rodeo the cowboy who's consistently done the best in an event gets the big prize."

Diana's next question set off a running commentary from Lefty as he explained the various technicalities of each event. He pointed out the string barrier that allowed the calf a head start before the roper was permitted to go after him. If the roping horse broke the barrier, there was a ten-second penalty added to his roping time. After the catch had been made, the calf had to be on his feet before the cowboy could throw him back on the ground and tie his legs.

It continued on through the bareback riding event, when Lefty told her that the rider had to have his feet above the horse's shoulders as the horse came out of the chute or else he was disqualified. The rider's free hand could never touch the horse, which was the reason he waved it in the air above him so the judges could see he hadn't touched the horse. Doing that also gave him a certain amount of balance.

"Why does Lije let the other cowboys ride his horse?" Diana asked as the steer wrestling began.

"He don't exactly 'let' them ride his horse." Lefty smiled. "You see, Lije's got himself a valuable piece of ee-quine ee-quipment there and he makes the most of it."

She nodded, enjoying Lefty's penchant for funny phrases. When his cowboying career was over, he could definitely be an announcer or auctioneer.

"Red is probably the best dogging horse around. Them boys pay to use his horse, so much for each go-round or a percentage of the purse if they win on him. That red horse of his makes Lije a pretty fair profit. I don't know how many offers he's had to buy that stallion, but the price just keeps going up and up. Masters has a smart head on his shoulders." He winked confidentially at Diana. "With that horse and Lije's know-how, those two could take it all this year and end up at the National Finals Rodeo."

Lefty fell silent during the bull riding event, sensing the reason for Diana's clenched hands and pale face. After Lije's successful ride, she smiled weakly at the older cowboy, who nodded and patted her hand comfortingly before signaling that it was time for them to leave to meet Lije.

Chapter Four

Lefty persuaded Lije that, even with his restricted mobility, he was capable of taking care of the horses. Lije agreed to the offer, although he unsaddled them before he left.

"Would you mind waiting a few minutes outside my camper while I change my clothes?" Lije asked as he and Diana walked toward some parked vehicles near the stables. He glanced ruefully at the dirt stains on his white shirt. "I forgot to tell the bull I was taking you out to dinner."

"I don't mind waiting," Diana said as they stopped beside a pickup truck with a camper mounted in the bed and over the cab.

"I won't be long," he promised, adding with a twinkle, "I would invite you in, but . . ."

"I'll wait outside." A rising tide of warmth started up her neck. She had been in those types of campers before and knew very well there wasn't any real privacy when it came to dressing and undressing. A smile crinkled his eyes as he nodded and entered the trailer.

True to his word, Lije was out in a matter of minutes. He hadn't just changed his shirt, though—more like everything. He had on a dark Western-cut suit with an open-neck shirt in cream that looked amazing on him, enhancing his rugged good looks. The subdued colors intensified the gray of his eyes and did something wonderful for his brown hair, and the cut of the suit really brought out the width of his shoulders and how his broad chest tapered into lean hips. Lije Masters looked every inch the commanding rancher, and the effect awed Diana.

"Will I do?" he mocked as she realized that she was staring at him.

"Now I feel like I should change." Diana laughed nervously, looking down at her serviceable denims.

"It's too late. I'm hungry," he decreed, taking her arm and guiding her to the front of the truck. "And you'll get noticed no matter what you have on. I don't think any man actually would remember your clothes. Just you."

"I think that's a compliment," she murmured, a little overwhelmed by the rough charm of Lije Masters. He was all man in a great, old-fashioned way and she just wasn't used to it.

"Good." He held open the door as she climbed into the cab. "That's the way I meant it."

There was a caressing quality to his softly spoken words that quickened her pulse. All day she had been wondering how she could get close to this remote and sometimes arrogant man, but Diana was learning fast that he set the pace of their relationship. She could only follow his lead. She had always resented anyone who was dominant or dominating to others, including herself, but this time she thought it would be kind of fun to let Lije be in charge.

The restaurant he took her to had a friendly, informal atmosphere and was decorated with Western trappings that were a perfect background for Lije. Last night Diana had discussed her past with him with ease and tonight she found herself doing it again. Lije Masters had the rare quality of being able to listen with sincere interest and draw people out with gentle questions, while somehow deflecting any questions about himself. Diane learned little about him than she had before. But after their meal was finished, she got a little bolder.

"So tell me how the son of a rancher came to be named after the biblical prophet Elijah?"

The corners of his mouth lifted in a half smile as he studied his coffee for a couple of seconds before meeting her gaze. There was a velvet quality to the color of his eyes that was oddly soothing.

"My father's name was Daniel, a common name, although it's from the Bible too, of course. But my mother, Naomi, was really religious. She'd had several miscarriages before I came along when she was in her thirties. Elijah was considered the messenger of glad tidings in the Bible and lived in the mountain wilderness, and she felt it was doubly appropriate. My father was the one who shortened it to Lije."

For the first time in many years Diana was struck by a sadness that she would never be able to recount personal stories like that. When she was left at the hospital there hadn't even been a note telling her name.

If she'd had one.

"Hey. Change of subject. You haven't said when you're leaving tomorrow," Lije stated when Diana didn't speak.

"I don't actually know." She gave herself a mental shake to force herself back to the present. "There's a chance we won't be leaving— Rick was thinking of getting more shots just to 'cover his butt,' quote, unquote."

"Beg pardon?"

"You always have to take about a million photographs just in case the client turns out to hate the concept they came up with in the first place."

"I think I understand." He laughed.

"Anyway, Connie was supposed to let us know this evening."

"Want to phone the hotel?"

"I guess she'll tell Stella if I'm not there." Diana glanced at her watch. "I probably should call Stella, though. That way she won't have to wait up for me to let me know."

"Couldn't she just text you or something?"

Diana gave him a goofy smile. "She hates to text. She's too afraid she'll crack a nail and it's not like we have a stylist following us around. This is a low-budget shoot. Even the photographer doesn't have an assistant, so we're responsible for our own hair and makeup."

Lije grinned. "How about that. I'd have to say that you do a fantastic job, Diana. You always look great."

"Aw, shucks. But thanks. Okay, I'm going to go call her room—she can never find her cell, anyway, and usually the battery is kaput."

"I'll take care of the check," Lije said.

Diana's face was radiating her inner happiness when she came back from making the call and nodded to the waiting Lije. "We leave on Sunday morning," she announced.

She wasn't quite sure of his reaction, although he was so stoic by nature she almost expected him not to react. But Diana was glad. With luck, it would mean another day in his company.

"Does that mean you'll be working tomorrow?" he asked as he went with her out the restaurant door.

"Not until late tomorrow afternoon, Stella said."

"Okay. Hey, have you been to the Alamo or along the River Walk?" Lije asked. He really did seem indifferent and, as before, it bewildered her.

"No."

The breeze caught a lock of her blond hair and blew it across her face. She swept it behind her ear in a graceful gesture as she picked her way over chunks of gravel in the parking lot.

"I'll take you there tomorrow, then."

They had reached the pickup when he said that. It was what she wanted to hear, but she wished he'd said something more—or been a little more demonstrative. Diana wanted to tell him how much she looked forward to going with him, but all the words that came to mind sounded so trite.

"What time?" she asked as calmly as she could.

"I'll give you a call around nine." His arm was resting on the pickup door, but he was making no attempt to open it. He was looking at the dark, clear sky above, filled with stars. "It's a beautiful night, isn't it?"

Diana had been studying his face, not the stars. Even in the near-darkness, she could discern that far-seeing quality in his eyes, which made it seem to her as if he saw beyond the horizon. Any moment now he would look down at her. She forced herself to look up at the twinkling brilliance of the heavens.

"The Big Dipper really stands out tonight," she said when she felt Lije's movement beside her. "But I've never been able to find the Little Dipper. Where is it?" Diana studied the sky. "And tell me how you got to be an astronomy buff."

"Told you, I read a lot. And you could really see the constellations where I grew up."

She nodded, her hands on her hips and her head thrown back. "Okay. So maybe you would know the answer to this. Don't laugh at me—"

"I won't."

"It is kind of a silly question, I guess. But when I was a kid, I thought the North Star was the Star of Bethlehem. It isn't, is it?"

"No. But there was a phenomenon in the sky around that time. A celestial event, they call it, like a supernova or maybe a comet. Nobody knows for sure."

She sighed with satisfaction. "Thanks for setting me straight. So, show me where the North Star is."

"The two stars that form the outer edge of the Little Dipper point to the North Star. You have to follow their imaginary line."

As Diana continued to search the night sky, Lije moved closer, bringing his arm around her shoulders so she could sight along it. The sudden contact with his lean hardness made her legs feel weak. His breath stirred her hair. A tightness clamped on her throat as she fought the feeling taking hold of her.

"I still don't see it." But then, he was distracting her.

She made the mistake of turning as she spoke and found herself at eye level with his mouth. The soft, sensuous curve of his lower lip was awfully tempting and Diana couldn't look away from it. His hand touched her cheek, the roughness of his skin rasping in a satisfying caress against hers before his thumb lifted her chin. She hardly recognized the burning darkness in his gray eyes.

Her eyelids fluttered shut as Lije moved closer. An unspoken invitation for his kiss was conveyed by her parted, glistening lips. He drew her into his arms. Her hands raised to rest lightly on the back of his neck where his hair waved over her fingers. Diana was torn by conflicting emotions of tenderness and urgency. Her mouth was moving in response to his as a sensual warmth began spreading over her.

The hands that had been holding her easily in his arms began slow, steady movements that brought her closer to him. The melting of her soft curves against the muscularity of his chest made the tentative kiss much hotter. There was fiery demand in his kiss now. Diana surrendered to it, enjoying every second of what was happening. The blood was pounding in her veins, heightening her senses until she was drowning in this new awareness.

Her fingers twined more tightly around his neck as she went on tiptoe to get closer to him. In only moments, Lije Masters had awakened the passionate side of her nature. His mouth began to press more kisses on her face and neck, and she responded with whispering gasps of pleasure. Lije pushed away her denim jacket so that only the thin material of his shirt and her top separated them. The growing heat of their bodies was intensely arousing to both of them. His hands were once more at her hips, pressing her against his thighs and revealing his rising need for her. Again his mouth claimed hers, doing away with the last of her resistance.

Then a sniggering laugh sounded from several cars away, followed by a male voice saying in a loud aside, "There's a guy who's got it made for tonight!"

Almost before whoever it was shut up, Lije was pushing Diana away from him and opening the door of the pickup. His breathing was ragged but his expression was filled with cold anger. He kept a steadying hand on her, since she was still reeling from the effects of his embrace.

"Get in," he said in a low voice.

Her shaking legs were slow to obey, but with the help of his supporting arm, she made it.

He wasted no time in coming around the other side, and starting the truck and driving off. They'd gone several blocks in what seemed to the surprised Diana like a freezing silence before Lije turned to look at her.

"Sorry. I was about to go find him and throw a couple of punches," was his explanation. "And I would've connected too."

"Calm down," she said. "So some joker said something rude. It's not that big of a deal."

Lije blew out his breath. "Maybe so. Actually, sure, you're right. But I—hell, I'm talking in circles, aren't I? You got to me, girl. I think that kiss went a little far."

"Did it?" She'd loved it. Why on earth was he having second thoughts?

"How about if I take you back to your hotel?"

That suggestion didn't make her happy, not in the least. "Look, that stupid comment really didn't upset me. I mean, it did ruin the mood but—" Not being in his arms was what ruined the mood. She studied the fingers knotted in her lap.

"It wasn't a casual kiss. Maybe we should think about that."

"No, it wasn't. Not for me," Diana admitted.

"Or me," he declared, braking to a stop in front of her hotel. He turned only his face to her, and it was shadowed by the light flowing in behind him from the streetlight outside. "Keep in mind, Diana, you're leaving on Sunday to go one way and I leave on Monday going another."

Blindsided by the pain she felt at his statement about the one thing she'd been trying to forget, Diana reached for the door handle, wanting only to run away. His hand reached out and grasped her wrist.

"I've learned a lot about you in the last day or so, Diana," Lije went on quietly. "You're not like the buckle bunnies that hang around the rodeos. As gorgeous as you are and as much as I want you, I can't treat you like one of them. If you want to call off tomorrow, I'll understand."

"I don't," Diana answered, keeping her eyes averted.

His hand took her chin and twisted her face around toward him. He was smiling now, a big, genuine, all-the-way smile.

"Then we're both a pair of fools, because I don't want to, either." He leaned over, his mouth brushing hers in a tender kiss before he settled back on his own side of the truck. "I'll call you tomorrow morning."

"Well, all right. Works for me. Good night, Lije."

Diana beamed at him as she slipped out of the truck. He nodded in reply. She couldn't see his expression too well but she felt sure he was still smiling.

* * *

The phone rang at nine o'clock on the dot the next morning. Diana, who'd been pacing back and forth beside it, lifted the receiver before it could ring a second time, ignoring the bubbling laughter from her roommate.

"Good morning," she said cheerfully, her heart pounding against her ribs.

"Good morning," Lije echoed.

Diana breathed a silent sigh of relief. He had called. Okay. No, better than merely okay. She felt like doing a happy dance, but didn't, since she wasn't alone.

"I'm dressed and ready. Just name the time," she told him.

"Ah, I was calling because a pal of mine— he's someone I do business with too—just got into town. So our date—"

"I see." Diana exhaled slowly, the enthusiasm in her voice dying.

"No, you don't see." Lije wasn't finished. "It's not an excuse. As a matter of fact, I want you to join us for lunch, at your hotel. Interested?"

"Yes," she murmured breathlessly, hoping she didn't sound pathetically eager.

"Meet me in the lobby at twelve thirty, then."

"I'll be there," she assured him.

There was only one dress in her suitcase, a wrap style in an interesting paisley print. It was a breeze to put on, and flattering, especially with her hair down and swirling around her shoulders, she thought. It took all her willpower not to go down to the lobby until the decided-upon time, since she was ready an hour before that.

When she finally walked out the elevator into the lobby, Diana saw Lije talking to a tall, dark-haired man who looked as rugged and forceful as he did. The instant Lije saw her, he excused himself and walked over to greet her. His eyes made a slow, approving sweep over her, and she felt warmed by his open admiration. Her heart swelled with pride when he took her arm and led her over to the other man.

"Diana, this is Cord Harris," Lije said. "He owns a spread over near McCloud, Texas. Cord, this is Diana Mills."

The man was about the same height as Lije, or maybe a little taller. His strong jaw was accentuated by high cheekbones and the resolute look in his eyes. There was approval in his gaze as he shook her hand and glanced over at Lije.

"My wife will be joining us shortly," he explained. "Our son needed a change of clothes before he was presentable enough to have lunch with us. She won't be long."

On cue, a woman stepped out of the elevator and walked to them, carrying a dark-haired and dark-eyed toddler. The little boy let out a squeal and held out his hands for his daddy, who gathered him into his arms with obvious parental pride. There was a loving exchange of looks between husband and wife that made Diana feel a wistful pang. She looked at Lije at the same moment that he turned his eyes toward her. There was a flicker of unrest in their gray depths before he looked away.

Cord introduced Diana to his family. "This is my wife, Stacy, and this is our son, Joshua."

An open, friendly smile brought out the other woman's dimples as Stacy offered her hand to Diana. Her shining chestnut hair cascaded around her shoulders and her olive green jacket was echoed in the flecks of green in her warm hazel eyes. Diana liked her immediately and she sensed that Stacy felt the same way toward her.

The men dominated the table talk, but Diana didn't mind. She picked up in a general way that Cord Harris raised quarter horses and that he was interested in breeding some of his mares with Lije's stallion. Diane assumed he meant the bay Lije used in the arena until Cord referred to Red as an excellent example of the stallion's potency.

"You wouldn't consider selling Malpais?" Cord asked, looking like he expected the negative shake of the head he got from Lije.

"No way. He's part of the future of my ranch," Lije said firmly. "I have a couple of his yearlings and two-year-olds I'd part with, but not Malpais."

"I'd like to look them over," Cord stated.

"Just contact Jim."

"I'll do that."

"Oh, these ranchers. They'll talk cattle and horses all day and into the night." Stacy gave her husband an indulgent smile.

"That's my business. I can't talk about clothes, hairstyles and babies," Cord said. "Not that those are the only things women talk about," he added hastily. "I was just trying to be funny. Sorry, ladies. Kick me. Get it over with."

"You're forgiven," Stacy said magnanimously.

"Well, Stacy, Diana is an expert on the first two things you mentioned—clothes and hairstyles, I mean. She's a model."

"That doesn't qualify me as an expert," Diana said, smiling. But she was immediately drawn into a conversation by Stacy that dissolved the last of her shyness.

About an hour later, Lije and Cord rose from the table. Cord leaned down and brushed his wife's cheek with a kiss and rumpled his son's dark hair. Diana glanced hesitantly at Lije, wishing she could inspire a look of adoration like the one Cord had given his wife. Had he seen it? She had to think so. A crinkling smile made lines at the corners of Lije's gray eyes.

"I'll see you tonight at the rodeo," Lije said. It should have been a question but he made it sound like an order.

"I'll be there," Diana answered warmly. His

hand touched her shoulder as he passed her chair, following Cord out of the restaurant.

"The three of you seem like a truly happy family," Diana went on, feeling just a trace of envy of the woman, who she figured was about her age.

"We're unbelievably happy," Stacy sighed, gazing in the direction her husband had just gone. "I don't think I would've said that about myself before I met Cord."

"How did you meet?" Diana asked. "You really don't have a Southern drawl or a Texas twang."

"Oh, I lived all over. My father was a photo-journalist and he took me with him all over the globe."

"Cool." Diana was impressed.

"I'd always loved the Far West so I headed out there after he died, renting a cabin that happened to be on Cord's land. We had an, um, stormy courtship." She grinned, apparently remembering things she didn't seem about to confide to Diana. "But all's well that ends well. How long have you known Lije?"

"Not long."

"I only met him myself last year at Cord's annual quarter horse sale. He bought three of our broodmares. Of course, Cord's known him for several years. They're a lot alike in some ways. Proud. Strong-willed. You know what I mean, right?"

Diana nodded. "I certainly do."

"You know, he always reminded me a little of an eagle. Remote. Watchful. High above the world—his world, anyway. Seems to me he's come down to earth some. Is that because of you?"

"I don't think so."

"Are you in love with him?" Stacy asked gently. "It can happen fast when it's the real deal."

Diana glanced at her sharply, her blue eyes guarded. She didn't want to reveal how many times she'd asked herself the same question in the past twelve hours.

"I know the symptoms," Stacy continued, taking Joshua out of his high chair and wiping his mouth. "It's easier to recognize in a stranger than it is in yourself. I like Lije and I like you. I couldn't think of anything better than for you two to find the same kind of love that Cord and I did. There's nothing like it."

Diana sighed. "You almost make me think it's possible."

"Anything is possible, Diana, if your love is strong enough," Stacy assured her. Her hazel eyes twinkled. "But there's one piece of advice I'd like to give. Neither Cord nor I guessed that we felt the same way about each other. We almost broke up because of that. Don't be afraid to tell him you love him if you do." Stacy paused, her expression growing more solemn.

"I'll try to remember that."

"Hey!" Stacy said with a beaming smile. "How

did we ever get so serious all of a sudden? Tell me about what you do. It must be really interesting being a model. My father never worked with any—oops, wait a minute, this is not going to be about me and my life. Your turn to talk, Diana."

And with that, the subject of Lije Masters was left behind.

Chapter Five

It was the last night of the rodeo. She'd shown up. She'd watched. Now Diana was leaning on the stable door. The last wave of nausea was subsiding, but she still felt unsteady. The vivid picture of Lije being tossed from the bull and falling under its hooves was still firmly implanted in her mind. She had stayed in the stands long enough to see him scramble to his feet completely unharmed before she fled from the arena to the stables.

The *clip-clop* of a horse's hooves sounded behind her, and Diana knew without turning that it was Lije. All the nagging doubts about whether she really loved him had vanished in those fleeting seconds when his life had been in danger. She could feel his eyes resting on her. Squaring her shoulders, she turned to face him. He studied her thoroughly, taking in the pallor in her fair complexion and the fear that still shadowed her eyes. She was looking at his white shirt stained with dirt from the arena floor.

"I don't make a very good rodeo fan." She laughed nervously. "My heart is in my throat too often. Are you all right?"

"A few bruises and pulled muscles." Lije dismounted and led the horse into the stall. "It's all a part of rodeo."

"Like Lefty's broken arms," Diana concluded for him. "Have you ever been hurt seriously?"

"Cracked some ribs a couple of times. Broke my wrist once." He unsaddled the bay and carried the saddle to its rack. His hand came up and touched the bump on his nose. "Busted this. But on the whole, I've been lucky."

Diana shuddered, visualizing the horror of seeing Lije carried from the arena on a stretcher. "I couldn't shrug it off that easily," she said. "I'm not that brave."

"You didn't panic until after it was over, I noticed." Lije smiled. "I saw you in the stands when I stood up. You were afraid but you waited until you found out that I was all right before you collapsed. Bravery is fighting back fear until there isn't any more reason to be afraid. You did fine, Diana."

There was comfort in his words even if she didn't look at the subject the same way he did. She had been terrified, pure and simple.

"Don't think about it anymore," he ordered

her, seeing right through her mask of composure. "You'll just get worried worse."

"I know you're right," she agreed weakly.

"While I'm brushing Red, you look out at those stars and see if you can find the Little Dipper without me to distract you." Lije winked at her.

That and the swift change of subject took her back to the night before when stargazing had brought her into his arms. The night was clear, making the stars seem so close that she could reach out and touch them. The cold spell was over and the air was pleasantly warm. After Lije's teasing and affectionate words, it was easy for Diana to give herself up to the magic of the evening. When Lije finished grooming the horses, she was even able to point with pride to the Little Dipper with its brilliant North Star.

"I'll have you finding all the constellations in no time." Lije laughed, pulling her down on a bale of hay next to the stable door. "Orion the Hunter—he's easy, with the big stars on his belt."

"Kind of like a rodeo buckle?"

He laughed, a rich, warm sound. "Yeah, come to think of it."

"What else?" she asked.

"Oh, the Pleiades, at the right time of year. They're in a bunch. And the Northern Cross and Cygnus and—"

"Okay!" She held up a hand to stop him. "One at a time. But I am looking forward to it."

"You mean you never slept outside on a starry night? Jim and I used to every summer when we were kids, except when it rained." He was leaning back against the building, staring out into the night. "My dad helped us pitch a tent near the house and he'd make a little fire, tell spooky stories. My mom did the ghost noises, usually. And she taught us campfire cooking. Like how to make s'mores without the marshmallows turning pure black. Oh, and how to make dough dogs."

"Enlighten me. I never heard of them."

"Get a thin green stick, put it through a hot dog, wrap it in biscuit dough from a package, and hold it over the flames until it falls in or you die of starvation, whatever comes first."

She had to laugh. "Sounds like you had a happy childhood."

"Yeah, we had a lot of good times. I think life was just less complicated then."

Diana leaned back too, studying the faraway expression on his face. Her contentment was blended with a hint of wistfulness.

"What do you mean?"

He thought for a minute. "Well, there just wasn't so much stuff that you had to have. We made do with what there was a lot of the time. Like what we found in nature or out in the shed that could be reused. I remember we usually made our own gifts for birthdays and Christmas and occasions like that."

"Really?"

"Yeah," he said, a note of amusement in his voice. "Going to the mercantile in the closest town, Ventana, was a big deal and we didn't get off the mountain that often, so we had to be ingenious."

"Where's Ventana? I've never heard of it."

"Oh, it's just a little town. Blink and you'll miss it as you drive through. But that's where the school is and the mercantile and the feed store and the bank and the newspaper. And a café and a restaurant, both owned by the same guy. We had everything we needed, as I remember."

"Sounds peaceful."

"It really was," he mused. "Except on the Fourth of July."

"What happened then?"

He grinned at her. She saw the white flash of teeth in the dark.

"Oh, just the worst marching band in the Southwest going up and down Main Street for hours. Kids from the schools, old soldiers, the town drunk and his best girl bringing up the rear, blowing on flutes and trumpets and banging on those slatted things—"

"Xylophones. I can imagine," she said, smiling.

"They made enough noise to wake the dead in the old cemetery. It was great. When they got tired, there was free watermelon and ice cream for all and then there were fireworks."

"Do they still do it?"

"Nah. People moved away and things change.

You know how it is. But Christmas, they still do that right."

"Tell me."

"There's lights all over town along the walks, you know, the candles in the bags—*farolitos*. You probably call them luminarias."

"Yes. But I know what you mean."

"And folks go caroling. Spanish and English songs. And they visit each other. That's about it. Not a big deal, but it's the best."

"It sounds wonderful," she said quietly.

"Do you mind all this memory lane stuff?" he asked her after a while.

"No. I love it. I—I don't have any traditions like that to share."

"Not your fault, Diana."

She could sense the compassion in his voice, but the subject was still closed. She'd said all she wanted to say to him for now about how she'd grown up.

"I miss the scent of pine that was always in the wind at the ranch," he said softly. "And the taste of piñon nuts. Jim and I used to spend hours gathering cones, then pick 'em apart to get at those little nuts. He'd give most of his to his mom, but I ate all of mine."

She smiled at him, imagining him as a boy. "Sounds like a feast."

"To a couple of perpetually hungry little boys, it was. We ran around all day out there."

"I guess you knew your way around the

wilderness," she said. "I sure didn't when I was a kid. And I don't now."

He nodded in acknowledgment. "Hey, it's not for everybody. There's always rattlesnakes, the odd mountain lion, the risk of getting lost if you're disoriented, or thrown from your horse and injured. Just your everyday life-threatening type of things." He chuckled.

"Is that all?" she asked, amused.

"You can get used to danger. This little boy grew up and joined the rodeo."

"You just be careful, Lije Masters. That's all I can say."

"I'm very careful." His arm went around her shoulders and drew her against his chest. She snuggled comfortably against him, relaxing when she felt the soothing caress of his hand stroking her hair.

"How did your meeting with Cord go?" she murmured.

"I think he'll probably buy a couple of yearling fillies I have," Lije answered softly. "That will really help, along with the stud fees to service four of his mares. I have a Hereford bull all picked out to improve the bloodline of my cattle. With Cord's payment and what I've earned so far this season, it will just about cover the cost of him."

"What else do you want to do at the ranch?"

"Well, I need another couple of wells sunk for water, a new tractor and a stacker for the hay. The list is endless." His lips brushed her forehead, and Diana gave a little mew of pleasure as she lifted her face for his kiss. It was tender and controlled, but still satisfying. Lije shifted her in his arms and she noticed his wince of pain.

"You're hurt!" she accused him, pulling herself out of his arms.

"Nothing that a little liniment won't cure." He smiled and shook his head at her disbelieving look. "My muscles are just stiffening up a bit."

"It won't get any better if you don't do something about it." The tone of authority in her voice seemed to amuse him, but she refused to let that deter her.

"Come on." Lije took her hand and pulled her to her feet. "It might be a welcome change to have someone other than Lefty rub my back and shoulders."

Blithely Diana followed him to the pickup. The camper on it was compact and the interior was amazingly tidy for a bachelor cowboy on the road. Lije's tall frame barely seemed to fit in the close quarters. Diana glanced around her, wondering where he found room to stretch out.

"The liniment is in the top right-hand cupboard," Lije told her as he unbuttoned his shirt and pulled its tails out of his jeans.

Diana averted her gaze. The sight of his strong chest and its fine, curling dark hair had an unsettling effect on her, to say the least. The bottle of liniment was at the front of the cupboard. Ignoring the way her heart was racing, she turned around and opened the bottle with calm briskness.

"Whew!" she exclaimed as the strong odor of it seemed to explode in the air. "This smells terrible."

"Well, it ain't cologne." Lije chuckled and turned his back to her, sitting crosswise on the couch that did double duty as a chair for the small table.

His broad, lean back displayed a sinewy ripple of muscle that she couldn't wait to touch. Diana stepped forward, pouring the liniment on her palm. The pungency of it acted like old-fashioned smelling salts, driving away her jittery nerves.

She took a deep breath and began.

There was something incredibly sensual about massaging the smooth, tanned skin of his back, she thought dreamily after several minutes of doing it. She could keep this up for hours.

"You're good," Lije said. "Real good. Do you do this often?"

"You bet. For every good-looking cowboy I meet."

"That's not funny," he mumbled.

"You knew I was kidding," she said. "Besides, you're the only cowboy in my life. My first, too."

"Let's keep it that way."

She was glad he was facing away from her so he couldn't see the pink in her cheeks. "Anyway, I'm just imagining what would feel good to me if someone was rubbing my back, and doing that."

Her hands and arms were beginning to ache, but the sensation was pleasurable and she was enjoying her unrestricted caressing of his skin. It was an intimacy that she wanted to prolong.

But Lije straightened up and moved away. "Any more of that and I'll fall asleep," he said. He shifted his position on the couch-seat-thing and took her hands, holding them between his own.

"Are you still sore?" she asked.

That breathlessness attacked her voice as she stared down at his strong face and bared chest. He shook his head, his gaze straying to her lips. Slowly, he pulled her down on his lap. His fingers captured a lock of hair that had fallen across her cheek.

"You're very beautiful, Diana," he said huskily.

"I'm glad you think so," she breathed as his mouth moved closer to hers.

He started with a soft, persuasive kiss, not matching the passion of last night. Yet its gentleness and tenderness was more satisfying and more sincere. It had the taste of honey and all the sweet things of life. Another dimension of emotion opened up as Diana discovered a different facet to her love for him. The golden skin beneath her fingers was more precious than any metal or material wealth.

Lije held her away from him, his gray eyes reflecting the mystery and awe in hers. A furrow cut across his brow and his eyes narrowed. When he curved his hand around the back of her neck to hold her where he wanted her, he kissed her with passionate hunger. His iron-hard arms held her so tightly she could barely breathe. Their hearts hammered as one.

Then his hands were digging into the flesh of her arms as he firmly set her feet back on the floor, easing her up and off his hard thighs. He raked his fingers through his wavy hair and rose himself, pushing past her to yank a shirt out of his closet.

Diana was startled by his abrupt moves. "What's the matter?" she asked as he got himself all buttoned up again.

"You get to me, girl. Isn't it obvious?"

She kept her eyes fixed on his face. "Is that bad?"

"You make it hard to be good, put it that way. Wait outside for me," he said crisply. "I think it's time we went out for coffee."

Diana didn't have much choice. If he was done kissing her, then he was done. Lije took another few seconds to run a comb through his messy hair and he was ready.

But she was feeling more than a little hurt. She told herself to just forget it.

The windows of the café they'd stopped at the first night were dark and the blinds were down. It was after midnight, the witching hour. She had been restless during the drive over, fighting the odd feeling that anything could happen tonight.

Lije veered away when he saw the CLOSED sign, driving the truck in the direction of her hotel. "It's just as well," he said grimly. The gray eyes were uncompromising as he glanced over at her. "We would only be prolonging the inevitable."

Diana swallowed as tears burned the back of her eyes. All evening she had been trying not to remember that this was their last night together. The blissful fooling around with Lije had succeeded in keeping it from her mind until now.

"When will you be in Houston? I thought I'd drive down to see you." It was hard getting those casual words past the lump in her throat.

"Nope. This isn't going to go anywhere," Lije said flatly. "So there's even less reason for you to put yourself through hell watching me do my thing at the rodeo."

Unable to speak to that, Diana blinked unseeingly at the lights of the hotel shining ahead of them. She still couldn't speak when he parked at the front entrance and sat behind the wheel.

"I guess I led you on a little, and that wasn't right. We have to say good-bye, Diana. And now's the time to get it over with."

Her chin quivered, but she made it stop. "Maybe I'll see you in Dallas, then," she said with forced brightness.

"I won't be going there this year." His cold

tone made it clear that he was suddenly ending their relationship before it had really begun. In one quick movement he reached across her and pushed down the door handle. The door swung open, creaking a little.

The sound made her feel so damn sad. But she felt worse when he spoke again.

"Good-bye, Diana."

"Good-bye," she answered in a choked voice as she scrambled out of the truck. Before she had time to turn around, Lije was driving away.

Diana didn't sleep that night, but she didn't toss and turn, either. She just lay there.

Lije liked her. He even cared for her, but not to the extent that she cared for him. Otherwise he couldn't have shoved her out of his life. Why hadn't she made a move or tried to persuade him? Maybe she wasn't as tenacious as she thought she was, but then, he was a whole new kind of man for her.

Fate had denied her many things: a home and childhood memories of family love. Would fate deny her the man she loved so well? Or had she grown so used to bad luck that she had no strength of will to fight?

Not until Stella called her did Diana open the eyes that had been feigning sleep. She went through the motions of packing until her continued silence got her a curious look from the other girl.

"Is your cowboy coming this morning to say good-bye?" Stella asked.

"I don't know," Diana replied with studied indifference. Just to see him once more was what she wanted more than anything.

A little while later Diana was standing in the lobby with Stella, waiting for Rick to bring the SUV around to the front. Her luggage was at the bellhop stand and her bulging cosmetics case was in her hands. In another few minutes she would be on her way to Dallas. Stacy Harris's parting words came back to Diana.

"Don't be afraid to tell him you love him."

"Bring your bags. We're ready to go," Connie ordered as she walked into the lobby and waved toward Stella and Diana.

Together the two younger women walked out the entrance. Rick took Stella's suitcases and loaded them somehow into the back, which was already crammed with his photographer's gear. Just ahead of the vehicle was a taxi cab. As Rick walked back to get Diana's bags, she stepped away from him.

"I'm not going," she said.

"What?" Connie began an on-the-spot interrogation, but Diana grabbed her luggage and was already hurrying to the taxi. There was no one in the backseat and she got in fast.

Her mind was made up. She was going to the rodeo grounds. She was going to find Lije and tell him that she was in love with him. If . . . if it didn't matter to him, then—well, she'd decide what to do then.

The first place she went after the taxi dropped her off was to the stables. The buckskin was in his stall, but the bay was gone and so was Lije. Diana paused to collect herself, then proceeded to the arena. He was there, standing next to a group of cowboys, his back to her as he tightened the cinch to his saddle. She walked slowly toward him, the big horse blocking her from the view of the other cowboys.

"Hey, Lije!" one of them joshed. "You gonna see that beautiful blonde again tonight?"

"No," Lije answered sharply, giving a hard tug on the cinch and causing the horse to move nervously.

"I'd be more'n glad to stand in for ya," another man said, drawing sniggering laughs from the rest of the group.

"Shut up, Rare." Lije's voice had a threatening note under its surface calm.

"He's been like that all morning."

Diana recognized Lefty Robbins's voice.

"That little gal put a burr under his saddle, I think."

"That's enough out of you too, Lefty." Lije gathered the reins to lead the horse away. As he turned, he nearly walked straight into Diana. His head came up as his troubled gray eyes surveyed her.

"Hello, Lije," she murmured. Her movement was frozen by the coldness in his gaze.

"What are you doing here?" he demanded. "You should be halfway to Dallas by now."

"I couldn't leave." Diana swallowed, feeling her courage heading for the hills. She took a deep breath and said what she'd come to say. "I'm in love with you, Lije."

He took a step toward her, then another. There was a smoldering, dark fire in his gaze that Diana mistook for anger.

"I didn't mean for it to happen." She hurried her words. "But it did. Love isn't something you can turn on and off at will."

Her eyes pleaded with him to understand, to stop looking down at her so arrogantly. His hands reached out and clasped her waist with all the strength he had. Diana steeled herself, for what reason, she didn't know. Then Lije suddenly lifted her into the air above his head, then slowly lowered her to eye level. With her feet still dangling off the ground, he proceeded to kiss her. He kissed her so thoroughly that when he lowered her to the ground amid the applause from the watching cowboys, Diana could barely stand on her shaking legs.

"Let's get out of here," he muttered, picking up her cases that at some point had tumbled to the ground.

"Lije?"

Her hand touched his arm and he smiled down at her. It was a miracle. That was love shining out of his eyes. His arm swept around her as he hustled her out of the arena.

Lije didn't stop until they reached his pickup camper, and then only long enough to open the door and help Diana inside. She would have gone back into his arms but he held her away from him.

"We have to talk first, Diana," he said firmly. "And I can't think straight when I hold you."

"There's nothing to talk about." Diana smiled, supremely confident in the face of his love for her. "I'll follow you all over the country or all over the world."

"No. I meant what I said last night. I'm not going to put you through the agony of wondering every time I was in the arena whether I was going to stand up in one piece."

"Then I'll wait for you. Two years, three years, whatever it takes."

"Diana, I can't wait that long for you!" There was no mistaking the reason for the burning look in his eyes.

"I'm in love with you, Lije. I don't want to let you go." Panic crept into her voice and involuntarily she moved closer to him.

"There is an alternative," he said, gripping her shoulders to get her to stay where she was. "But it won't be easy. I can quit the rodeo and go back to the ranch. It'll mean some lean years when we'll have to do without a lot of things, but we could make it."

"You said you needed another two years at least," she murmured. "How can you do it?"

"I can sell Red," Lije sighed. "I had hoped to keep him for a second stallion. As it is, I'll get only half of what he's worth, but it'll give me the money to make necessary improvements to the ranch. We can get by for a couple of years."

"I can find work, Lije," Diana offered. Most likely not as a model, though. She'd told him some about her modeling—but not that her gigs had decreased in the past year and would dwindle down to none at all soon enough.

Somehow taking this step—it was more than a step, hell, she'd jumped into his arms—had emboldened her. She was ready to quit that world and go where life took her for a while. The thrill of modeling was gone and so was the fun, and she'd had a longer career than most girls. It was high time she did something else. Something real.

There were really important things she wanted to do with her life. And one of them was so close to her right now, she wanted to kiss him, especially because of the sacrifice he was willing to make for her.

"It's a hellacious drive from where the ranch is just to Ventana, you know," he said hesitantly, "and that's a tiny town. The nearest city is hours away."

"I don't mean modeling. Something else, where I'm not considered old at the age of twenty-five."

"Okay." He hesitated. "We talked about it for a bit but—"

"We can figure out the details later. And I have some savings—"

"Like I'd take a single penny," he said indignantly. "Absolutely not. You hear me?" He paused. "Sorry. I didn't mean to talk to you like a caveman."

"A cave cowboy," she teased him.

"Yeah." He seemed to like the concept and thumped his chest. "*Mastodon* rider, that's me. Anyway, I am old school about some stuff. Like wanting you with me, Diana. We could make it work. Together."

"That's the way I want it to be," she whispered earnestly.

"I love you, honey." The hands that had held her away now drew her to him as Lije proceeded to rain kisses on her face and neck. "Tonight will be my last rodeo," he murmured against her cheek. "Tomorrow we'll drive to El Paso. We can get married in Juarez. By Tuesday we'll be at my ranch . . . our ranch . . . our home. Is that too long to wait?"

"I would wait a lifetime if you wanted me to," Diana breathed, her happiness knowing no limits when he held her like this in his arms.

"Not a chance. I'm not that patient," he growled. "Why wait?" His mouth covered hers quickly, letting her know without words how he felt.

With a shaky laugh of exaltation, Lije lifted his

head from hers. "The first thing we'd better do is get you checked back into a hotel for tonight."

"Do I have to?" she asked impishly.

"Yes. This afternoon you can go out and buy yourself a wedding dress while I handle a few other things."

"You're the boss."

"No." He kissed her and took his time about it. She was breathless when he stopped and not really listening to what he said next. "We're equals. I don't want a woman who's meek and mild. I expect you to raise hell when you're not happy, you hear?"

Her blue eyes twinkled up at him demurely. She was rewarded with another kiss and a promise of more.

Chapter Six

"Well, Mrs. Masters?" Lije looked at her lovingly. "You're now in New Mexico, the Land of Enchantment. Are you happy?"

"Very happy," she answered, snuggling closer to him as she gazed out the window of the pickup, noting absently that there were fewer and fewer roadside businesses and houses as they drove on down the road.

She didn't care. It was all too wonderful to believe it had happened, Diana thought, sneaking a glance at the man who last night had become her husband in every sense of the word. She still marveled at how tender and gentle he had been with her when he discovered she'd never gone that far before. He'd taken her there and beyond. And she had been astounded by her own response. From the beginning, Lije had been able to arouse her with something as ordinary as a kiss—not that there was anything ordinary about his kisses or all the rest of his expert lovemaking. But Diana had never believed she could be transported to that level of heaven.

"Baby, are you sure you don't mind not having a honeymoon? We could spare a few days in El Paso. We aren't that far away that we couldn't turn back." The concern and desire to please showing in Lije's gaze made Diana's heart leap with love.

"I'd rather go home, Lije," she assured him.

"I hope you won't be disappointed," he said quietly. "If you're dreaming of an enormous house with plush furnishings, my home on the range won't measure up. It's just a one-story frame house that's seen better days."

Diana placed her hand on his mouth to hush his proud apologies. "If you're there, it'll seem like a palace to me."

His arm circled her shoulders and pulled her closer while he drove with one hand on the wheel.

"With you, right now I feel like a king," he said, taking his eyes from the empty highway for the fraction of a second he needed to give her a quick kiss. "There are so many places I want to show you. Where I used to hike when I was a kid and hide out sometimes where no one could find me. We'll sleep under the stars sometimes too, when it's warmer. I hope you grow to love the ranch the way I do, Diana."

"I will."

When they turned to the northwest out of Socorro and left the valley of the Rio Grande behind, the landscape began to change. The few towns they passed were minuscule compared with the rapidly growing and merging cities of Dallas and Fort Worth where Diana had lived all her life. That area was pretty much flat for miles around. Here there were real mountains, rugged and forbidding even with their pine-covered slopes. Diana was beginning to realize that she was going to be living on the other side of nowhere.

She wouldn't let that bother her, not even when Lije turned off the main road onto a dirt one and several miles later turned off that one too. Now they were on a dirt track that led off into the mountains.

"This is the ranch," he announced. His gray eyes left the land around them to look at his wife. There was so much pride and contentment in his gaze that Diana had to smile.

"It looks like something out of a Western movie."

There was not a cloud in the azure sky or a telltale mark of civilization anywhere in sight. Snowcapped mountain peaks sloped down to plateaus, mesas and rolling plains where patches of snow melted slowly in the shadowed areas of grass. The rutted track stretched endlessly into the hills without a sign of any buildings. The emptiness, the isolation, the immense space— everything she saw struck Diana simultaneously. Gone was the security of tall buildings and crowds of people that had constituted her life. Lije had told her that his ranch was miles from anywhere, but the impact of that just hadn't sunk in until now.

At last they topped a rise and the buildings of the ranch were ahead of them. As they got closer, Diana could see a weathered one-story house standing away from the outbuildings. The fact that it had more windows than the others was the only difference. The house and the other structures were the same dirty white, their paint chipped and peeling.

Lije seemed to be seeing the scene through her eyes. "The first trip into town, I'll buy some paint," he said grimly. "But rest assured the roof over your head won't blow away. The buildings are sounder than they look."

"You don't get tornadoes up here like the ones in Texas, do you?"

She meant the question to be lighthearted but he gave her a serious look. "Once in a while, yeah. And thunder and lightning and gully-washers and hailstorms and snow and even blizzards once in a while."

"But it seems so dry."

He held up his hands in a who-knows-why

gesture. "We get a lot of crazy weather in New Mexico. Nothing I can do about it."

"Oh. Well, just tell me what to do when the time comes. And about painting the house— that can wait. And don't do it for my sake," Diana said quickly, wondering how much of her disappointment had shown on her face. "If you need the money for something else, you don't have to make an impression on me."

"I have enough to cover it. Just because the ranch isn't as prosperous as I intend it to be someday doesn't mean it has to look run-down." Lije smiled at her, gradually slowing the pickup and stopping near the first of the buildings. "Let me put Buck away, then we'll go up to the house together."

Diana slid out of her side of the pickup, then followed Lije to the rear where the horse trailer was hitched. This was a homecoming for her husband, she reminded herself. She could tell by the light glowing in his eyes when he looked at the corral and the horses inside. They were his. Obviously.

Everything on the place belonged to him and he was entitled to that look of proud ownership. But Diana felt out of place, as if she didn't belong here at all. She touched her gold wedding band to reassure herself. Lije had enough to worry about without her yapping about her insecurities. She'd always been able to adjust to anything. And now, as his wife, she was going to get used to this.

But it was nothing like the million-dollar spreads that had sprung up not all that far from here. It was remote, as if it had never changed and never would.

The breeze whipped around her, carrying an edge of biting cold from the mountaintops. Diana held her jacket closed as she followed Lije to the corral. While he was seeing to the horse, she took the chance to study the ranch yard, determined to become familiar with everything. Then, out of the corner of her eye she saw something move—a man, walking out of a nearby building. He had jet-black hair that hung over his forehead and his cheekbones were wide and prominent, setting off deep-set dark eyes. He wore a heavy, flannel-lined denim jacket and jeans, a variation on a theme around here, she thought. At first she thought he was Mexican, but as he came closer Diana could tell he was Native American.

"Lije?" Her voice raised to let him know that someone was coming.

Lije was just shutting the corral gate when she called to him, and he walked past her to the stranger. She braced herself, expecting to see Lije order whoever the guy was off the property, then stared curiously as he clasped the other man's hand in his and shook it warmly.

"Diana, come here," Lije called, a grin

spreading across his face. "I want you to meet Jim Two Pony, my friend and foreman."

"Oh, hello. Nice to meet you." Diana felt a little awkward. She'd hoped to be all alone with Lije and hadn't bargained on there being another person when they came home to his secluded ranch. He had mentioned Jim, of course.

There was no welcoming light in the dark eyes that looked back at her, only taciturn reserve. The barest nod of his head was the only indication that Jim Two Pony had even heard her before he turned back to Lije.

"Good to have you back, man," Jim said.

"I didn't expect you to be here when we arrived," Lije said, smiling and seemingly taking no notice of Jim's lack of attention to Diana. "I thought I'd have to go into the mountains to find you."

"The jeep broke down again. I was fixing it," Jim replied. There was no discernible change in his expression.

"Got it. Okay, I'm taking Diana up to the house, then I'll come down and give you a hand. It's good to be back, Jim." Lije clasped the other man's shoulder for a brief moment before he turned to Diana. "I might as well get to it right away," he said to her.

"Of course." She had to force herself to smile. If Jim Two Pony wanted to make her feel like an outsider, he'd succeeded.

"Hey, you're awfully quiet." As they reached

the house, Lije turned her to him and warmed her lips with a kiss. "I think it's time for the groom to carry the bride over the threshold."

He opened the door leading into the house, then gave her a gallant grin. The coldness that had begun to numb her swiftly disappeared under the adoring look in his eyes.

"I love you, Lije," she whispered fervently as he swept her up in his arms.

"You'd better, Mrs. Masters." He walked through the door with Diana's arms entwined around his neck. "That's part of the deal."

She clung to his hand as he set her down on the yellowed vinyl flooring of the kitchen. She glanced around at the old-fashioned white metal cabinets and the heavy porcelain sink. A square wooden table and chairs sat in the middle of the room. The white paint that had covered them had turned a dingy yellow too. Against the side was an electric stove from the 1960s, which looked like it hadn't been scrubbed since then, she thought. There was a refrigerator of the same vintage, and it was just as grimy. Faded gingham curtains hung at the window above the sink and the one near the cabinets. The walls were covered with a glazed paper with a nondescript design of flowers.

"Okay, it's nothing special," he said right off the bat. "And it sure could use a woman's touch. Meaning yours. Whatever you want to do is fine with me. I've let it go for too long." Lije gave her a comically hopeful look. "Besides, I'm a rodeo cowboy. What do I know about decorating?"

"Not much," she said truthfully, and he laughed.

"Let me show you the rest of the house."

The living room was spacious, but it had an austere look—to be expected with only guys in residence. But she noticed a toppling pile of magazines that made it clear the house hadn't always been an all-male preserve. Diana looked at the top one, running a fingertip through the dust on it. "These look like they've been here forever."

"My mother believed in always having something to read," he said offhandedly. "And she didn't think it always had to be great literature."

Diana grinned. "I'm with her on that. Reading is entertainment. Or it should be, great or not."

He seemed a little relieved that she thought that way. "I remember her saying that my grandmother started that pile back before she was born. Then my mom brought it all over here when they married, and it grew."

She peeked at the titles of the magazines, noticing that they were all vintage and that she'd never heard of them. *Heart and Home. Our Day. Ranch Romance. Movie Star.* "How far do they go back?"

He looked abashed. "Decades. I wasn't

allowed to use them for kindling, and they just kinda stayed there."

"Good thing. I actually want to read some of these." She pulled out a crumbling newspaper, a small one. "Hey, look at this. The *Ventana Bee-Gazette*." She examined the date. "Before I was born. You're a pack rat."

"That's our local paper. There used to be two, but there wasn't enough advertising for both of them, so they merged."

She opened it carefully. "Let me guess. Your mom kept this because you were mentioned in it."

"You know something, it could be." Lije thought about it, looking a little surprised by her astute comment. "Let me see that."

She handed it to him and he leafed through it just as carefully. "Sure enough. There's me: 4-H champion."

Diana looked over his arm and saw the old photo of Lije as a boy with a gap-toothed grin, his hair much lighter and topped with a cowlick. "Now that's a treasure," she said.

"You found it, Diana."

"Luck of the draw."

He kissed her lightly on the cheek, folding the old newspaper. "Let's keep this somewhere safe."

She turned around and saw glass-doored bookcases, not fancy but serviceable and definitely antique. "How about there?"

"Good idea." She went with him and watched as he flipped the small latch and put the newspaper inside, on top of a row of books that looked to be about the same vintage as the old magazines.

"Is this your library?" she asked.

"Was. I haven't had time to read the way I used to, not for years. But every one of them is an old friend."

She looked quickly at the titles, seeing several by famous authors of Victorian England along with some classic Westerns. Jack London's books were there too, mingled in with natural history reference works. And, not surprisingly, there were books on stargazing. On the lower shelves were how-to's on everything from home sewing to car repair. Most of the books, from the top shelves to the bottom, had worn spines and a friendly, beat-up look, showing that they'd been read over and over.

"Well, maybe I'll get a chance," she said softly. Knowing that the books were here, as if they'd been waiting for someone to open them again, was comforting to her. And that her rugged husband valued them as he did was a revelation.

She leaned her head on Lije's shoulder when he closed the door of the bookcases with a quiet click of the latch.

"I'm glad you want to," he said, and gave her

a kiss on the top of her head. "Okay. Back to the tour." He turned her around.

She saw a fireplace on the outside wall, its hearth blackened, smelling of old ashes. There was a nook that had been intended to be a dining area, by her guess, but Lije had installed a desk and office files.

"This is where I keep the records for the ranch and transact business," he said.

"No computer, huh?"

He shrugged. "The answer to that question is *yes and no.* I do have a laptop and sometimes I can pick up a wireless signal. But until they can run Internet service through the power lines, which is in the works for remote areas, it's not a sure thing."

"Are you even on the grid?" If there'd been power lines, she hadn't seen them on the way up. But, then again she hadn't been looking.

He nodded. "Yeah. But I've got backup. As in a propane tank and a generator that hooks up to it. I've been thinking about installing solar power, but those panels are way too expensive."

"So I've heard."

"But don't worry. You aren't going to be doing the laundry in a zinc washtub or anything. The washer and dryer are on the side porch, right around that way, if you walked through the wall."

She looked through the doors of a small bedroom opposite a main bedroom. Both were sparsely furnished with no art or anything else on the walls. The bathroom was large, with an old claw-foot bathtub that looked deep enough to swim in.

Nothing in the house remotely resembled the bright and cheery apartment and all its conveniences where Diana had lived for the past few years. She tried hard not to let her lack of enthusiasm show for the drab little house. After all, it was Lije's home and he had a lot of warm memories associated with it. Diana would be the first to agree that designer décor did not make a house a home.

"Well, I'm sure you want to unpack and prowl around a little," said Lije, leading her into the kitchen again.

"Yes, I would," Diane agreed quietly. She walked to the window over the sink and gazed out. From there she could barely make out Jim Two Pony working in the shadow of one of the buildings. "So he's here all the time?"

"You mean Jim? Pretty much. Not that you'd always know it. He goes into Ventana to see his girl and have a good time. But he likes the ranch a lot more than he likes town. He's Navajo, you know. Full-blooded. They're proud people."

She nodded. The brotherly bond between Jim and Lije had been clear to her. She just hadn't expected to get the silent treatment from someone who had been brought up with Lije.

"Anyway," Lije was saying, "Jim is my friend, the closest thing to a brother I'll ever have. I don't expect you to feel the same way about him right from the get-go, of course."

"Thanks," she said. "I don't think he considers me part of the family, either."

"Aw, honey." He looked at her warmly, and she realized that he had noticed Jim's reticence, which made her feel a little better. "Give it time." He stretched out his arms. "You feeling blue? Come on in."

She went into his enfolding embrace, pressing her nose into his shirt so she could inhale his wonderful smell.

Lije lifted her chin and gave her a long, slow kiss that left her clinging to him, wanting more of that.

"Be a little mean to me," he said teasingly. "Otherwise I'll stay here all day."

She tucked her head under his chin, enjoying his caresses and the feel of his warm body next to hers. "Promises, promises, that's all I ever get," she murmured, smiling up at the passionate gleam in his eyes.

"You just keep that thought in mind." Lije touched the tip of her nose. "And we'll find out how true that is tonight. Right now, Jim is probably wondering where I am."

"He can probably figure it out." Diana laughed, moving out of her husband's arms.

"Go. Your jeep needs you. And I can get a few things done myself."

"I have half a mind to stay and teach you who gives the orders around here." He reached over and swung her playfully back into his arms. "But I'll save that for tonight too."

"Mmm. I have a lot to look forward to."

"You make it hard for a man to leave." This time it was Lije who moved away first.

"In case you and Jim are busy all afternoon, what time is dinner?" Diana asked as he opened it and headed out.

"With all the work I have to do, you'd better make it early. Say, around six," he said. His eyes shone when he looked at her.

"Yes, Mr. Masters." Diana's laughing deference didn't seem to fool him for a second. Lije was smiling as he walked out the door.

Unpacking didn't take long since most of her things were still in Dallas. She'd gone back to the hotel to get her suitcases, then dropped them off at her apartment somewhere in the middle of the whirlwind of getting married. She'd brought only what she needed up here, figuring she would deal with the matter of her lease and call the landlord as soon as she had a chance. But there was no big rush to do all that—she was in the habit of paying her rent in advance because she traveled so much, and she was currently ahead by two months.

And maybe . . . maybe she hadn't cut all her

ties because there was a part of her that insisted on a backup plan. Even when she didn't think she'd need it. She hoped she wouldn't. Diana wanted this to work more than she'd ever wanted anything. And she wanted a home.

There was something pleasant and intimate about rearranging the clothes in the one and only chest of drawers to make room for hers. The act of folding her husband's clothes—he hadn't bothered with that, just kinda rolled them up out of the dryer and stuffed everything in every which way—made their marriage seem more real and less like something that had happened in a dream. When she'd dawdled over that uncomplicated task to her heart's content, she reluctantly went to the kitchen.

No matter how dreary it looked, it was her kitchen now. Not being able to fix jeeps or well pumps, she'd already decided that her contribution was going to be cooking and housework. The sooner she learned where everything was, the more at home she'd feel. Looking around at the old appliances and shabby furniture, Diana realized that the only way to improve the kitchen's appearance was to take most of it to the town dump, and start over with a complete remodeling. The money from Lije's rodeo winnings and the sale of the blood bay horse wouldn't stretch to cover that. She would just have to suffer with it the way it was, and try to figure out a way to earn a little money up here herself.

And just how do you plan to do that? she asked herself. *Raise chickens or something?*

Diana was not actually sure how eggs were laid, if it came to that. Nests were involved, she knew that. And maybe a rooster. Maybe not.

She realized that there was probably a book on the subject in the old bookcases. Now that she'd moved up here, it wasn't like she could look everything up on the Internet. But browsing in her own personal little library was going to be fun.

Dinner was on the stove when Lije came in a little before six o'clock, smelling like axle grease and the great outdoors. Diana was setting the table with the ironstone plates from the cupboard. Lije planted a kiss on her cheek without touching her otherwise, then started into the other room to wash up.

"You only need two place settings," he said.

"Isn't Jim eating with us?" Diana held the third plate in her hand.

"Not tonight." Lije's voice carried from the small hallway. "I think he figured we would want to be alone."

"Is that what he said?"

"Not in so many words."

It occurred to her that maybe Jim just didn't

want to eat dinner with her, but she quickly banished it. Lije was undoubtedly right, and Jim was just trying to be thoughtful. Still, Diana had gotten the distinct impression that Jim didn't like her. It was a feeling that wasn't easy to shake. Whatever. She wasn't going to make a big deal of it, and things would probably work themselves out eventually.

The first meal she ever cooked for Lije was an unqualified success. He confided after he devoured it that he hadn't had the nerve to ask her if she could cook before he slipped a ring on her finger.

"Well, to make up for doubting me," Diana said with mock anger, "if you did doubt me, that is, you can help with the dishes."

The rest of the evening was idyllic, just as she'd hoped. Later, after Lije had helped with the dishes, they went into the living room where Lije built a fire in the darkened fireplace. The cheerful flames enlivened the room and chased away some of its dreariness or at least camouflaged it in dancing shadows. They sat on the brown tweed sofa comfortably wrapped in each other's arms.

"Feel like home to you yet?" he asked.

"A little. Not quite," she answered honestly.

"Tell you what. We never had a wedding dance. Feeling up to it?"

"Sure."

She hadn't investigated the other shelves

that held a mix of vinyl LPs and CDs. A lot were from his parents' younger days, by the look of them. Lije pulled out a record and chuckled. "Conway Twitty. My man. Look at that pompadour. So natural looking."

Diana looked. "As a former model, I can tell you right now that he used hairspray. A lot of it."

"No. You think so?"

"I know so."

Lije slid the record out of its cover. "My mom and dad used to dance to a song on this one." He hummed it. "You know it? The one about the man who made you a woman?"

"Nope. Before my time."

Lije turned on the stereo and put the record on the turntable. He switched a rounded lever and the record began to turn, then he carefully picked up the tone arm and placed the needle in the second groove. "You watching this?" He laughed.

"Of course. It's interesting."

He came back to where she was and took her in his arms as the singer's soothing baritone filled the room, and they danced.

"Oh, those old love songs," he murmured. "Nothing like them, is there?"

"No," she whispered. They danced and they kissed . . . and then ended up on the sofa again, dreaming in each other's arms, utterly at peace.

From some distant place outside came a

series of howls that penetrated the walls of the house. The lonesome sound made Diana shudder and curl tighter against Lije's broad chest.

"What was that? A wolf pack?" She looked at the windows that reflected only the light inside the room.

"Nope. Coyotes," Lije answered.

"They aren't dangerous, are they?"

"Not unless you're a sheep or a lamb." Lije moved restlessly, finally getting up to poke the fire again.

"Are you worried about your flocks?"

Lije sighed heavily. "Sure. With good reason. We've lost more lambs than I'd care to count to coyotes."

"Who takes care of your sheep?"

"I hire a sheepherder for each flock, and they have dogs. Their own. They're mostly from South America now. Used to be a lot of Basque guys, but I guess they found easier ways to make a living."

"Oh. So do the dogs keep the coyotes away?"

Another yelping howl drifted eerily into the room, answered by an echoing call. It was another reminder, not a welcome one, that Diana's new world was very different from the one she'd so blithely left behind her.

"The shepherds and dogs do the best they can but coyotes are very bold. Now, mountain lions flee to the high country and have it to themselves, but they're a lot more wary. The coyote doesn't have that fear of man. He treats people with a little respect, I have to say, but not much. But they get less and less afraid all the time, and that means they're more of a menace than a nuisance. Especially to ranchers—whoa. How did we get on this subject?"

In answer, she threw her head back and let loose a pretty good howl.

Lije laughed and walked back to her. "Born to be wild, huh?"

"Maybe," she said, grinning.

He leaned over Diana and kissed her passionately, then pressed her down against the cushions with his whole long, strong length and nipped at her neck.

That was just the beginning.

Chapter Seven

Diana felt Lije nuzzling her ear and she turned sleepily over for his kiss. Bright sunlight tried hard to penetrate her closed eyelids. His mouth was warm and moist against hers.

"Good morning, sleeping beauty," he whispered. "It's time to get up."

Diana moaned, slowly blinking her eyes while she focused on the man sitting beside her. He was wearing a plaid shirt in yellow and dark blue with a pair of worn jeans. Then she noticed the cup of coffee in his hand.

"Need something to help wake you up? Here you go." He handed the cup to her, waiting as she plumped the pillow and pulled herself into a sitting position. "Fresh brewed and strong," he added.

"Thanks," she murmured, taking the cup and sipping from it. "What time is it?"

"Nearly seven. I've been up for a couple of hours, but I thought I'd let you sleep this morning." Lije smiled.

"You shouldn't have done that. But I do appreciate the coffee. I'll make you breakfast, how about that?" She took another quick sip as she started to pull back the bedcovers.

"Too late—I've already eaten. But I left the dishes in the sink for you." He kissed her again and let his mouth trail along her neck.

"Aren't you sweet," she gasped as his attentions caused havoc with her heartbeat.

"I wouldn't know." He raised his head and looked at her fondly. "I don't get called that a lot."

She picked up a pillow and gave him a friendly wallop with it. Lije caught it and set it aside. "I'll be out with the horses for the rest of the morning, but this afternoon we're going into town to pick up supplies. Make a list of the things you need." After bringing her hands to his mouth, Lije rose from the bed.

Being in Ventana was a nice break. They'd gone through it so quickly she hadn't had a chance to really look at it. The storefronts were only one- and two-stories high, made of clapboard and painted in cheerful colors. The town was small, but it was clear that the people who lived in it took good care of the old buildings.

Even with signs of modern life everywhere, it still probably looked a lot like it always had, she thought.

"How old is the town, Lije?"

He slid his hand over the top of the wheel as he made a turn. "About a hundred and fifty years old. Sprang up overnight like a lot of them did. Served the miners and ranchers and lumbermen for miles around. Somehow it survived."

"It seems so authentic."

"It is." He pointed to a pink and white house with flower boxes. "That's a bed-and-breakfast. Rumor has it that it was the local bordello."

She nodded. "Miners and ranchers and lumbermen had to have company."

He gave her a wicked grin. "Rumor also has it that the leading families of Ventana are descended from some of those 'ladies of the night' and the company they kept. But no one's talking."

"Just as well. It doesn't matter a hundred and fifty years later, does it?"

Lije laughed. "I can tell you never lived in a small town."

He dropped Diana off at the mercantile with the daunting reminder to buy enough to last two weeks when they would make another trip in. For Diana, that was a tall order, since she had no idea what her husband's likes and dislikes were and only a rough idea of his appetite. About Jim Two Pony she knew nothing.

She went through swinging doors into a cavernous wood-framed interior. So this was an honest-to-God mercantile.

Long rows of deep shelves held all kinds of goods. She found a shopping cart and wandered the aisles, seeing only a few people browsing here and there.

Good. That gave her more time to really look around.

She passed the hardware and household fix-it aisle, heading for bright pyramids of canned goods. On the way were folded flannel shirts and rows of galoshes. One-stop shopping, she thought happily, with everything you needed. A mercantile was sort of like a small version of a big-box store.

But the food items weren't anything she was used to. The categories were clear—stuff for baking, meals in a can—but it was the brands and some of what was offered that were new.

Sorghum? What on earth was sorghum? She looked at the container. Something you put on pancakes, evidently. Next to it was blackstrap molasses in glass jars. Granted, that was nothing new, but she'd never seen any this thick. Diana picked up a jar and tilted it, watching the viscous black goo inside flow slowly from one side to the other. Lije had a plastic bottle of lubricant with his automotive stuff that looked just like it. She put back the jar and reached for several cans of pineapple and peaches she could use in cakes.

Then she loaded up on flour, cornmeal, baking powder, sugar and salt. Oil too. So far, so good. She felt awfully domestic, looking down at it all. The feeling wasn't bad or good, just different.

She did wonder what Stella and Vanessa would think if they saw her now. They'd probably pity her. But it didn't matter. She felt happy in her new life, even though she knew there were more things she was going to have to get used to.

The next aisle held a strange surprise.

Bacon in a can.

Diana looked at it uneasily. She was willing to admit that anything could be put in a can, but somehow bacon was going too far. The label photo of fatty pink-and-white strips wasn't very appetizing. But she took a deep breath and into the cart it went. If Lije didn't like it, she could return it.

She covered it over with a heap of smaller cans of evaporated milk. There was a Deep-freeze at the house in a utility room off the kitchen, but the items she saw on the shelves were giving her the idea that it wasn't necessarily easy to keep things fresh out here and also that electricity wasn't a sure thing.

In other words, this was the kind of store that sold stuff for when you couldn't get to the store.

Stuff that kept. Through . . . what had Lije said?
Tornadoes, hailstorms, thunder and lightning,
snow and blizzards. She told herself sternly that
it all wasn't going to happen at the same time,
but she added more canned goods to the cart.

That left meat and fresh fruit and vegetables.
There were large hunks of frozen venison in
the glass-topped case and she averted her eyes,
taking the frozen hamburger instead. Not
much of a selection in the fresh bins, but she
took what looked best and topped off her cart.

Then she went to the ATM machine, pushing its little buttons and checking her balance.
Not bad. Her last check from Connie had
cleared. She was going to pay for this whether
or not Lije liked it.

The proprietor was talkative without being
nosy. He seemed to take her, vaguely, for someone on her way somewhere else, driving through
just to look at the scenery. Diana didn't set him
straight, just made small talk as she paid.

Lije had told her where he would be parking
his truck and that when she was done he would
meet her at a local restaurant. So she unloaded
the bags into the truck from the shopping cart,
returned it with a wave at the proprietor and
went off to look for him.

Diana checked out the storefronts as she
walked, noting a bigger, more comprehen-
sive hardware store and the offices of the *Ventana Bee-Gazette*. She was tempted to go inside

and see if the offices of the local paper were as old-fashioned as the rest of the town, but she felt too self-conscious. As far as her idea of writing, she wasn't sure what she even wanted to write. So she settled for a free copy of the paper from the rack at the front.

Diana read as she walked, amused by the funny bits of town news and skipping the articles about the town selectmen. She had just opened the paper to its inside pages to look at the classified ads when she heard a rapping at a window. She looked up and through the glass of a restaurant's bowed front.

Lije was sitting at a table, gesturing her in. She made her way through the door and the tables inside, tucking the paper under her arm. Rising, he held out the adjoining chair for her.

"Are you all done?" he asked, signaling the waitress for a cup of coffee for Diana.

"I hope so," Diana sighed, shrugging off her jacket. "I put everything in the back of the truck. No one steals stuff around here, right?"

"I hope not. We can head back."

"Okay. I have an awful feeling that I forgot something important at the mercantile."

"I'll look over what you got. The place is fun, isn't it?"

She nodded. "Something for everyone. You have to explain what some of that stuff is, though."

Then the restaurant door opened and a

young woman in pigtails came in, slender and boyish in tight blue jeans and a denim jacket. Her buoyant way of walking got Diana's attention even before the other woman's eyes lit up when she saw Lije Masters.

"Lije? Lije Masters?" The woman hurried toward them, her cowboy boots clicking on the floor. "You're supposed to be in Houston! What are you doing here?"

As she reached their table, Lije rose to his feet and she threw her arms around his neck and gave him a huge smooch on the cheek. Diana watched in stunned silence. Whoever this woman was, she hadn't noticed that Lije was with *her*.

"What are you doing here, Patty?" He calmly removed her hands from around his neck, as if he got that all the time, and offered her a chair at their table.

"Libby was a little off his feed when the tour started. I came back to pick him up for the Houston rodeo." Her bright brown eyes finally turned to Diana. "Hi, I'm Patty King."

"This is my wife, Diana," Lije told Patty before Diana had a chance to reply. "Patty is a trick rider in the rodeo, Diana. And Libby is one of her horses."

"Your *wife*?"

Diana noticed the flicker of pain in Patty's eyes before it was quickly concealed.

Then Patty darted a provocatively playful look

at Lije. "I let you out of my sight for two weeks and you get yourself married!" She turned to Diana with an impish smile on her face. "You just can't trust a man for a moment. But anyway, congratulations to both of you."

"Thank you." Diana smiled. Although it was obvious to her that Patty had a major crush on Lije, she couldn't help liking her. All that youthful exuberance was hard to resist.

Patty turned to Lije. "You still haven't told me why you aren't in Houston. Have you left the rodeo?"

"Yeah. For good." Lije glanced Diana's way, letting Patty know the reason why without saying the words. "I sold Red and I'm going back to ranching full time."

Patty changed the subject. "How is Jim? I haven't seen him in ages."

"He has his hands full, but he's fine," Lije answered.

"Tell him I said hello. Well, I imagine you two newlyweds would rather be alone, and it's time I hit the road." Patty rose to her feet. "It was really nice to meet you, Diana. Sorry if I sounded so surprised, but—"

"It's okay. And thanks. Same here."

"Take good care of Lije. You've got one great guy here. I know."

"She's sweet," Diana commented after the good-byes had been said and Patty left.

"There isn't anyone quite like her," Lije agreed. "She's always got a smile for everyone."

"Her face lit up when she saw you." Diana's comment was meant to find out what Lije felt for Patty.

"Oh, we've known each other a while. Plus we have a lot in common. Are you ready to head back to the ranch?"

That was all she was going to get out of Lije, Diana realized. The two of them undoubtedly did have a lot in common from being on the rodeo circuit. She had to wonder if things would have turned out the same for her and Lije if Patty had been at the San Antonio rodeo.

Her second day at the ranch Diana struggled out of bed before the sun. She wasn't at her best early in the morning, and it wasn't even morning yet. Lije was very patient with her fumbling attempts to be organized and efficient. Streaks of pale light were just showing on the horizon when breakfast was done with.

"What are you going to do today?" Diana asked with forced brightness as she poured herself another cup of much-needed coffee.

"I'm going to check the east pasture. The cattle have pretty well grazed out the winter field and they'll have to be moved soon." Lije rose from the table and went to the small closet just to the left of the door leading outside.

"Most likely I'll be late for lunch, so don't worry about me."

After shrugging into his heavy sheepskin jacket, Lije reached into the closet and took out a rifle, its metal barrel gleaming menacingly to Diana's eyes.

"Wh-what are you doing with that?" she stammered.

"I'm taking it with me." He gave her a look over his shoulder that said he was wondering why she asked.

"Why? What for?" Her hesitation ended when she got up and rushed to him. "Oh, Lije, you don't have to take that gun, do you? I can't stand guns."

"Guns are a fact of life out here. Better get used to it." He reached back inside the closet and extracted a box of shells, which he stuffed in his jacket pocket.

"What do you need it for?" she persisted, her pale face turned up to him.

"I always have a rifle in the rack of my pickup when I'm on the ranch." His steadying hand held her shoulder firmly. "There are times when you need it."

"When?" she cried.

"I told you last night that coyotes aren't at all like the funny critters in the cartoons. They can have rabies. They can be hurt or starving too. The thing is, they're just too many of them because they don't have natural predators.

Sometimes it's best to not let them suffer. And that goes for my sheep too," he added. "Real ranching means you gotta do some things you don't necessarily like."

"But—"

There was a bite of irritation in his voice at her naïve fears, followed by a brisk kiss directed at her cheek. "I have to go."

As he put on his Stetson and walked out the door, Diana wondered unwillingly whether Patty would have reacted the way she had. No. Most likely Patty King could shoot as well as Lije. But no matter what, Diana loathed the violence and killing that were automatically connected with guns. And her husband had more than one.

Don't worry. Hah.

Diana was a nervous wreck until he drove into the yard in the early afternoon. It was all she could do to keep from rushing out the door and flinging herself in his arms, but this time she controlled her anxiety and greeted him calmly when he entered. Later, judging by their conversation during lunch, the subject seemed to have been forgotten.

But the strain and tension didn't ease for Diana. During the next few weeks her senses and emotions were overwhelmed. The profound silence of her new world was the first thing she noticed. No more vague hum of the city, even though she hadn't really noticed it until it wasn't there. It was a hum that meant people were all around her. Here, especially at night, the silence was broken only by the sounds of wild animals that she never saw and, more often than not, that sent an eerie chill down her spine.

Lije had explained that most desert animals woke up and hunted and prowled around at night to avoid the heat of the sun, but she hadn't found that particularly reassuring.

The days were long and lonely. Lije left the house at sunrise and often didn't return until sundown. Diana tried to fill the empty hours with busywork that she knew was sort of pointless. The house was spotless. The furniture gleamed from repeated polishing. All the rooms were permeated with the smell of lemon oil from her efforts, and over that, the sugary fragrance of baking and the savory smell of casseroles, stews and soups. She didn't actually want to eat any of it. It was just that cooking and washing up kept her hands busy.

Nothing she did eliminated the feeling that the house was an island surrounded by an ocean of unending grasslands and dark, scowling mountains.

They matched her mood, she thought gloomily. She told herself not to be melodramatic but it didn't help.

The qualities that had drawn her to Lije—strength of purpose, natural dominance and driving ambition—were exactly what were keeping them apart. It wasn't in him to slack off, ever, if there was work to be done. For Diana, that meant almost no time in his company. Not even the nights were sacred anymore, as Lije spent more and more of his time at the desk in the living room alcove.

As Diana found the adjustment harder and harder to make, Lije thrived on it. He stepped up to meet the challenges of the unforgiving land he loved, and all she wanted to do was shrink away from it. The dimness inside the house depressed her, but the sun seemed nearly blinding when she ventured out. Which she did less and less.

She seemed to be stuck in a dangerously domestic mode, feeling lost unless she had a rag in one hand and a bottle of furniture polish in the other. Or a spatula and a bowl. She didn't know quite how she'd transformed herself into a compulsive housewife, but that's what she was. She hoped that Lije got something out of it.

Diana knew how important it was to their future that this year be successful, and she knew that Lije was determined to make it that way for their financial security. Ranches didn't run themselves. After getting a little hysterical about his guns, even though they were, as he'd said, a fact of life out here, she didn't feel like complaining about something else and adding to her husband's burden. But now the isolation and strangeness were getting to her. She kept silent about her loneliness, her failure to find any beauty in the harshness of her environment and the empty feeling that nagged at her that again she didn't belong.

That last was intensified by Jim Two Pony's attitude toward her. He did concede to take the evening meal with Diana and Lije, but all other meals he had at his small cabin in the low woods some distance from the rest of the ranch buildings. He never directed any conversation toward her and he replied in monosyllables to everything she said. Lije's air of remoteness was a lot more pronounced out here, and Diana felt sure now that it came from a long association with Jim Two Pony. That knowledge made it harder for her to try to reach out to Lije.

After more than three weeks on the ranch with only a second trip into town to break the monotony of her days, the drab walls of the house closed around her like a prison. She rarely went out except to accompany Lije and say goodbye before he left. She'd never been the outdoorsy type, and the cool mountain breeze always seemed too brisk to her for walking. But this afternoon she felt there was no other alternative and she did realize she was getting stir-crazy. There were enough pies, cakes and cookies in the freezer to last a month. Soups and stews too. The house was immaculate. She'd started on the stack of vintage magazines, which was probably why she felt like she was in a time warp, and decided which books in the house she would read when she felt like reading.

At the moment, none.

Her hair was washed. Her nails were polished. And it was barely two o'clock.

With an air of resigned indifference, Diana changed into clothes that would do for a walk and looked good enough to improve her morale. Minutes later she was buttoning her jacket and going out the door. The sun had climbed in the sky until it was almost exactly overhead, soon to begin its downward journey to the west. The constant breeze was gentle, carrying a mingling of wild scents, from the fragrant pines and hay to the earthy smells of horse and sheep and cattle. But the odors were unfamiliar to her and somehow irritating.

The house had no lawn, just a continuance of the yellow grasses that covered the hills. There were no hedges, no flowering shrubs, no shade trees, except for the pines behind the house and a scrubby-looking tree of some kind in front of the house.

The white paint that Lije had brought to spruce up the buildings was in the storeroom of the house. There had been too many other things to get done before spring, so that time-consuming and arduous task had been set aside.

First Diana strolled toward the fenced pasture where some horses had gathered. For a while she leaned against the wooden rail, watching the shaggy-coated animals as they quietly grazed. A distant, smaller enclosure held a lone horse, which, Diana knew from the talk between Lije and Jim, was his stallion, Malpais. At this distance, he looked solid black, although Lije had said the horse was a bay with black points.

The yearlings in the corral where Diana was became curious about this human who made no move toward them and began heading en masse in her direction. Before they could reach her Diana stepped away. She couldn't think of them as casually as Lije and Jim seemed to, as if horses were overgrown dogs.

Something moving near the barn caught her eye. Jim Two Pony was putting gear into the back of the pickup before returning to the barn. Diana hesitated. Lije was out somewhere on the range and wouldn't be back until dusk. Here was her opportunity to talk to Jim, even if he seemed determined to ignore her presence.

Resolutely she walked into the dark confines of the barn, which was illuminated only by the sunlight filtering through the dusty windows and the open door. Diana knew that Jim had to have heard her come in, but he didn't glance up.

"Hello, Jim," she said with determined brightness.

"Hi" was his clipped reply as he walked over and took a saddle from its rack near the door.

"Is Lije around?" Diana asked, knowing that if it was up to Jim, the conversation would have just ended.

"Nope."

He walked to the door, the saddle carried effortlessly over his shoulder. Diana followed a few steps behind.

"Do you know where he is?" she persisted.

"Nope."

"It's a nice day, isn't it? The sun feels really good." Diana stubbornly refused to give up, but she felt kind of guilty about being so annoying. Obviously he had work to do.

"Yeah, it does." Cold, dark eyes flickered over her.

"How much longer before spring comes?" There was the barest trace of a challenge in her voice as she silently dared Jim Two Pony to find a one-word reply to that.

"Soon."

Diana pressed her lips together. "Why don't you like me, Jim?" she asked, hoping her bluntness would make him speak his mind too.

"You are very beautiful," he said.

Okay. That didn't follow. But it was a start of sorts. "Is that the reason? But I can't help what I look like." Diana hoped she didn't sound whiny, but she had a feeling that she did. A little.

"Beauty is as beauty does." His flat tone didn't change when he said it.

Diana thought it over, not sure she could puzzle out what he meant by the familiar phrase. Then she spoke but hesitantly. "I guess what you're really saying is that you don't think I'm right for Lije. That even though we both love each other, I don't belong here. Am I right?"

She lifted her chin with proud sadness. The light breeze coming in through the wide barn door flowed over her face and caught at the silken strands of her pale hair.

He gave an almost inaudible sigh. "Maybe there's a better way to explain it."

"Go ahead."

"When I first came to this ranch after Lije's mother died, there was a place by the house where she had tried to grow roses. But they withered and died. They couldn't exist without her fussing over them."

The offhand way Jim was talking would have led a stranger to believe that he was recounting a story instead of answering Diana's question.

Yet Diana understood his analogy perfectly. She was the rose who needed too much attention—from Lije. And Lije was her only reason for being here. Diana didn't comment. She had a feeling Jim Two Pony had more to say, now that the semisilence between them had been broken.

"There is a plant that grows wild around

here called the yucca. It thrives—it doesn't just live."

She gave him an encouraging nod but she didn't smile.

"It has leaves shaped like swords—they have strong fibers that Indians used to use to make baskets and clothes. In the spring, it has a tall stalk"—he showed her the height with his hand—"about this tall, and there are flowers on it, like bells. It's pretty but it's tough too. What I'm saying is that it belongs."

And I don't. Well, thanks for the botany lesson, she thought silently.

When Jim headed for the near corral, Diana was left standing alone. Not that she was very surprised by what he'd said. She had guessed at how he felt about her, but now she knew why. There was some truth to his words. Granted, she did the housework and the cooking, but that didn't seem on a par with the men's endless, generally grueling, labor. And she'd shaken up an established way of life and no one ever liked that to happen. Anyway, if it wasn't for her husband, she never would have ventured into this harsh country, let alone thought she'd be able to live happily in it.

She really was a city girl and she did like her comforts, and all Jim Two Pony had done was point that out.

* * *

At supper, Diana picked at the food she'd prepared so carefully. She more or less followed the conversation between Lije and Jim, but there were too many terms she didn't understand. Her fear of not understanding Lije himself stole her appetite. She kept wondering how long it would be before Lije noticed the serious differences between them.

Usually Diana waited until the guys finished their coffee before clearing the table, but tonight she couldn't sit passively in her chair. If she didn't do it now, she would snap at them to carry their own damn plates to the sink. Not that it would kill them, but it would give away her emotional state. She got up. Gray eyes watched her thoughtfully as she made the trips back and forth between the sink and the table. Even after Jim left the kitchen to check on a sick mare, Lije stayed at the table, not retreating to his desk in the living room as he usually did.

"Anything the matter?" he asked her quietly when the silence continued.

She became conscious of a tear slowly wandering down her cheek, and she wiped it away with a soapy hand as she shook her head.

Of course not. What could possibly be wrong?

As if she'd screamed the words instead of just thinking them, Lije got up and came quickly to the sink.

"Then what's that teardrop doing on your

cheek? Running a race with the other one?" A finger touched the new arrival.

Diana moved her face against his hand, seeking the comfort of his caress. She turned her jewel-bright eyes to look at him.

"Why are you crying?" Lije asked gently.

She swallowed the lump in her throat, then gave him a wobbly smile. "Um, because I'm not a yucca plant."

He gave her a puzzled but patient look. "Huh?"

"Oh . . ." Diana hesitated. She didn't know whether or not she should tell him about her conversation with Jim. For some reason, she was afraid to. "Never mind. Just thinking about something someone said. It was silly."

"Yeah? I'm not so sure."

"What, don't I get to be silly? I think I can tell the difference between myself and a yucca plant. Unless I've been out in the sun too long."

"Gotta watch out for that. In New Mexico, it's fierce." He smiled. "Try not to bake your brain, okay?" His arms circled her waist as he nuzzled her ear. "Let those dishes be for a while. We can do something else—start with a fire in the fireplace and go from there."

"Don't you have paperwork to do?"

She was held tightly against him, but she continued to stare at the sink and the clutter of dirty dishes in it. They both had work to do, but it sure as hell could be done later.

"Not tonight," he whispered in her ear.

Hearing those beautiful words, she turned in his arms to face him, her love shining brilliantly in her eyes. She needed him so much.

"Hold me, Lije," she whispered fervently.

Chapter Eight

A few days later Cord Harris phoned and made arrangements to fly up in his private plane the following weekend. Lije and Jim both spent extra time with the yearlings Lije wanted to show Cord. When Cord learned of their recent marriage, he said that he wanted to bring his wife, Stacy, with him. Not until Diana heard that did she realize how much she'd missed contact with other women.

When the morning came for the Harrises' arrival, Diana's eagerness had her hearing the drone of an airplane engine half a dozen times before the red Cessna actually flew over the ranch. She raced out of the house to intercept Lije, who was just getting into the jeep to go out and meet them.

"Can I come with you?" she asked breathlessly. Her face was aglow with excitement.

"Hop in." His gray eyes shone as Diana quickly took the seat behind him.

They rattled over the track leading to the flat stretch of pasture where a lone red windsock marked the landing area. Diana could barely conceal her impatience as the plane slowly taxied to where they were parked. She followed Lije when he got out and walked to meet the man and woman getting out of the plane.

Stacy's twinkling brown eyes sought out Diana immediately. As she gave Diana a quick hug, Stacy whispered, "I feel like a matchmaker. Congratulations—although I think I'm supposed to say that to the bridegroom."

"Thank you." The warm feeling of having found a true friend brought a sparkle of happy tears to Diana's eyes. "I'm glad you could come."

"Cord is very thoughtful that way." Stacy glanced at her husband, who was talking to Lije, before she smiled back at Diana. "He knew this trip would break the monotony of ranch life for you as well as me, although I'm already getting homesick for little Josh."

All the way back to the ranch yard, the two women chattered about everything under the sun while the men sat in front wrapped up in ranch talk. When Lije stopped the jeep near the corrals, Cord turned around to look at Stacy.

"I want you to see the stallion Lije has, Stacy. Malpais is a one-in-a-million animal."

"I'll have Jim bring him out of his paddock so you can have a closer look," Lije offered, signaling to Jim Two Pony, who was just walking out to greet them.

The big, barrel-chested bay was led out for their inspection. Diana watched with envy as Stacy led the discussion, admiring the muscular haunches that could spring the horse into full speed in one bounding leap and the beautifully formed head with its dignified, intelligent eyes. Diana wished she knew as much about quarter horses as Stacy did. But it was obvious that Cord's wife was a horsewoman, while she, Diana thought ruefully, was a housewoman.

The stallion was led back to his enclosure and the yearlings were paraded for Cord one at a time. Diana watched, not understanding why three were singled out from what seemed to her equally beautiful horses. When Cord and Lije became engaged in a purely business discussion, Stacy suggested that she and Diana walk over to the corral to look at the older horses.

"That's a beautiful chocolate-colored mare!" Stacy exclaimed excitedly.

"Which one?" Diana asked. She could tell a mare from a stallion, but all horses were a variation on brown to her.

"That one there," Stacy pointed, "with the star on her forehead and the white front foot. She's a dainty little horse. Cord, come and look at this mare!"

The two men walked over to where the women stood near the corral. Diana had finally been able to determine which horse Stacy was talking about and admitted silently that it was a pretty little horse with soft, long-lashed eyes. Lije opened the corral gate and walked over to the mare, taking her by the halter and leading her to the railing where Stacy waited.

"How old is she?" Cord's keen eyes trailed over the mare.

"A coming four-year-old," Lije answered. "Would you like to ride her, Stacy?"

"Would I ever!" Stacy cried.

Lije turned to ask Jim to saddle the horse.

The brunette's gaze took in Diana and Cord. "I have a horse of my own, but Cord doesn't want me to ride him because he's a bit wild, so I don't. I've been trying to find another horse that's spirited enough for me and gentle too."

"She looks like an ideal ladies' mount," Cord agreed as he watched the mare stand quietly when Jim tightened the saddle cinch. "I wouldn't get too enthusiastic about her, Stacy. Lije might want to keep her for Diana."

"Oh, no." Diana spoke quickly as Lije turned a questioning look on her. "I don't ride."

"You'll have to get Lije to teach you," Stacy

said, putting her foot in the stirrup while Jim held the horse's head. "There's nothing like exploring this rugged country on the back of a horse."

Diana smiled but didn't reply as she watched Stacy expertly put the horse through its paces with the wild landscape as a backdrop. The thought of going alone through that country intimidated her, horse or no horse. Her mind conjured up all kinds of images—rattlesnakes, coyotes, mountain lions, jagged cliffs.

"She's perfect!" Stacy dismounted and hugged the mare's neck briefly before dancing over to her husband. "You do like her, don't you?"

The way he looked back at Stacy gave Diana the impression that if she and Lije weren't there, he would have taken his wife in his arms. As it was, Cord just smiled and nodded. "As if I could refuse you."

"Diana and I will go up to the house while you persuade Lije to sell her." And Diana was swept away with the exuberant Stacy toward the house.

"I wish I were more like you," Diana sighed after she had put the coffeepot on and joined Stacy at the kitchen table.

"What do you mean?"

"You're so at home on the ranch. You know one end of a horse from another."

"The important thing is the middle. That's where you sit." Stacy laughed.

"That much, I know. But the only other thing that's country about me is my jeans," Diana said, trying to laugh at herself. "How did you make the adjustment from big-city life?"

"I traveled all over the world with my father and a lot of the time we were headed to the far side of nowhere," Stacy explained. "My dad had a real love of nature that he passed on to me."

"Is the part of Texas where your ranch is very different from here?"

"It's not quite as untamed as this." The glowing look on Stacy's face revealed her admiration for the quality about her new home that Diana most disliked. "Only a really rugged guy could carve out a place for himself in this kind of wilderness. Lije is tough enough for ten men."

"Don't you get worried sometimes when Cord goes out on the range?"

"Sure." Stacy grinned. "I know it's foolish, but I think it's natural to worry about the one you love."

"Lije goes out by himself a lot." Diana stared out the window, remembering the long, lonely hours she spent watching for him to return safely. "We're so far away from any kind of help. It worries me just thinking how critical that could be if there was ever an emergency."

"Don't borrow trouble, Diana." Stacy touched the hands clutched so tensely on the tabletop.

"The coffee's done." Diana nervously hopped

up from the table. Yet it seemed so natural to confide in Stacy, especially since she understood so well. "I made a coffee cake. Would you like a slice?"

"No, thanks," Stacy refused with a smile. "I still have a few pounds I'm trying to shed after the baby."

"You look great. I wouldn't worry."

"Well, there are still some clothes that are a little tight. A reminder that my girlish figure isn't quite back to where it was."

"I've put on a couple of pounds too." Diana glanced down at her tummy, sliding a finger into the waistband of pants that were relatively snug. "I've been overdoing the baking lately and sampling the results. I got some of the recipes out of those old magazines over there." She pointed toward the living room.

"On you it looks good," the other woman commented as she got up and went to look at them herself. "Being a model you probably had to stay as skinny as you could for the camera's sake."

"It was getting harder and harder to do," Diana called to her. "I kept developing curves."

Stacy came back with several of the magazines and a couple of ancient *Bees*. "Oldies but goodies. These are so much fun. Life was simpler then."

"Yeah. Men were men and women tended their ovens," Diana said wryly.

Stacy leafed through a magazine as she sat down, putting the rest on the table. "Do I detect a note of restlessness?"

"More than a note," Diana said.

Stacy raised her head and made a quick, sympathetic study of Diana's expression.

For her part, Diana didn't know what to say. Complaining was just not her style, and she really didn't know Stacy.

"So if you had to change one thing about your life right now, what would it be?" Stacy asked in a soft voice, looking at the magazine again.

"I'd buy a car," Diana blurted out. "Something used. But with four-wheel drive."

Stacy nodded and looked at her again, expectantly.

"But I can't afford it. And I can't ask Lije. He doesn't have the money, either, and he needs his truck. Jim's got the jeep."

"You would think the guys would figure out that was going to be a problem before you got here," Stacy said with a small sigh.

"Well, we got married in a fever, like the song says. I didn't think about it, either, so it's not all Lije's fault or anything. Please don't mention it to him, Stacy." Diana hated the idea that he would think she talked about him behind his back.

"I won't," Stacy assured her.

Diana fell silent, reasoning with herself in a

not very logical way. She had to talk to somebody about her life, and Lije was a part of her life, so he was bound to be part of the conversation. She let it go at that, feeling confused and irritable.

"Got a couple cups of that coffee for us?" Lije demanded in a teasing voice as he and Cord walked in the door.

"Of course." Diana was quick to place two more cups on the table along with plates for the coffee cake that she set in the center.

"That mare is yours now," Cord said quietly as he sat beside his wife.

Her mouth formed the words "thank you" and curved in a glowing smile at the same time.

"I have to pick up the Hereford bull I bought, so I've agreed to trailer the horses Cord bought to his ranch. Then I can bring the bull back in the empty trailer." Lije's statement was addressed to both women, but Diana knew it was specifically meant for her.

Although since that day in San Antonio he hadn't mentioned the possibility of Cord buying any of his yearlings, Diana had known instinctively that Lije had counted on it. Without the money from that sale, he had been reluctant to buy the bull he needed for his herd. It would have bottomed out their bank account. So, while she silently rejoiced with him, she was also afraid of what would happen during the journey. It would be their first separation, which in itself would pull on her heartstrings, but

it was being alone on the ranch that she
dreaded more.

It was some time later when Cord rose from
the table, signaling his wife that it was time for
them to be on their way. Diana insisted on refill-
ing their thermos of coffee and preparing sand-
wiches for their plane ride home, stating that it
was the least she could do since they weren't
able to stay for a meal. Neither Cord nor Stacy
put up any argument. Stacy stayed with Diana to
lend a hand while her husband and Lije went
out to do a preflight check of the plane.

"Think you can persuade Lije to let you come
with him when he brings the horses?" Stacy
sliced efficiently at the cold roast beef while
Diana cut generous portions of her homemade
bread.

"If I asked him, he would. But as much as I
would like to, I won't." Her blue eyes turned
apologetically to Stacy. "Without me along,
he'll probably drive right through, settling for
a nap in the cab of the truck. If I was with him,
he'd feel obligated to stop at a motel. And I
would know no matter how well he would hide
it that he was anxious the whole time to get
back to the ranch." Diana gave a heartfelt sigh.
"I'll stay home like a good little ranch wife, I
guess."

"Diana." Stacy laid down the knife. What
she saw was Diana's blond hair, because she'd

bent her head down in resigned acceptance of her decision.

"I'm feeling sorry for myself," Diana mumbled. "Sorry about that."

"First things first. Quit apologizing for how you feel. I know this life and this country must seem strange to you. It's mostly because it's so different from what you've known. It's perfectly natural for anyone to be scared and even dislike things they don't know about. This ranch and all that land out there must seem like a godforsaken place to you."

Stacy's words were so accurate that an ironic smile tilted the corners of Diana's mouth. "Godforsaken" was the right word.

"It isn't." Stacy's voice lowered in an effort to get her new friend to understand. "The people who know it best call it God's country. Nothing is what it seems on the surface out here. You have to get close to it, really try to understand what it takes to live here and thrive."

"I know what you're saying is probably true, Stacy, but I'm not like you. I don't ride and once I'm out of sight of the house, I'm lost. The only vehicles we have are the jeep and the pickup. I doubt whether I could drive either one," she answered.

"Have you ever been outside the ranch yard?" Stacy asked with sympathetic curiosity.

"No."

"Then you gotta ask Lije to take you around

and show you the land he loves so much. He'll do it, believe me." Stacy gave her a touch on the arm that communicated nothing but kindness. "This is your home now."

"Lije is so busy. He has so much to do that I don't want to interfere with his work." Diana shook her head.

"You wouldn't. Don't you see? There would be things he could do along the way. Check on fences, see if the waterholes are full and not getting trampled. A hundred things. Oh, and chase cows—that's a given. At the same time he'd be showing you the country. Promise me you'll do it, Diana," Stacy implored. "And just accept the strangeness of the land. It really is beautiful once you know it."

"I promise," she said, unable to do anything else when she was looking into those caring brown eyes.

Immediately a grin spread across Stacy's freckled face, an impish one.

"I hope you were cutting some of this bread for yourself, because Cord and I can't possibly eat that much," she said, laughing.

Diana looked with surprise at the towering stack of bread slices, joining in with Stacy's laughter. The lightheartedness of the moment relaxed the tension that had built up inside her. She was still smiling when Cord and Lije returned from the plane, but with their entrance, depression settled once again. Stacy was leaving and Diana had no way of knowing when she would see her again.

The ride from the ranch yard to where the plane was parked seemed extremely short. The smile on Diana's lips was forced, as was her cheerful wave to the couple in the plane. A lump rose in her throat as the plane turned and made its run down the grass strip. When the wheels left the ground, she felt her last contact with civilization had been broken and she was left behind in this desolate land.

As the red Cessna flew out of sight, Diana turned to the man standing beside her, taking in the harsh, uncompromising lines of his face. It was during moments like these that the alien quality of the austere landscape overwhelmed her—she had nowhere to run and nowhere to hide. Right now her husband seemed like a stranger to her and not the man she snuggled against at night.

"Well, the excitement's over. It's back to just us now," Lije said quietly.

Diana sighed. "Yes."

Lije moved toward the jeep.

"I . . . I think I'll walk back to the house."

"Don't be ridiculous. It's way too far to walk from here."

"But—"

"Get in the jeep." The sentence was snapped out like a command.

Lije was already behind the wheel when

Diana made slow, reluctant movements to join him. An awkward, stony silence fell between them as he drove. Diana didn't want to voice her thoughts. She had been so sure of her ability to adjust to her new home and her surroundings, and in Stacy's presence, she'd been more than hopeful that her new friend's advice would work. Now, looking at the emptiness of the horizon, she doubted that anything could bring her to like this barren land when she couldn't even do it with the strength of her love for her husband.

"I can't make it any easier for you, Diana."

The jeep halted in the yard. His words forestalled her movement to get out as she jerked around to face him.

"What are you talking about?" The murmured but sharp question was in response to the cold glitter in his eyes.

"I can't count how often I've been shut out by you lately. You know exactly how to put on an expression that keeps people from knowing what you really think and feel."

"Oh, that? It's a model's trick," she said icily.

"I don't doubt it. But it's getting in the way of—of us."

Diana winced inwardly at his cutting tone. He didn't sound like he wanted to be part of the relationship one second longer.

"I thought this visit would help, but it's only made things worse."

"Lije?" The apology was forming but he didn't give her a chance to get the words out.

"Why don't you just admit that you're homesick for city life and stop trying to fake it here?"

"All right, I am homesick," she retorted, stung by his jab about faking it. "But that doesn't change anything. I'll get over it."

"Will you?" He raised an eyebrow and shot her a look that said he doubted it. "Some women never adjust. They end up full of resentment about their isolation and end up hating the men who won't leave their land. Or their way of life. It's not for everybody, that's for damn sure. Divorce court is next. And the land gets sold to pay the lawyers or something else awful happens. It's just ugly."

"Is that what you think is going to happen with us?" Diana asked in shocked but suppressed anger. Lije's carved profile was turned to the distant mountains, so she couldn't see the expression on his face.

"Why couldn't you talk to me about the way you feel?" Lije's voice was as cold as a mountain stream. "Stacy's practically a stranger to you."

"She's a woman! She would understand how I felt, because she had to make the transition herself," Diana said, wishing she didn't have to defend herself for it. Who the hell did Lije think he was, anyway? She took several deep breaths, willing herself to see it from his side. "Look, Lije, just keeping the ranch running has been very tough for you and it could be tougher going forward."

"You got that right."

"I didn't want to worry you or add to your burden. But how did you know I'd talked to her?"

"Guess what. I had a feeling that things were tough for you too," Lije said, but not in a kind way. "And I've been around enough married couples to know the compassion that springs into a woman's eyes when the wife confides what a rotten life she has."

"Rotten life?" Diana exclaimed angrily. "You never heard me say that, because I never did. And I wouldn't. For some strange reason, I love you, Lije Masters!"

He was silent. No, she decided, just sullen. She jumped a little when he spoke again, although his voice was soft.

"Love can happen at the wrong place and time, even when it's real," he said.

A vast distance suddenly opened between them even though they were only inches apart in the jeep. She didn't reply, couldn't think of what to say.

"And there's something else. You knew before we were married how much this ranch meant to me. I love you, Diana, but I would *never* give it up. Not even for you."

"I—I did know that." Did she? she asked herself. Or had she unthinkingly hoped that someday she might be able to persuade him differently? She was so upset and confused she couldn't think straight. She hated fighting and this argument was making her feel physically ill. She seized on the subject of the ranch in a last attempt at placating his cold anger, however justified. "I—I've never really seen the ranch. I mean, you've never taken me around and shown it to me. Would you?"

"I'll be too busy the next couple of weeks with the horses and so on, but Jim will be checking the fences. He can take you with him if you really want to go." Lije's hand was rubbing the back of his neck as he ground out his reply.

"No." Diana refused too fast, bringing the sharp look back into his eyes. "I'd rather go with you when you have time."

"What have you got against Jim?" he asked in an irritated voice.

"Nothing," Diana protested. "It's just that he doesn't like me."

"Hmm. You sure?"

"Oh, Lije," she began. "I don't know him well enough to like or dislike him." Her shoulders lifted in an uncertain shrug. "But I do have an idea of what he thinks about me. So I'm not that comfortable around him. Besides, this is the ranch where we live and I want you to show it to me, not some guy who works for you."

"You make him sound like a hired hand instead of my friend." His eyes had narrowed.

"You're misunderstanding everything I say!"

"Am I, Diana?"

"Why are you acting this way?" She swallowed hard around the growing lump in her throat and a sudden pain squeezed her heart. "What the hell did I ever do to make you so damn cold and remote?"

For all the attention Lije was giving to her questions she might as well not have asked. Exactly zip.

"Why did you tell Stacy things you should have discussed with me first?" he demanded.

"Is that what's bothering you? Just that I asked Stacy about what had helped her to adjust to ranch life?" She stared incredulously at him. "Last I heard, this is a free country and I'll ask anyone I like about whatever I want. Got that?"

He made no reply to any of it. "Guess Stacy prompted your sudden interest in seeing the ranch after you've been here more than a month," he muttered.

His sarcastic comment brought scarlet color to her cheeks. Put that way, it seemed like an unforgivable sin on her part. The ranch, with all its drawbacks, was his pride and joy, and she should have shown more interest, although Diana was too hurt to concede that.

"I don't understand you," she said softly.

"How could you?" There was a coolness in Lije's voice, and his expression could only be described as arrogant. "I guess I can answer that myself."

"Go ahead."

He gave her a defeated wave. "Out of the three days before we were married, we were only together exclusively about eight hours. So I can't really blame you for not figuring out whether you really want to spend the rest of your life with me. We hardly know each other and that's a fact."

"Are you trying to say that I made a mistake?" Her words were clipped and her tone was as cold as his.

"Maybe you didn't think it through, is all. Now, riding in rodeos, a man gets used to making split-second decisions that he doesn't get to take back."

She nodded slowly. "I understand, Lije. But I meant what I said when I married you. I'm not just going to blow out of here."

"I hope not. But telling Stacy you needed a car was over the line."

Diana was taken completely aback. "But I didn't—"

"Oh, she didn't say you'd said that, only that she had a friend who was going to donate a car to charity. She was chattering away." He made an airy motion with his fingers. "As if she just happened to think of someone who happened to have an extra car with four-wheel drive. It may not be new and shiny, but apparently it runs. She was sure her friend would have no problem with giving it to us instead."

"What?" Diana didn't know whether to be mad at him or Stacy.

"You know, that's the word that came out of my mouth too. But Stacy is the kind of gal who likes to get things done when they need to be done. So we are now officially a charity case."

"We can't turn it down, Lije." She wouldn't let him. Wheels of her own? She wouldn't have to rely on the guys for rides, wouldn't have to feel like she was imposing. Just because he thought the womenfolk were scheming behind his back was no reason to—that had to be what he was thinking.

"She's right, of course. And Cord thought it was a great idea. It just rankled me a little that I couldn't make that happen myself." He wearily rubbed a hand over the back of his neck. "But you need a car. So I guess we have to accept it when it gets here."

Diana didn't want to exult over something that he clearly had mixed feelings about. But she silently thanked Stacy about a million times in her head. Lije would get over his pride.

Chapter Nine

The morning sky was an immense stretch of startling blue that seemed to belong to an artist's canvas. The sun was a glaring yellow orb suspended over the distant mountains, casting long black shadows over the uneven terrain. A hawk soared lazily overhead, its wide wingspan catching the unseen wind currents. The coolness of the mountain night lingered, turning the warm breath of the horses in the corral to smoky puffs.

Diana's hands were shoved deep into the pockets of her jacket as she stared at the strange landscape. She felt an odd resentment that such a vast amount of space could constitute her prison walls. It wasn't as if she could escape. Lije had the pickup truck and Jim had the jeep.

The car still hadn't arrived, but Stacy's friend

had called. She'd let them know as soon as she fixed the—whatever it was that needed fixing.

Exhausted from nights of restless sleep, Diana had circles under her eyes, giving them a haunted look. Diana couldn't relax during the day, constantly driven by nervous energy that kept her physically active.

She stared at the weathered house and outbuildings in silence. A debate went on inside her as to whether to take the paint out of the storeroom and get started on the backbreaking job of painting them herself just for something to do. She vetoed it. Her husband probably had very particular ideas about how it should be done, and she couldn't just go sloshing paint on a whole damn building by herself just to show him that she knew how to do something useful.

She wandered to the rear of the house. Diana glanced down at her shiny brown shoes, the toes already showing a covering of pale dust.

Something like a smile came to her lips as she realized how out of place she was in this rugged, remote country.

The shoes were flat-heeled, practical enough for walking long blocks on city sidewalks, but they were useless in this terrain. Rocks and thorny bushes would scratch and permanently mar them in seconds. Even her pants wouldn't cut it out here—the material would snag on the first prickly twig she brushed against.

Okay, so that was easy to fix—all she had to do was go back into the house and change. But she felt an unreal sensation of wearing the right clothes against the wrong backdrop.

Her restless pace carried her to the rise in the land behind the house. A distant, spiky-leaved plant caught her eye, an instant reminder of Jim Two Pony's comparison of a yucca plant and a rose. His description certainly fit the plant she was looking at and she walked toward it for a closer inspection. There were no bell-shaped flowers on the stalk, only barely formed buds.

Farther on, there were a whole lot more of them, tough roots gripping a rocky hillside. Diana went that way, pausing once more to look back to make sure the house was in sight. The dark roof was plainly visible. A long-legged jackrabbit *boinged* away as Diana came close to a thick stand of brush. His hasty departure made her think of her own wish to flee her un-friendly surroundings as soon as possible.

With a resigned sigh, she continued on. The top of a larger hill promised a more encom-passing view of the land she was trying to per-suade herself to accept as home.

When Diana got to her new vantage point, she gazed out over the awesome expanse of wild land. Far, far away, she could see dark specks of slowly moving animals. Vaguely she remem-bered Lije saying that cattle were still pastured near the house and assumed that what she saw was part of the herd. Tiny against the vast landscape, the faraway cattle made her even more aware of her own insignificance, and a chill sent a shiver through her body despite the warmth of the sun. She again glanced back at the square building that was her home, so very different from what she'd dreamed of.

Diana had wandered as far from the house as she dared, and realized that now was the time to turn back, but she just couldn't face returning to the drab interior. It would only make her depression worse.

By nature, Diana had never been adventurous, even though she wasn't timid, but her situation seemed desperate. Stacy had suggested exploring the ranch, of course, but Diana hadn't wanted to all that much. Now she felt almost driven to do it, just to have a reason to stay outside. She went down a small draw at the base of the hill, sure she would only have to retrace her steps to be back at her starting point.

Nothing she now saw seemed familiar to her, except for the yucca plants that Jim Two Pony had described to her. The clumps of underbrush were a mystery to her. Ditto the birds—there wasn't a sign of a robin or blue jay or sparrow, or any other bird she knew. And she could only guess that the scrubby-looking trees she saw were some kind of pine.

The landscape was painted in earth tones,

from the dull dark green of the pine needles on umber-colored branches to the cinnamon- and ochre-colored rocks that studded the pale, sandy soil. Distant mountain peaks were a purple-brown, and the vivid blue of the sky and the yellow glint of the sun in her eyes were the only bold colors in the otherwise drab and somber land.

An animal trail led from the base of the draw to its rim some five feet above. Diana made her way warily up the steep incline, her mind on the critters that might have used it before her. Thinking of hungry coyotes and even mountain lions, Diana got something of a start when she reached the top and found herself staring at a white-faced cow. She took a hasty step back, nearly losing her balance before she stopped. The cow eyed her suspiciously for several seconds more, then it turned and trotted away. Not until it seemed like there was no chance of it returning did Diana expel the breath she'd unknowingly been holding.

It's just a cow, she thought. Not exactly dangerous and probably heading off to lie down somewhere out of the heat after the nasty surprise of seeing her pop up. She didn't turn back.

But the muscles in her calves were aching from climbing. To the right of where the cow had been standing was a jumble of rocks. One flat rock looked inviting, offering a relatively comfortable seat compared with the baked earth covered with scattered pebbles and stones and the prickly things growing among it all. When Diana climbed onto the rock, she discovered that while the rock rising behind it was jagged and rough, she could maneuver to avoid the sharper parts and settle into a backrest of sorts. The rays of the sun beat down and warmed the stone, which made it doubly relaxing. Leaning back, Diana closed her eyes and basked in the steady sunshine.

A tiny fly touched down on her cheek. Her hand moved up and brushed the pesky insect away, but it buzzed determinedly around her face. Blinking, Diana realized she'd dozed off. She glanced at her wrist before she realized that she'd left her watch on the counter by the kitchen sink.

It couldn't be that late, she thought. The sun didn't seem to have changed its position very much, hanging a little higher in the sky. A vague gnawing in her stomach confirmed her sense that it was right around lunchtime.

The path leading back down the draw was farther away than she'd thought. But the sun that had been over her shoulder during the first part of her hike was now shining in her eyes as she began to retrace her steps. Her legs were still a little stiff and she felt the beginnings of a blister on her heel. The nagging discomfort increased as she kept going down the draw, not seeing the hill that would bring her in sight of the house. If it wasn't for the sun shining reassuringly in front of her, she would have been willing to believe that she'd taken a wrong turn and was lost in this rough country.

The teasing breeze carried a sound to her. At first Diana had the strange feeling that someone had called her name, but then she chalked it up to a bird call. A little while later, the rhythmic and muffled hoofbeats—of a wild horse? a cow?—coming her way from behind reached her ears. With the memory of her encounter with the cow still fresh in her mind, she paused and turned. She brushed feathery strands of blond hair away from her eyes as she peered in the direction of the sound.

The walls of the narrowing draw gave the illusion of leaning in. But maybe it wasn't an illusion. That she was an obstacle in the path of an unknown critter that was definitely on the big side made her panic a little. Diana raced to the side, looking desperately for a foothold or handhold that would take her to the top, but her inexperienced eyes saw none. Glancing nervously over her shoulder at the bend in the draw, she saw a horse and rider come around it. Her thudding heart finally slowed.

"Lije!" she called, relieved to see him.

"What the hell are you doing?" he barked, reining his horse to a stop beside her and glowering down at her upturned face.

Startled, Diana couldn't bring herself to tell

him that she'd been about to claw her way out of the draw. He wasn't in a mood to laugh anything off.

"I was going for a walk. It turned into a hike, I guess." In spite of her resolve to keep things light, a defensive note crept into her voice.

"Any particular destination in mind?" Lije asked grimly. "Or were you just wandering in the wilderness? That's not a good idea, in case you don't know it."

"As a matter of fact, I was just on my way back to the house." She realized that sounded a little ridiculous, as if all she had to do was stroll on neat blocks of pavement to get there, instead of scramble over arid, unforgiving land that held too many surprises for her.

"The house is that way." He pointed in the direction he had just come.

"That's impossible." A troubled, disbelieving expression creased her forehead. "The sun was behind me when I started out and now it's in front of me."

"What time is it?"

"I . . . I left my watch by the sink."

He gave a slight, disapproving shake of his head. "It happens to be two PM. The sun moves to the west in the afternoon."

Her mouth opened and closed as she tried to think of some reply that wouldn't make her sound as ignorant as she was.

"Do you have any idea how close you came

to being really lost?" Lije demanded. Mutely, Diana nodded as the realization began to sink in. "If I hadn't come back to the house at noon—or if I hadn't been able to find you—" He left the thought hanging in the air. "Damn it, Diana! What if I'd come back after sundown? Didn't you even notice that you weren't going back the same way?"

"Everything out here looks strange to me." She cast her eyes down, suddenly feeling like she was going to cry, hating the powerless feeling of being scolded, even though he was right.

The creak of saddle leather announced that Lije was dismounting. Diana didn't feel any safer as he towered beside her.

"Hey . . ." He said the one word softly and put a hand on her shoulder.

She shrugged it off, hard. "Don't touch me!" All the emotions she'd been holding back— and her frustration—gave an edge to her curt reply.

He stepped back as if she'd slapped him. "I haven't touched you for nearly a week."

She gave him a mutinous glare, taking another jab at what was obviously a sore point. It was kind of nice to know that the mighty Lije Masters actually wanted something from her.

"It's amazing you could suppress—" Diana began sarcastically, only to be interrupted by a muttered curse from Lije before his mouth covered hers.

The strength of his embrace didn't hold the slightest hint of passion or desire. Diana was right up against the granite-hard muscles of his chest and her arms were pinned to her sides. There was no escaping that kiss. It was an odd sensation, and she was pretty damn sure she didn't like it.

Done with whatever he was trying to prove, he let her go. Then she was standing free, breathing hard.

"Don't you ever do that again," she snapped.

"What? Kiss you? I don't understand," he said blandly.

"You know exactly what I mean. Don't kiss me like that."

"Yes, ma'am. Sorry about that. Never again."

She thought of a few angry, spiteful comebacks, but somehow the words got stuck in her throat. Turning quickly, Diana stalked off, not thinking about which way she was going or the terrain.

"Unless you're running away, the house is still in the opposite direction."

His soft voice brought her up short. But her pride refused to let her turn around. It was foolish to keep on going and get herself lost.

"Diana, we've both been under a lot of pressure in the last few days. And we both exploded. Let's leave it at that." Even though his tone was quiet, it was commanding all the same. "I want you to walk back to the house with me."

She knew it was the closest to an apology she was going to get under the circumstances. She had to admit that a lot of her anger had been caused by tension and frustration. But all the logical thinking that her brain did was offset by the smoldering resentment still seething in her heart. Diana walked back to him anyway, refusing to meet his eyes or look at him even when he turned away from her to take the reins of his horse, leading it as they started back.

The silence between them was magnified by the shuffling sound of the horse's hooves on the sandy ground. The stubborn set of her chin and her squared shoulders were physical reminders of the way she'd acted as a child, when she'd been hurt by those she had wanted to please. A capricious wind played with the long, silken strands of her hair while someone's gray eyes watched.

"The next time you go for a walk, I suggest you pick out landmarks. Could be a mountain peak, a rock formation or a twisted pine tree, just so long as you remember it. Then when you've walked past the thing, turn around and see what it looks like from the opposite direction. Leave a note for me to say which way you're headed too. As in north, south, east, west. Just don't go wandering off like that again, Diana."

She nodded briskly. It wasn't necessary to add that at the moment more explorations were the last thing on her mind.

"Everything's done for my trip. I have to pick up the health certificates on the horses this afternoon, which means I'll be leaving the day after tomorrow to deliver the horses to Cord," Lije went on. "Will you be all right while I'm gone?"

His solicitous question seemed kind of funny. She let her gaze move up to his.

"I managed by myself for quite a few years." Her voice sounded colder and more independent than Diana meant it to be, but she didn't regret it, not even when he regarded her through narrowed eyes.

"When I get back, I'll take you on that tour of the ranch." He didn't seem any more enthusiastic than she was. "Oh, and I almost forgot. Stacy's friend is going to bring the car. She'll call you. Or you can call her. I took down the number. You two figure it out." He reached in his pocket and handed her a torn piece of paper.

Diana felt almost like flinging it back in his face when suddenly a voice came from the hilltop where her walk had started.

"You found her already," Jim Two Pony said.

"She hadn't gone very far," Lije replied. Diana looked at the two in tight-lipped silence. "She was walking along the wash."

"It isn't good for her to wander out of sight of the house." The Navajo fell into step beside

Lije as they topped the rise and started down toward the dark roof of the house.

"I think she learned her lesson."

"Will you two stop talking about me as if I weren't here?" Diana demanded. "Or do both of you really think that I'm clueless?"

Not waiting for a reply, she quickened her pace, getting ahead of them. Any moment she expected Lije to catch up with her and tell her what he thought of her rudeness, but he didn't.

A dreary gray dawn muted the morning calls of the early-rising birds as Lije rechecked the lashings of the horses in the van before locking the door. What was left of the night's nip in the air made his actions hurried.

Keep moving. That sounded like a plan.

Diana watched his progress from the kitchen window, her quilted robe clutched together tightly with one hand. When he turned toward the house, she busied herself with the coffeepot, pouring herself a cup and retreating to the table. A rush of cold air raced in as Lije came in the door.

"Do you want another cup of coffee before you leave?" Diana asked quietly, observing the unspoken rules of their truce.

He stood just inside the door, his cynical gaze taking her in. "No." He reached for the thermos sitting on the counter near the door. "It's time for me to leave."

Yet he made no move toward the door. Diana knew what he was thinking—that she didn't have the nerve to carry out the mockery of their good-bye to its final stage. Striving to seem unemotional about it, she got up and walked to him for what she hoped would be a casual farewell, but wishing he would take her in his arms and kiss her the way he used to do.

"Drive carefully, Lije," she said, rising on tiptoe to brush her lips against his.

Before she could step away, his hand came out to rest on the side of her neck, tilting her chin up. The kiss he gave her was possessive and sensual, as if he wanted to remind her that she belonged to him for more than one reason.

"I'll be back in about four days. Try to miss me while I'm gone."

There was another rush of cold air and Lije was out the door, striding briskly to the pickup truck and its horse van hitched behind. He didn't give her a backward glance or final wave as she watched him leave. It was really hard to ignore the aching void he left in her heart, regardless of any petty quarrel they'd had. Both of them just had too much pride.

Surprisingly the morning hours passed rather swiftly, mostly because Diana tried to convince herself that Lije was only out on the range and not journeying away from her. After a lunch of a green salad with cheese and crackers, she spread out a jigsaw puzzle that she'd found several weeks ago in one of the trunks in the attic. It was a gigantic picture of a European cathedral, with myriad tiny pieces in tan and gold.

In only a matter of moments, Diana was completely engrossed in the puzzle's complexities, so completely that she didn't hear the arrival of a car in the ranch yard. The loud rap on the door startled her right out of the chair and she walked hesitantly to the door. In all the time she had lived on the ranch there hadn't been a single visitor other than Cord and Stacy. People calling for business reasons—a rare occurrence— usually met Lije out in the ranch buildings, discussed whatever it was that had brought them and then left.

So it was with a mixture of excitement and curiosity that Diana opened the door. A man of medium height and build, dressed casually, stood with his back to the door surveying the ranch buildings. A cream-colored Stetson was pushed back on his head.

"Can I help you?" Diana asked. Her question brought the man around with a start.

He had a wide, friendly face with dancing brown eyes, in his late twenties by her guess.

"I heard Masters had married, but no one told me his wife was so damn pretty," the man drawled softly as his gaze roamed over her in respectful admiration. He reached up and deftly removed his hat while he extended his right hand to her. "My name is Ty Spalding. I own about the only well-drilling rig around these parts."

"Pleased to meet you, Mr. Spalding."

"I stopped out to let Lije know that my rig will be free all this week."

"I'm sorry, he isn't here."

"Maybe I could check with him this evening. I know he wanted a new well drilled in the turtle-back out in the south section."

"Actually, Lije is out of town. He won't be back for a couple of days," Diana explained. "I'm sure my husband probably discussed it with our foreman, though."

"You mean the Indian?"

Diana found herself flinching at the man's condescending tone. "Yes, Jim Two Pony. He's in charge while Lije is gone."

"Well, where could I find him?" He frowned as he looked over the ranch yard.

"Not sure. He's out on the range somewhere checking fences. He might or might not be back for supper."

"Here's my card with my contact info." He reached in his pocket and handed it to her. "Have him give me a call when he gets back."

Diana smiled, glancing down at the card. "I'll do that, Mr. Spalding."

"The name is Ty, ma'am." The cream hat was set back on his head at a rakish angle. "Very nice to meet you. I hope I get to see more of you in the future."

Diana realized the man was flirting with her. But he'd been fairly discreet about it, so she didn't feel creeped out. More like complimented. Her ego had been a bit deflated, but this stranger had just given it the boost it needed.

She stood in the door until Ty Spalding got behind the wheel of his car and drove off.

Chapter Ten

Stacy's friend, whose name was Lisa Griswold, didn't call until later that night and promised to bring the car around ten AM. That meant more waiting, but Diana didn't care. She got up early the next day, feeling good about life, and got busy. Not with the housework. That could wait. She did some basic stretches and aerobic moves that she remembered from her gym classes, then found some music with a beat and put it on, jumping around until she was sweaty.

She was determined to get in that car and drive off this mountain by herself and do what she wanted and then . . . come back. Just thinking about it was heaven.

There were two cars, of course, when Lisa finally arrived at eleven, at the wheel of the first one. She seemed genuinely nice, but that was no surprise, considering how nice Stacy was.

"Sorry it's so banged up," she said, patting the hood. "But it runs good. If it ever gives you trouble, I'm sure Lije or Jim can fix it for you."

"I'm sure too. I can't thank you enough, Lisa. I've been out here on my own and—"

"Oh, I know what it's like to be stuck out in the boonies," she said cheerfully. "Stacy does too. You can go nuts, especially if you didn't grow up around here and didn't know what you were getting into."

Diana felt a little guilty but not all that much. She gave an inward sigh of relief that it wasn't just her and it wasn't all in her head. "If there's anything I can do for you," she began.

Lisa grinned. "Stacy said you were a model. Maybe you can give me a makeover someday."

Her friend in the other car, a plump woman with carrot-colored ringlets, hollered, "Me too!"

"Sure," Diana said.

"All right, now, simmer down," Lisa called back. She extracted the registration and the title and the rest of the paperwork—including a thick, battered owner's manual with work receipts falling out of it—and handed the bundle to Diana. "I think this is everything. I shoulda used an envelope to hold it all, but we were already so late—"

"It's no problem," Diana said, holding the papers and manual tightly together so the wind wouldn't blow it all away.

"Oh, and the insurance on it is good for

another two weeks. I put you on as an alternate driver. So you can go ahead and make the transfer. There's an insurance agent right in town, that's her card right there clipped to the manual. Just drop in. If she's not in the office, she's at the mercantile or in the café. Give a holler in both places."

"I will. Thank you—you don't know what this means to me." Tears welled in Diana's eyes.

"Actually, I do," was all Lisa Griswold would say. She gave Diana an awkward hug that enfolded her and all the papers she was now holding, then headed for the car where her ringleted friend was waiting.

She turned around, lifting her closed fingers high in the air. "Forgot to give you the keys!" She tossed them and Diana didn't fumble. The keys were spiky and heavy in her hand but it was a great feeling.

"Come on!" the other woman yelled. "Getting up that dirt road was hard enough. I'm not looking forward to the ride back down and I'm late for my appointment."

"What appointment?" Lisa asked her, getting in and waving to Diana.

"With destiny," her friend teased her. "We all have an appointment with destiny every day, whether we know it or not."

Diana stood there and listened to Lisa laugh, with her friend joining in raucously until the sound disappeared.

Then she went in, put the documents in some kind of order, shoved them into an envelope, grabbed her purse and went back out to her brand-new old car.

She dashed back in to leave a note for Jim, telling him where she was going. No sense in looking for trouble, as Stacy had said.

Then she got in the car and just sat there in the enfolding warmth of the interior, soaking it up for a minute. Freedom felt *good*. She wasn't going to waste a minute of it.

Just like the two women who'd departed before her, Diana found the rutted road was tough to drive on. She had to hang on tight to the steering wheel to keep the tires where they should be, meaning not too close to the steep-walled side and not too close to the crumbling shoulder. She lurched in and out of ruts, braking hard.

You can do this, she told herself. What goes up must come down. At one point, after she had slowed to go around a turn, the car stalled, and her heart sank. She put the lever in PARK, waited for a few minutes, then started the engine again. It rumbled to life with no problem.

"Good car. Nice car. I love you, car," she said, patting the dashboard before putting the lever in DRIVE and resuming her bumpy ride.

She felt a twinge of nervousness wondering if Lije would change his mind and get upset because she'd accepted the car without him getting a chance to look it over. But hey—Lisa Griswold had gotten it up here and Diana couldn't see ever telling her thanks-but-no-thanks for the wonderful gift. She squelched her misgivings. Lije would have to get over himself. This car wasn't a luxury. What if something happened to him and Jim wasn't around or vice versa? They needed a third vehicle, period.

Without one . . . She reminded herself of what Lisa had said: *"You can go nuts, especially if you didn't grow up around here and didn't know what you were getting into."*

When the road got easier she sang, softly at first, then on the loud side. The occasional bump provided an interesting effect, like a hiccup, that made her grin. She knew she was getting giddy, but it sure beat sitting around and feeling sorry for herself.

Eventually she jolted onto a road that was paved, feeling very grateful to whoever had invented asphalt. Diana headed for Ventana, not seeing anyone else on the road.

She made a mental list of everything she was going to do. Insurance first.

The older woman who handled the transaction was as kind to her as the proprietor of the mercantile had been. She did have to ask Diana a lot of questions, but the requisite forms were quickly filled out and she told Lisa where to file the transfer of title with the New Mexico Department of Motor Vehicles, and that she could apply for a new driver's license while she was there.

That she decided to leave for another day, because it involved a fair amount of driving and she was happy just to be off the ranch.

She was going to do ordinary things that seemed suddenly wonderful to her. Walk down the street. Shop for five or six items, treats for herself that she could carry easily, not ten tons of canned goods and frozen meat. Look in windows of the one gift shop and not buy anything.

When she was done with all that, she realized she was walking by the office of the *Bee-Gazette* again, and took a free paper, sitting down to read it this time. Nothing much had changed since she'd read the last one. In fact she suspected that she might be reading the exact same paper.

Diana opened it to the middle pages, looking for the classifieds again. It was amazing how interesting they were, maybe mostly because there was no Internet. She perused the listings of *"Cute-kitten-free-to-good-home"* and *"Sofa-like-new-must-sell"* ads, and then glanced at the personals just out of habit.

Dear Momma: Thanks for taking care of that herd of grandkids for me and Jeff. You earned

*the vacation of your dreams ten times over. Stop
in at the travel agency and get the details. Your
loving daughter, Janey.*

Aww. She could just see Momma and Janey
hugging each other. The next one made her
laugh out loud.

*Rugged outdoorsman looking for a reliable
woman. Can you gut a trout and portage a
canoe? Heading way up north to the Boundary
Waters for fun 'n' fishin'. Reply with photo to
Fred, Box XYZ at the* Bee-Gazette.

She had to wonder if there would be any
takers and felt sorry for Old Reliable, if she existed.

Love out here in the sticks was a little different, that was for damn sure. But at least Lije
didn't expect her to carry canoes around,
not that there was any water deep enough to
paddle around in. Besides, she doubted he'd be
comfortable in a canoe, or anywhere except on
horseback.

Diana thought about the first time she'd seen
him—man and horse had seemed like one.
She'd fallen head over heels in love with a hard-
riding, independent-minded cowboy, and he
wasn't going to change.

She might have to. Yes, she and Lije had had
a rocky go of it after their whirlwind romance

and tearing out here, but maybe that was to be expected. Just this small taste of freedom gave her a better perspective on all that.

She closed the paper and turned it over, noticing the advice column on the back: "Ask Aunty Bee." She scanned the advice on relationships and marriage.

Aunty Bee had a pretty good sense of humor, Diana decided after she read it. She looked at the picture of an apple-cheeked woman with her hair in a short brown bob and smiled.

The column answers were short and snappy. There couldn't really *be* an Aunty Bee, she thought. Then she looked up and around, remembering how close she was to the newspaper's office. She could just go in and ask. Ventana was that kind of town.

Diana got up, swinging her car keys but keeping her thumb securely through the ring so she wouldn't lose them. The newspaper she tucked under her arm, grabbing her shoulder bag and putting it on first. She walked to the storefront that was the newspaper office and went in.

The interior had been meticulously restored. Its hardwood paneling and trim gleamed around her and reflected the inlaid marble floor. She didn't see or hear anyone, so she walked around the foyer, looking at the framed front pages of important dates and events in New Mexico history. Sometimes the old front pages were from the *Bee,* sometimes the *Gazette,* and at a certain point, they were from the merged version of the two papers.

"Thought I heard somebody out here. May I help you, miss?" a gruff voice inquired.

Diana nearly jumped out of her shoes. "Oh— I just wandered in. I was looking at your front pages. They're very interesting." She looked at the man who had spoken. He was probably about eighty, but clearly he had once been a cowboy. She knew enough about the breed by now to make an accurate guess on that. He had pure white hair and eyes that were light brown behind his glasses, and was strongly built for all his years, with broad shoulders and a barrel chest.

The man laughed. "You think so? That's nice to hear. They're about the only things in this town older'n me. Thank you, young lady."

She smiled at him and reached out a hand to shake, which was when she saw what his hands gripped. A walker.

"Sorry, can't let go," he said without a trace of self-pity. "But come on in. I guess you must want to place an ad."

"Um, no—" she began. But he had already turned and was evidently heading for the office she hadn't seen him come out of.

She followed him, watching as he seated himself again with some difficulty, using his arms more than his legs. "I have MS," he explained.

"It's a bear. But what can you do? It ain't too bad in my case."

"N-nothing, I guess." She didn't know what to say or much about MS, for that matter, but she sure as hell admired his fortitude.

"So." He took a pencil from an old shaving cup that was full of them. "What are you selling?"

"I'm not selling anything"—she glanced at his nameplate. Herbert Bigelow. She finished with, "but it's very nice to meet you, Mr. Bigelow."

"Nice to meet you. You can call me Herb."

"I'm Diana Mills—I mean, Diana Masters."

"Aha." His eyes twinkled. "You the one who married that Masters boy?"

"Ah, he's not a boy, but, yes, I did."

"Guess I still think of him as a wild kid," the old man said with gruff fondness. "But he done all right. We're proud of him around here, winning all those rodeo purses. Of course, he hasn't been around much in the last several years." He eyed her shrewdly. "Guess that's changed, now that he's got you. Welcome to Ventana, Mrs. Masters."

She blushed. How long would it be until she got used to hearing that? Coming from Lije, it had sounded so sweet at first. And then . . . well. She straightened in her chair, not wanting to dwell on that aspect of their life together.

"Thank you. I like it here." The newspaper fell out from under her arm and she reached down to the floor to get it. "And I really enjoy this little newspaper."

Oops, wrong word, she thought instantly. Never tell a man that anything about him is little. Even if he's a hundred and five.

But Herb Bigelow seemed pleased with the comment. "Well, we try to make it an enjoyable mix of local news and human-interest stories."

"It works. And that column in the back— I was laughing over Aunty Bee's answers to everybody," she said. "Actually, that was why I came in. I was going to ask if she was real."

"Of course she is."

He gave her a look of mock indignation and Diana wasn't sure if he was pulling her leg.

"You mean—" she began hesitantly.

"I'm Aunty Bee. I took over the column from the gal who wrote it, when she retired to Key West."

"You?"

He nodded and laughed. "Why not? A man my age has seen it all and done it all. And I like to hear myself talk, or so says my darling wife, Dottie. She encouraged me to do it."

"Oh." Diana was still surprised.

He leaned back in his chair, folding his arms over his midsection. "It's easy to write. People aren't getting any smarter. They make the same mistakes over and over, so my side of it is variations on a theme."

"I see."

He laughed in a kindly way. "So how do you like married life?"

"Oh, I like it just fine," she hastened to assure him. "We're adjusting to each other and—and to our new lives."

"I happened to hear that he was giving up rodeo," Herb said.

"That was the plan. The ranch means so much to him. When we first met, he told me all about growing up out here and how much he loves the wilderness."

The old man gave her an appraising look, as if he were wondering whether she did too.

"New Mexico is beautiful," she said quickly. "Where we are is kind of lonesome sometimes, but I'll get used to it."

"That can take a while," Herb said sagely.

"Well, there's lots to do," she assured him, not wanting to sound like a whiner. "Mostly I've been cooking and reading and trying to decide which project to tackle first as far as fixing up the house—"

She stopped herself, not wanting to chatter too much.

"Do you ride? That's the best way to see the country."

"No, I don't. Lije just about lives in the saddle, of course. He's gone most of the day."

Herb Bigelow nodded thoughtfully.

"But I expect he'll teach me as soon as he can," she said firmly. "I'd like to learn. Although

I'm not ever going to be on his level—I've seen him in action." She laughed.

"So you two met at the rodeo?"

"Yes, we did." A sudden thought occurred to her. "You're not going to put this in the paper, are you?"

Herb Bigelow chuckled. "Not unless you and Lije want me to. This is just a friendly conversation, not an interview. Though I would like to run a formal announcement of your marriage, even though everybody's heard of it, anyway. Just send me the particulars."

She gave him a worried look. "Oh. Well, we just drove down to Juarez, so it, uh, happened in a hurry. We hadn't known each other that long but we were crazy in love . . ." She trailed off, not wanting to say the words in her mind.

It seemed like enough. And it was real. Is real. But once you're married, things change.

That was true enough. But at the moment she was feeling a lot more hopeful. Diana just couldn't explain everything to Herb Bigelow, who, after all, had known her husband longer than she had. A lot longer.

"That's how it was for me and Dottie," he was saying. "We've been married for fifty-four years." His eyes twinkled warmly as he glanced at a picture of an older woman with beautifully styled white hair and sparkling eyes. "I still don't know what she sees in me."

Diana envied the Bigelows a little. Was it

possible that what she and Lije had would last that long? Maybe their marriage was too new to tell.

"Anyway, the women of Ventana would be happy to read all about it," Herb said. "But that's up to you."

"I'll talk to Lije," she promised vaguely.

He picked up his pencil and twiddled it. "You could place a little personal ad for him, send him a message if you like. He'd get a kick out of it."

She nodded her head, smiling faintly. "You know, he might." Diana didn't think Lije had a free minute to peruse the paper, but why hurt Mr. Bigelow's feelings? "Sure, I'll think about it."

"On the house," Herb offered. "Newlywed special. I'd bet my last nickel you two don't have a dime to spare."

Coming from him, the blunt comment seemed kind.

"Well, no, we don't." She took a deep breath and an explanation rushed out when she let it go. "The ranch house needs a lot of work and I just acquired a car for free but I paid for six months' insurance in advance. That put a dent in my bank account and I'm not sure how I'm going to make it up, because it stalled on the way down the mountain, so it's probably going to need repairs—"

"Whoa." He looked at her curiously. "You

sound like you've been dying to tell someone all that."

"Oh. Did I? Sorry to bend your ear."

"I don't mind," he said amiably. "I was just thinking that you must not get out much, that's all."

"No. Not lately. I mean, I haven't been at the ranch that long, but that's why a—a friend of a friend gave me the car." More words tumbled out in a cheerful rush. This nice old man didn't need to hear any complaining from her.

"Makes sense to me. You don't want to get too isolated, that's not good for anybody. You know, Lije's momma used to drive a truck that was one of the first Fords around here, up and down that dirt road, going like blazes. She was fearless. Whatever it was, she did it with all her heart. Raising her boy. Throwing barbecues for a hundred people. Growing roses where roses weren't meant to grow—yep, she saved bathwater and lugged it out there by the side of the house—" He stopped himself, winking at her. "Just listen to me, going on and on. I expect Lije told you all that, anyway."

She pressed her lips together. "Not so much. But I guess he will. Well, I'd better be getting back. I'm taking up too much of your time." She got up, and this time he extended both his hands and clasped hers.

"No, you ain't," the old cowboy said indignantly. "You stop in again, whenever you like, and tell Lije to do the same. Dottie's baking this week. If he wants a slice of peach pie, he better hustle over an' get some before I eat it all. You come too."

"I will, Mr. Bigelow."

"Herb! The name is Herb!" he barked.

"Herb. Thanks again. Don't get up—"

Oh, geez. Why had she said that stupid catch-phrase?

"I had no intention of it. But you know I would if I could," Herb said. "Hell, I'd do the Texas two-step with Dottie until the sun comes up if I could. But I cain't."

He grinned at her and she waved good-bye, feeling like she'd made a friend. Something about his indomitable spirit and twangy voice reminded her an awful lot of Lefty. "See you soon."

Chapter Eleven

The next day . . .

It was after seven o'clock before Diana saw the jeep parked near the barn, a sign that Jim Two Pony had returned. The dinner had been kept warm on the stove for the past half hour. From the kitchen window, she saw that Jim was preparing to feed the horses, which meant nearly another hour before he was done.

Okay. She got the message. With a sigh of irritation, she walked to the closet and took off her jacket.

Her temper was simmering when she walked into the barn where Jim was methodically measuring grain into a collection of buckets. She stopped a couple of feet away.

"Dinner's ready, Jim," she said, striving to keep her voice calm.

"I thought it would be best if I ate at my place while Lije is gone," he replied, not a break in the rhythm of his work.

"Lije didn't mention that." She mused, looking at him, about how difficult it was to talk to someone who refused to look at you. Relying on Jim for casual conversation wasn't going to happen. Well, at least she knew a couple of other people in the area now.

The thought made her feel like she could at least cope. There was Lisa Griswold and her friend, who she didn't think was named Destiny, but it was an easy way to remember her. And Herbert Bigelow.

All of whom were in Ventana at the moment and not here. Diana reminded herself that there were worse things in life than not getting everything she wanted at the second she wanted it.

Jim still didn't look at her. "It was my decision," he said.

"I wish you'd told me. I made a ton of food and I can't eat it all by myself."

"That's what refrigerators are for," he said quietly. "Besides, the horses have to be fed first. They can't just walk to a table and pick up a knife and fork."

She fumed. It did no good. "When you're done, the food is on the stove." Exasperation edged her voice. "In another forty-five minutes it will be dried up."

"The horses have to be fed. They should

have been given their grain an hour ago," Jim answered stubbornly.

"What has to be done? Maybe I can help." Diana didn't know what prompted her unchar-acteristic offer, but the sudden gleam in Jim Two Pony's dark eyes led her to believe that he expected her to take it back.

"You can take these portions of grain and put one in the manger bins at each stall," he suggested.

Diana hesitated for only a second before reaching down and picking up two of the buck-ets. Eager, tossing heads leaned as far over the stalls as wood partitions permitted. The simple task of emptying the grain from the buckets into the square bins required that Diana put her arms in the stalls, brushing against the horses' heads as they pushed and butted to get their meal.

She eyed the first horse nervously. It looked gentle enough. Taking a deep breath, she pushed the bucket past the inquiring nose and dumped it into the bin. The horse completely ignored her in favor of the tasty grain. Diana was filled with triumphant glee when she re-turned to get more buckets of grain, but Jim didn't seem to notice. He had finished measur-ing the nutritious mixture and was busy tossing hay into the larger manger bins.

"Hey, I almost forgot. A man named Ty Spal-ding stopped by the other day to see Lije," Diana said to Jim, raising her voice a little since he was several feet away. "He said something about drilling a well here on the ranch? Wants you to call him."

"Spalding was here?" Jim looked at her thoughtfully.

"Yes. I got the idea that he was expected. Didn't Lije mention it to you? About the drilling?"

"We talked about it, yeah. Spalding told him that his rig wouldn't be available for another week," Jim answered, resuming his distribution of the hay.

"Oh. Well, he told me that it was going to be free all this week." Diana emptied the bucket of grain and turned with a flourish. "Is there a problem?"

"No. It just woulda been better if Lije were here to talk to Spalding." Jim shrugged, as if that were all he had to say about it.

"Okay, well, I guess they'll connect at some point. Are we ready to eat now?" Diana cocked her head. There was a trace of defiance in her stance.

"There's still the stallion to be fed."

"While you do that, I'll go see if I can save the food."

There was the faintest trace of a smile around Jim's mouth as he nodded. "I'll be up when I'm finished."

Keeping the conversation going had been an

effort. Diana had thought for a moment or two that being in the barn and working in harmony might close the distance between them.

But no. Not yet. Maybe if they talked about something else . . . something besides the ranch or Lije.

Later, as they sat at the kitchen table eating, "Do you have any family, Jim?" she asked, looking at him to see if the question made him uncomfortable. She wouldn't pursue it if so, but it didn't seem like it. His expression was about the same. "Brothers? Sisters?"

"Nope. Got a passel of aunts and uncles and cousins, though."

"Where do they live? Do you get a chance to visit them very often?"

"They live on the rez, out in Arizona." He didn't specify which one. "I haven't seen them for several years. Not since my mother died."

Slowly, asking questions that weren't phrased like questions so she wouldn't seem too nosy, Diana was able to get more information out of Jim Two Pony. None of his answers was ever specific, but she did get an idea of his early life. It was after his father's death in a truck crash that he'd come to this ranch, where his mother worked as a housekeeper and cook, as well as looked after Lije. Jim seemed disinclined to reminisce the way Lije did, summing it up simply that they had grown up together. Diana didn't learn much that was new, but she did manage to get through his reserve, and that was a start.

When the meal was finished—he seemed to like it and he ate a lot—and she was clearing it away, Jim went into the living room to call Ty Spalding. He was quiet as usual, very quiet. She didn't hear him hang up the phone or walk into the kitchen and out the door. Only the click of the latch signaled that he'd left— apparently not for good, because a few minutes later Diana heard him pounding away with a hammer outside. Wiping her hands on a dish- towel, she walked to the door to see what he was up to. He was standing on a ladder hanging something on a heavy-timbered, open frame- work that projected from the side of the house.

Puzzled, Diana went to get her jacket, then joined him.

"What are you doing?" In the dusky twilight, she tried to discern what was in his hands.

He didn't answer until he'd finished what he was doing and was heading down the ladder. Then she saw the thick rope dangling from a large bell mounted on the framework.

"The sound of a bell ringing carries a long way out here," he said quietly. "If you ever need Lije or me when we're out on the range, you just ring that bell. You don't need to holler and you don't need no electricity. It works every time."

For a moment Diana was at a loss for words. It

was such a simple gesture of practical kindness on his part that she didn't know quite how to react. Here was her bond to them, a reliable means of communication when she was left alone for hours at the ranch house. Even though she had the car now, knowing the bell was there gave her a deep sense of security.

"Thank you," she whispered, her emotions obvious in those two little words.

His bronze hand touched his hat, then he gathered his tools and the ladder and faded into the darkening twilight. Diana felt infinitely safer just looking up at the faint, burnished gleam of the silent bell. She was still smiling serenely when she walked back into the house.

The morning sun broke with brilliant radiance on the eastern horizon. Its rays warmed her. She took in the glorious sight, thinking of it as a promise of happiness, renewed and strong.

Rolling clouds of dust acted like old-timey smoke signals to announce the arrival of a vehicle in the ranch yard. Matching the eagerness of the sun to rise, Diana looked toward the car, recognizing it almost instantly as Ty Spalding's.

She didn't mind. It was nice to have visitors, especially someone as affable as Ty. Only in passing did she wonder why he'd come to the house instead of joining his crew at the drilling site.

"Good morning!" she called out as the car slowed to a stop a few feet away. "And isn't it a beautiful one?"

"It does make you believe spring is just on the other side of that mountain." He'd gotten out, but he seemed to want to look at her more than he did the gold-splashed sky.

"Jim told me that he was meeting your crew to take them out to the drilling site."

"Yeah, he is. I was just heading out there myself, but I thought I'd stop and—" He looked her over. "The truth is I stopped because after I left you I really couldn't believe you were as beautiful as you appeared to be. Thought afterward you could be a vision. Things like that happen in the Land of Enchantment, you know."

What a sweet-talker. But she still enjoyed hearing it. His open admiration was a balm, compared to the enigmatic remoteness of her husband, who wasn't here to scoff at Spalding's obvious flattery.

"Aw, shucks." She couldn't think of anything remotely intelligent to say. But she didn't want Ty to get too carried away, either.

"You know, I can't bring myself to call you Mrs. Masters."

"Why?" There was no harm in playing along.

"In the first place, because you're married, which I would prefer to forget. And second, because I'd like to find out what name goes with that face."

"Diana."

"Aha. The name of a goddess. Why am I not surprised?" Ty widened his eyes.

Wow. He was laying it on thick, Diana thought. But what the hell. Words were harmless. Let him talk. No, let him flirt, she corrected herself. You do know the difference.

"Well, Diana, you can put Ty Spalding on the list with all your other admirers."

"Hey, I'm sorry, Ty, but I can't do that." She put on a fake-regretful expression for his benefit. "Since I got married, I only keep a list of my friends."

"That's a pity. So I'm relegated to the fence?"

"It's either the fence or the gate."

A rueful yet respectful gleam entered his eyes at her statement. "In that case, you tell those other fence-sitters to move over, 'cause I'm climbin' on."

"Sure will, friend." Diana smiled, holding out her hand to him, which he shook with a warm grasp. "Do you know that when you stopped by the other day, you were the first person I've met from around here?"

"That's a shame! But I count myself lucky, real lucky."

"Well," she said, smiling, "I have met a few people in town, though."

He nodded, not asking her who they were or

why she'd been in Ventana. "Come spring and summer is when the social whirl begins here, and you're bound to get caught up in it. New girl that you are."

"I can't imagine anything much going on around here." She laughed.

"Okay, I exaggerated some," Ty admitted. "But in our country way, we do all right."

"In that case, come up to the house and have coffee and sweet rolls while you tell me all about it."

As they walked there, Ty gave her an obviously embellished account of the doings in the area. She'd thought at their first meeting that Ty Spalding could really turn on the charm when he wanted to, and she'd been right. Over coffee, his lighthearted talk kept a smile on her face, and Diana felt more at ease with herself than she had since the first day she'd set foot on the ranch.

"Pardon the pun, but how did Lije manage to 'master' you, Mrs. Masters?" His engaging smile was easy to return.

"He just swept me off my feet," Diana replied mischievously, the glow that only Lije could give her lighting her eyes all over again.

"I should say how lucky he was." Ty chuckled. "But Lije Masters is a man who makes his own luck. Ever since I can remember he's always been king of the mountain. Guess it was inevitable that he would come home someday with a fair-haired queen." His eyes flicked around the kitchen. "Got any plans to redo the castle? It sure could use it."

Diana suddenly remembered exactly how ugly it'd seemed to her when she first saw it. Pride wouldn't let her say that they couldn't afford to rip it out and start over from the walls out. She said something noncommittal in reply.

"You could do it. Women amaze me. Give a girl some paint in a pretty color and fabric to match, and you got yourself a whole new room. On any budget, mind you."

His casual statement inspired her. She looked around the kitchen, trying to visualize the freshness of new paint and crisp curtains. Her mental redecorating was interrupted by a knock at the door. When Diana recovered her wits enough to get up to answer it, she was surprised to see Jim Two Pony standing outside. He never knocked. The question in his dark eyes puzzled her even more.

"Come in." She stepped aside.

"I noticed Mr. Spalding's car outside." Jim ventured no farther than just inside the door. His gaze moved from Diana to the man leaning back in his chair. "I thought maybe he wanted to talk about the drilling."

"Actually, I was just on my way out to the site." Ty smiled in a condescending way. "But Diana invited me in for coffee." There was annoyance in his eyes when he saw Jim glance at the empty cup on the table.

"I have to check on the herd near there. I'll follow you out." Jim's face remained impassive despite the crackling tension that was suddenly present.

"Why don't you have a cup of coffee, Jim?" Diana glanced from one man to the other, looking for a reason for the undercurrents she felt but couldn't define.

"Nope. I have a lot to do with Lije gone." His gaze softened just a bit when he looked her way, then turned blandly back to Ty.

Diana could sense the other man's reluctance and irritation in the slow way he got up from his chair. He hadn't taken one step in the direction of the door when Jim held it open for him.

"Be there in a sec," Ty told Jim, his hat in his hand.

Jim only nodded, then glanced at Diana, closing only the screen door behind him. The smile on Ty's face held a hint of anger as he looked at Diana.

"I shoulda known Lije wouldn't leave you here alone without a faithful watchdog to guard you," he said sneeringly.

That unnecessary comment, and the patronizing way he'd talked to Jim Two Pony, suddenly got on Diana's nerves. This was the second time Ty had made a disparaging remark about Jim.

She hadn't liked it the first time and she liked it even less now. But Ty took no notice of her silent disapproval.

"Thanks for the cup o' joe, Diana." He set the hat firmly back on his head. "I'll be seeing you." A wink emphasized the promise in his voice, then he went through the door, walking ahead of Jim.

In those last minutes, the golden aura of happiness that had been with her all morning vanished. As Diana put the dirty coffee cups in the sink, she tried to make sense of her unsettled feelings. They weren't caused only by Ty's rudeness to Jim, although that had definitely lessened her enjoyment of his company.

She turned, leaning her back against the sink, and let her pensive gaze wander over the kitchen. It had been Ty's offhand comment about a woman's ability to redecorate on a budget. For the life of her, Diana couldn't see how fresh paint and new curtains would transform this sorry excuse for a kitchen. The white enamel on the stove and metal cabinets was badly chipped and scratched, and repainting wouldn't do much for them. In her opinion, the answer was new appliances and custom cabinets made from wood, none of which they could afford.

Yet the conversation bothered her all the rest of the day. The reason why escaped her, something that proved just as disconcerting as the conversation.

The evening meal of meat loaf, baked potatoes and baked beans was in the oven, and the coleslaw and strawberry pie were in the fridge. The table was set. The prospect of waiting until Jim arrived demanded more patience than Diana possessed.

There was no sign of his jeep outside, and with the memory of the previous night's delay in feeding the horses still fresh in her mind, Diana put on her jacket and walked down to the stables. Questioning whinnies from the rows of stalls greeted her as the horses stuck their heads out. There was something rather welcoming about the sound. With their graceful heads turning toward her, and their large, luminous eyes watching every move she made, Diana found them less intimidating than she had before.

A soft, inquiring nicker from a sorrel horse right near her made her look at it. It pricked its ears forward in anticipation as it stretched its neck toward her. Hesitantly Diana extended her hand, letting the velvety-soft nose nuzzle her palm. It tickled wonderfully, what with the few stiff hairs among the velvet and the breathiness of the contact.

She smiled at her new friend. The strip of white that raced across its delicate, gazelle-shaped face accented the shimmering brilliance of its red-brown coat. The soft brown eyes blinked, an incredible gentleness in their expression.

"You look like Bambi," she commented as she stroked the satiny smooth neck, then added with a quiet laugh, "a great big Bambi."

She glanced at the storage bins where the grain was kept and wished she'd paid closer attention last night when Jim had been measuring out grain and supplements for each horse. There was really nothing to feeding horses, as she had discovered. With Lije away, it would have made one less chore for Jim.

Her wandering gaze rested on the bales of hay stacked near the barn door. That was something she could give them without having to measure it out. All she had to do was toss some hay into the mangers. Before the decision was fully thought through, she moved to carry it out. She had one side of the rows of stalls done when the clamor of a ringing bell shattered the peaceful contentment of the barn. It took a second for Diana to remember the bell that Jim had hung at the house. She left the horses to their snack of hay and went to the door.

"Jim, I'm down here!" she called, waving to the dark-haired man standing at the house. She waited in the doorway as he walked to meet her. "Is anything wrong?" she asked.

"I thought you might've gone for one of your

walks," Jim said with just the suggestion of a smile.

"Not after the last time." She shook her head ruefully. She didn't want to remember that other walk and swiftly changed the subject. "I was just giving the horses some hay. I would've given them grain too, but I didn't know how much they're supposed to have."

"I'll show you." Jim was already walking by her into the barn. "The phone was ringing when I walked into the house," he said over his shoulder. "It was Lije calling to let you know he would be starting out in the morning."

"When will he get here?" Diana asked eagerly, her heart sinking a little at not being able to talk to him herself. In spite of the strangeness and misunderstanding of their parting, she missed him terribly.

"The day after tomorrow, probably in the morning," Jim answered.

"Did you mention that Ty was here to drill the new well?" Now why had she asked that? Diana wondered.

"Yeah. And I told him about the car Stacy's friend brought. He wanted me to look under the hood, make sure it wouldn't blow up on you. I said I would when I got a chance." Jim glanced at her before opening the grain bins and instructing her in the amount of grain and vitamin and mineral supplements to feed the horses. Diana was happy to confirm that there really wasn't anything difficult about feeding them once she knew the right amounts.

And it was nice to know they appreciated her efforts, or at least that was how she interpreted the way they *whuffed* at her through flared, velvety nostrils. This time, secure in the knowledge that nothing was burning in the oven, she stayed with Jim Two Pony when he fed the big bay stallion, Malpais.

He was a beautiful animal, sleek and muscular with graceful lines, like a Greek statue come to life. Yet for all his size, the stallion was light on his feet, moving playfully around Jim when he entered the paddock. The full mane and tail and all four legs were jet-black, but the rest of his body was the deepest, darkest shade of brown possible without being black.

"How did he get the name Malpais? Does it mean something?" Diana asked when Jim had emptied the grain and hay into the stallion's manger and walked over to stand beside her.

"Did Lije tell you about the lava beds on the north border of the ranch?"

Vaguely Diana recalled him making some comment about the area when they'd first met, but she hadn't thought about it since.

She nodded. "I think so, but I have to admit that I wasn't curious about them until now. What do they have to do with Malpais?"

"Malpais is the Spanish word for badlands," Jim explained, "and it's a good description for that twisting, black river of rock. Runs for miles—guess you didn't get that far."

"No, I didn't."

"It's ancient lava."

"Really?"

He smiled a little at her surprised tone. "Cool now, of course. So it's black, or, like this horse, nearly black."

"I had no idea there were volcanoes in the Southwest," she said.

"Mount Taylor and El Tintero are dormant but they did erupt about eight hundred years ago."

"How come nobody tells me this stuff?" she asked with mock annoyance.

"Just didn't have a chance, I guess."

As if. Diana's head rose proudly but she didn't deny what he said. If that was his version, then that was that. Let it alone.

"Okay, tell me all about it now."

He nodded, talking more than she'd ever heard him talk. "Lava is like liquid fire, killing every living thing in its path and destroying anything else. You can still see where it flowed. Here and there the river of lava split into two and made an island of green trees and grass, but that was all. Eventually the lava cooled and hardened, of course, but usually from the surface on down. So there was still molten lava beneath that, creating caverns. Some of them got filled with ice."

"Fire and ice, huh?"

He gave her a nod. "Strange but true. In places, the roofs of some of the caves are very thin. One step and a man could fall through and there'd be no way out, even if he survived. You can't see the difference between solid rock and a treacherous spot."

Diana shuddered expressively at the picture he painted.

"But it's only one small part in the whole of New Mexico." There was quiet amusement in his voice. "There's a lot you haven't seen."

"I'm looking forward to doing more exploring," she said, adding, "if that car doesn't stall out on me."

"Me and Lije will check it out and keep it running."

"Thanks," she said, meaning it. "So what else should I go see?"

"Just a few miles from the malpais is Acoma, the Sky City—that's an ancient pueblo. And not far from that is El Morro National Monument. There's a place there called Inscription Rock where the early Spanish explorers carved their names. I suppose you could call it an early form of graffiti."

Laughter rolled easily from Diana and with more freedom when Jim Two Pony joined in with her. Her blue eyes registered friendliness when she met his dark gaze.

"It gets scorching hot out that way in summer. So maybe you should go now, in the spring."

"Okay, I will."

This new camaraderie was a welcome change and one that she enjoyed very much.

"How do you get through the summer around here?" she asked, feeling like she was on a roll.

"Ice-cold beer," Jim answered, giving her a wink.

"Got it. Okay, I'll make sure the fridge is stocked. But I might lie low myself. I like the fall and winter seasons best."

Jim nodded. "We get snow up here."

"Lije told me that. In fact, he mentioned hail-storms, tornadoes and blizzards. Not all at once, right?"

"No," Jim said, smiling just a little. "But we have had more than one white Christmas in the last ten years. It's real pretty when that happens."

"I would love to see that," she answered sincerely, wondering what this rugged land would look like draped in soft, pure white.

Chapter Twelve

The barrier had been lowered between Diana and Jim. The first tentative steps toward friendship and respect had been taken, though there was still a measure of reserve on his side.

He was Lije's friend first and hers second, if that, she reminded herself. Total acceptance of her presence here on the ranch that both men had grown up on and knew so well might be a while off, but for the first time in weeks a lot of things were looking hopeful to Diana. Her smile was warm when she turned to him, liking his strong Navajo profile and the way his straight black hair fell over his forehead. She didn't doubt that he had a girl in town, as Lije had said.

"I'll feed the horses for you tonight if you don't mind," she offered, raising her voice to make sure she could be heard over the grumbling of the jeep's cantankerous engine.

"Okay. But leave Malpais to me." Jim put a finger to his broad-brimmed hat in a farewell salute before he put the jeep in gear and drove away.

After watching him disappear, followed by slowly dissipating clouds of dust, Diana turned her gaze the opposite way, looking at the rutted track her husband would return on. She was looking forward to that in every way, feeling like a lot had changed even though not much had happened at all.

Late that afternoon Diana left the stillness of the house for the more companionable atmosphere of the stables. She'd had more than enough of her own company and she didn't want to be sitting there twiddling her thumbs when Lije finally got home. Just the anticipation of his arrival made the minutes drag interminably.

An ecstatic whinny greeted her as she paused at the end of the individual enclosures that extended from the outside stall doors. A faint smile of surprise curved her mouth as she saw a sorrel head with a white stripe stretch inquiringly over the rails. The welcoming eagerness in the horse's face made her laugh.

"Hello to you too, Bambi, if that's what you were saying." She climbed the main fence and made her way down the path to the sorrel's pen. The horse lowered its head for her caress, blowing gently against Diana's bare arm with what seemed like contentment. "If I were really sure that you're as gentle as you seem, I might be persuaded to learn to ride. Not that I'm afraid of horses"—she stroked the shining, arched neck— "but you have to admit, Bambi, that your back is awfully far away from the ground."

The perked ears of the horse swiveled alertly to catch every nuance of Diana's crooning voice. She perched herself on the fence rail while the sorrel explored her arms and legs and face with its nose, inhaling deeply as if memorizing her scent for future reference. Diana continued talking to the horse, unmindful of what she was saying. The exact words didn't seem to matter to the horse, either. It was just soaking up all the attention.

When Diana glanced at her watch, nearly an hour and a half later, she was stunned that the time had passed so swiftly. But she was on the dot as far as her promise to Jim to feed the horses as she'd promised. The sorrel whickered forlornly when Diana climbed down from the top rail.

"Chow time, Bambi." She laughed as the horse pushed its head against her chest and kept it there for more gentle caresses. She gave the strong, silken neck one last hug before going back to the main fence, then on to the barn.

The clanging of the metal buckets as Diana prepared to measure the grain was a clear signal to the rest of the horses that feeding time was imminent. Instantly they moved into their stalls, heads hanging over in anticipation of their evening meal. She was nowhere near as efficient as Jim, so it took her longer to fill all the buckets. But soon her satisfied customers were all contentedly munching the grain while Diana went in search of the bales of hay to top off their meal.

Usually there was a stack of bales near the door, but it had been depleted to only two, not enough to feed all the horses. Diana had just placed a foot on the first rung of the ladder leading to the hayloft when a car horn sounded in the yard, followed by a man's voice calling out, "Hello? Anybody here?"

She walked quickly to the open barn door, brushing away the wisps of loose hay that clung to her jeans. Ty Spalding was standing beside the driver's side of his car, his gaze searching the house and yard before spotting Diana standing in the open double doors of the barn.

"Hi, beautiful!" he called, his lithe stride covering a lot of ground fast.

"Hello, Ty." She answered calmly, purposely not matching his by-now familiar enthusiasm. "What brings you here so late in the day?"

"I was just out at the drilling site." He stopped in front of her, taking in her reserved expression. "I thought I'd stop by and let you know we hit water."

"Lije will be glad to hear that."

"Yes." But there was an uncaring note in his affirmative response. "I stopped up at the house first. When you weren't there, I was about ready to decide that these wide-open spaces had finally swallowed you up."

"Not yet. But sometimes . . . I know what you mean," she said a little wistfully. "I really am a city girl."

"Well, you wouldn't be the first woman to not like this land or this life," he said.

"What makes you think I don't like it?" she asked noncommittally.

"Call it an educated guess. And maybe"—his gaze did more traveling around than she was comfortable with—"it's just that you seem so out of place here. You're too classy to live out here in the sticks."

"I guess that's a compliment. Not to my intelligence, though. Sometimes I find it hard to believe that I came out here of my own free will."

"Now, don't beat yourself up over that. You do sorta have to be born in the saddle to like it here and you don't strike me as the horsey type, Diana."

"Good guess. I'm not." Her laughter was a little reluctant.

There was no doubt that Ty Spalding had charm, although it was wearing thin. Even his somewhat tactless teasing was better than nothing, though. His attention wasn't that unwelcome, but she hated to think of how low her standards had sunk if she was willing to listen for lack of other diversions. Heck, it didn't matter. The guy kept on talking no matter what. She guessed that he wanted attention too.

He grinned as he spoke again. "But some girls Lije knows definitely belong in the horsey group."

"Such as?"

"Such as Patty King."

"I met her," Diana murmured, blinking at Ty with some bewilderment. That was the girl who'd flung herself at Lije in the restaurant. "She's pretty. You could hardly describe her as horsey."

"Really? You met her?" His question was purely rhetorical. "I'll be damned. Patty had her lasso out and spinning, ready to throw the loop over Lije."

"Uh-huh. I did get the impression she had something of a crush on him."

"More than that," Ty hooted. "That girl joined the rodeo just to be near him. Finding out that he married you must've blown her mind."

The thought came to Diana that if Patty had married Lije, she probably would have been out on the range working right beside him instead of sitting in the house waiting for him to come back.

"It did seem like a surprise to her," she said, straightening a little as she spoke. Enough of this, she thought with some exasperation. "Ah, I haven't finished feeding the horses yet, Ty, so if you'll excuse me, it's getting late."

"What's left to do? I'll help." He was already starting through the double doors of the barn before Diana could reply.

"There's no need. Really." He wasn't listening. She sighed and followed him into the dimly lit barn.

He smiled. "I insist, pretty lady." He reached out and captured her hand. "I don't like the thought of these lovely hands getting dirty."

Ick. She pulled her hand back. "Don't be silly. A little dirt never hurt anyone."

"Well, I'll help all the same." He was half-teasing and half-serious and one hundred percent in her way. It was obvious to Diana that nothing short of ordering him to leave was going to work. What the hell. He was a friend of Lije, as far as she knew, and she had to be polite to him, as long as he stayed within the limits of appropriate behavior. She wasn't sure he would, but, with a resigned sigh, she accepted the situation.

"I've already given them their grain. All that's left is the hay."

"Those two bales won't be enough," he observed, glancing at the hay near the door.

"I know," she said, feeling a little annoyed. "I

was just going up to the hayloft to get more when you came."

"Hey, I'll do that for ya. Ration out what's down here."

Reluctantly Diana nodded in agreement, walking over to the bales of hay as Ty climbed the ladder to the loft. The horses stamped restlessly in their stalls and the sound made her pull hard on the twine around the bales. Above her she could hear Ty walking toward the far end of the loft and she could see some of the chaff he was kicking up fall through the floorboards of the loft. By the time she'd distributed the first two bales Ty had tossed down more. Diana had just freed one bale from its twine and was turning to carry the hay to the horses when her feet became entangled in the wiry rope. With a gasping yelp of surprise, she went tumbling down. Ty skipped the ladder and swung from the hayloft opening to drop on the floor beside her.

"Are you hurt?" he asked, worried. "Anything broken?"

"No," she answered with a shaky laugh, getting back the breath that had been knocked out of her in a whoosh. The hay that had been in her hands was strewn on and around her. "You look like a scarecrow with all its hay falling out," Ty said, laughing once assured that she was unharmed.

Now that her surprise had diminished,

Diana was able to join in his laughter a little. She willingly placed her hand in the one he extended to her. His hold tightened to pull her to her feet, but the silhouette that loomed in the doorway, blocking out most of the light, stopped them cold. It took Diana only a second to recognize him.

"Lije!" she gasped, scrambling to her feet without Ty's aid.

Lije ignored Diana. "What the hell are you doing here, Spalding?"

"Uh—I was giving Di—your wife, I mean—a hand with the horses." His breezy confidence vanished as he faced Lije.

"I'll help my wife if she needs help, you useless son-of-a—"

Ty raised his hands. "Don't take this the wrong way, pal."

Lije took a step toward him and Ty swallowed hard.

"Hey. Calm down, Lije. Did you just get back?" Her question sounded a little ridiculous given the free-floating testosterone in the air, but she had to say something. It was clear that Lije was putting the wrong spin on the innocent scene he'd just witnessed. "We didn't expect you back until tomorrow." She realized how that sounded and bit her tongue.

By "we" she'd meant herself and Jim Two Pony. At the narrowing of her husband's gaze, she felt herself reddening.

"That's rather obvious, isn't it?" he drawled coldly.

At his insinuation, the hair on the back of her neck began to rise with her temper. For a moment she stood silently in front of him, stiff with anger. "Ty was helping me," Diana said sharply.

"Is that what you call it." There was no question mark on the end of his comment. "I think you should go back to the house." His own anger was barely in check.

"Uh, it's getting late," Ty said uncertainly. "I'd better be getting along. Listen, Lije, nothing happened here and you shouldn't blame Diana if it seemed like—"

"Shut up," Lije growled.

Ty straightened and gave him a level look, then studied Diana for a long moment. "Do you honestly feel safe staying here? Because if you don't, just get in my car and I'll take you to the sheriff's and this hothead can go to—"

Lije made an extraordinary effort to really control his temper. "She's totally safe. How long have you known me?"

"A while," Ty said grudgingly.

"And have you ever heard of me raising a hand to a woman, let alone hurting one?"

"No, but—"

"There isn't going to be a first time. I have to hand it to you, Ty. You sounded like a real man for once. But it's probably a good idea if you don't wear out your welcome any more than you already have."

Diana folded her arms across her chest, sorry that it had come to this. But she did trust Lije, as angry as he was.

"It's okay, Ty," she said quietly. "Just go."

"If you're sure," Ty said.

She nodded.

He went to his car and started it up, giving them one last look where they stood. Together but apart.

They turned in silence and walked back to the house, leaving it to Jim to finish haying the horses.

Once inside, she took off her jacket and flung it into a corner. She had to do something, anything, to work off her tension and her anger.

Cooking was about it for something to do around here, she thought savagely. She hated this kitchen all over again. Throw in the whole house. The desolate land around it. And Lije Masters, for pulling a fast one on her and dragging her out to the back of beyond, all in the name of love. Most of all, she hated herself for being so damn needy that marrying a man she'd known only a few hours had seemed like a great idea.

There were problems, big problems, with this relationship that having her own car wasn't going to fix.

The pots and pans clattered and clanged as she slammed food into them. There was no way he could miss hearing it. Not in this . . . this shack that he called a house, she thought furiously.

"Damn the supper!" He came into the kitchen and spun her around to face him. His expression was cold with anger. "What I want is an explanation."

"I don't owe you an explanation," she said through gritted teeth. "Not for that."

"No? I'm gone for three days. I rush back here to apologize for not understanding all your problems, even though you won't talk about them—"

"Hey, I tried!"

"And then I find you stretched out in the hay with another man—I think you do owe me an explanation, Diana! So let's hear it!"

She retorted in language he'd never heard from her before, and his eyes widened. Diana's flashing blue gaze clashed with the thunderclouds in his, and it was only going to get worse.

"I knew you were lonely out here"—an ominous quiet crept into his voice—"but I never dreamed you were so desperate for attention that you'd do something like that."

Diana never thought she would see so much contempt on the face of a man who supposedly loved her—but she was seeing it now. All the little happy moments she'd had since he'd been gone seemed to have never happened at all. She was fooling herself with her girlish hopes that she and Lije were meant to be, if *that* was all he thought of her. And the pain it caused her heart was unbelievable. She had to strike back.

"Yes, I've been lonely! Who wouldn't be, in this godforsaken hole?" she cried. "Nothing to see, nowhere to go, nobody to talk to, just nothing! Until Stacy found a way to get me a car, which was really kind of her, although it sure seemed to stick in your craw—"

"That's not so," he retorted with some heat.

"No? Prove it isn't!"

"I don't have to prove anything to you, Diana—not when I work so damn hard so that you and I can—ah, what's the use!"

His distrust had triggered an answering emotion in her that burned up every green sprig of hope. She put her hands on her hips and glowered belligerently at him. When he broke off, she let him have it.

"Listen, Lije, while you were gone, I actually thought I could—we could—make it somehow. But I was so wrong, because the second you got back, I felt bad all over again. And I hate it! I hate this damn ranch too! Do you hear me? I hate it!"

Now both of his hands were gripping her shoulders, but he kept his superior strength in check. "It's not the ranch. You knew what it was like before you got here. You wanted to come."

"No, I didn't know. How could I possibly?"

"I—I told you."

"I got the happy childhood version, not the grown-up reality. Being here is no picnic!"

"Whatever you think of it, it's still my land and my home. And it always will be."

"Not a problem," she said sarcastically. "You and Jim are welcome to it."

"I was wondering when you'd get around to him. He said you were doing okay. But that was about it. I wish I knew why you two didn't take to each other—"

"That's not true!" She wasn't going to launch into a long explanation of how she and Jim had come to some kind of understanding during his absence. Lije wouldn't believe it—or he would think she was just trying to distract him from the subject of Ty Spalding.

The hell with it. The Lije she'd been in love with had been nothing but a creation of her imagination.

"So what is true?" he asked icily. "What you say? What I say? What?"

"I can't stand any more of this." Her anger gave way to sobs of frustration as she twisted to free herself of his grasp. "You don't really try to understand how I feel! You don't even care!"

"And I suppose Ty Spalding does." He released his hold as if he didn't want to touch her at all, ever again.

Cheap shot. But to be expected from him in this ugly mood. "Ty's not like you. He's human."

"Don't try to make him look good, Diana. Ty is a jerk and you know it," Lije said with impassive finality. "And that's being kind. I'm sure he didn't impress you. But I bet you wanted to get back at me, didn't you?"

"That's neither here nor there." She didn't want to answer his question. "What I meant when I said he's human is that—that he's capable of making mistakes."

That assertion seemed to irk him more than anything else she'd said. "Oh? He shouldn't make them with other men's wives."

"He didn't—"

"Does it really matter, Diana?" he interrupted her with savage swiftness. "I think I made one hell of a mistake when I married you."

It felt as if a knife had been plunged in her heart and Diana gasped at the pain.

"Do you blame me for that too?" she asked bitterly. "After all, you tried to say good-bye before anything much happened. You were ready to move on to another rodeo!"

"No—"

"Or some other girl," she said bitterly. "Someone who wasn't so starry-eyed and stupid."

"Diana—"

She wouldn't let him get a word in edgewise. "I was the one who refused to accept the obvious."

"And what the hell would that be?" he shot back. "I've been gone a few days. I think I missed all the soul-searching. Fill me in."

Stung by his dismissiveness, she flung a choice curse his way.

"Nice to know how you really feel about me," he said in a flat voice. "But you still haven't told me just what exactly is so obvious to you."

She paced back and forth, her arms crossed over her chest. Diana didn't want to say the words, but she had to admit the truth of them. Her dreams were just that—dreams. They didn't have a chance.

"That a rodeo cowboy isn't exactly husband material," she said with finality.

"Hell, I know I tried," he said. "I gave it everything I had and I haven't given up yet."

"Are you still trying?" Her eyes blazed with fury. "Going the full eight seconds? Lucky me. If you win, you get to walk away and I get to go back home to Dallas."

"Is that so bad?" he asked. "Isn't that what you really want?"

She went at him with her fists clenched and he caught her wrists with ease. "No!" she screamed.

"Then what do you want?" He struggled to hold her.

"I don't know!" she sobbed. "Not this—not fighting like this. And not the loneliness."

After a long minute, he spoke in a whisper. "Is that my fault?"

"It doesn't matter whose fault it is." She sagged against him, then straightened. "I—I honestly don't know if I can make it. Maybe I shouldn't have ever tried."

He stiffened and walked away from her.

"Yeah, well, hindsight is always sharper. But all the what-ifs in the world don't do any good."

"Meaning?"

"The big question here seems to be what if we hadn't gotten married. Well, we did and we are. The only thing that remains to be done is to get unmarried." Lije said it casually and matter-of-factly. "Go ahead and pack your stuff tonight and Jim will take you into town tomorrow. Whoa, I almost forgot. You can drive yourself."

"Is that rattletrap car something else you resent? Who do you think you are, Lije Masters?"

He answered slowly, "I almost don't know anymore. Not the man I used to be, I can tell you that. Not even the man I was while coming up our road. I wanted to see you—more than I've ever wanted anything."

"Like hell you did," she muttered.

He threw up his hands. "That's enough. Have your lawyer get ahold of me. You do have one, right?"

"No," she whispered, tears in her eyes.

Diana was still standing in the same place when Lije walked out the door.

Chapter Thirteen

Lije didn't come back to the house that night. Diana could only assume that he was staying in Jim Two Pony's cabin. Pride wouldn't allow her to go in search of him and beg his forgiveness when she was guilty of nothing—except maybe loving him too much and having too much pride. And, in spite of the accusations she'd flung at him, she did love him. But did it do any good? Had she and Lije come up against an obstacle that not even their love could overcome? Like the old song said, maybe it was love at the wrong place and the wrong time. Nothing more.

Diana went through the motions of preparing her own evening meal and even sat down at the table with the intention of eating, but her fork succeeded mostly in pushing the food around on her plate. Very few bites actually made it to her mouth. It was doubly strange to clear the table and wash the dishes with the thought that this was the last time she would be doing it. The kitchen that had always seemed so slapped-together and raw to her aesthetic eye suddenly seemed . . . homey. She'd started a new life here. Letting go of that cherished hope wasn't necessarily easy.

She wandered through the rest of the house, telling herself all the time how lucky she was to be able to leave its dismal interior, but she did a terrible job of convincing herself. It didn't seem true that she was really leaving.

Not even when her suitcases were dragged from the closet and lay open on the bed did it seem possible that she was. The whole thing seemed like a bad dream. Diana kept thinking that Lije would walk through the door at any moment and the cold ache in her heart would melt away at the sight of him. But he didn't come.

Mechanically she filled the suitcases, her thoughts going in every direction and on some odd tangents. When she removed a long hostess skirt from the closet, she wondered why on earth she'd brought it here to the ranch.

It wasn't as if she'd been married in it. No, she'd settled for a simple, knee-length white dress with bell sleeves and a bouquet of lilies from a Juarez street vendor. The white dress had stayed in a vinyl bag, carefully zipped up to protect it from the red dust of New Mexico.

She set aside the skirt and looked in the closet for her wedding dress, realizing that she must have already packed it in a different bag, because it wasn't there. Well, she wasn't going to unpack everything and look for it. She would probably burst out crying all over again.

Diana picked up the gold skirt, running her hand over the hand-woven silk it was made from. Had she honestly ever thought she would wear it to a dinner party at the ranch?

She exhaled a sigh. The silk skirt was something Connie had passed along, a designer original featured in an upscale magazine spread on Taos, worn by the wife of an investment banker for a feature on second homes of the wealthy. Or maybe it was third homes.

And here, in her anything-but-glamorous first home, Diana hadn't ever worn anything but jeans. How ridiculous.

But its rich golden color made her wonder what the pillows on the living room sofa would look like covered in the muted but brilliant shade. Before she realized what she was doing, she had carried the skirt into the living room to wrap it around one of the pillows. The effect against the brown tweed sofa was amazing. There was just enough light yellow in the material to add brightness to the room and still blend with the existing furniture. Why hadn't she thought of it before?

And again, a few minutes later, she picked

up a blue silk scarf that had a border of white daisies around it. The simplicity of the flower design sparked an instant inspiration to decorate the metal cupboards in the kitchen by edging the cupboard doors with a decoration of flowers.

Nesting instinct or temporary insanity? It was hard to tell. But it was too late for the first and she didn't think that she actually had gone crazy.

Whatever. Maybe it would be a good idea to not judge every little thing she did, she told herself. If she felt like letting her mind wander, that wasn't going to be the end of the world.

She could even bring a little of what she did like about this house back to Dallas somehow. It wasn't like he could kick her to the curb, emotionally speaking, because she had kept a place to go back to.

So, she thought absently, redoing the kitchen table and chairs wouldn't be difficult. New curtains at the window and fresh paint on the walls would . . . Diana put a firm brake on her irrational thoughts. She was leaving. Lije had told her to go. Their brief marriage was over. Why was she thinking about redecorating a house she would never see again after tonight?

Very slowly, a tear trickled down her cheek, then another. Soon enough, there was a deluge. She kept dashing them away, telling herself she was entitled to a good cry as she clicked shut the last suitcase. Hell, she had a *right* to cry. Hadn't her husband, the only man she could ever love, accused her wrongly of being unfaithful? He hadn't exactly agreed with her low opinion of him, but he didn't seem to have much faith in the relationship, either. He'd just about ordered her off his precious ranch.

There was nothing she could do. It wasn't as if she could ask Stacy to fly down with Cord and have her smack some sense into Lije. Or ask Jim to set Lije straight on what had actually happened during the days he'd been gone. She thought of old Herb and his darling Dottie, and wished them well, vowing to stop by when she passed the offices of the *Bee* on her way out of town, just in case he happened to be outside. Fifty years and counting—that wasn't going to be her and Lije.

It was just too bad, Diana thought, although with a measure of guilt, that she'd lost it, big-time. The look on Lije's face when she'd shrieked that she hated the ranch and her life on it hadn't given her a trace of satisfaction.

For a while, though, that had been totally true. He hadn't wanted to acknowledge her withdrawal, as far as she could tell—or maybe he hadn't even noticed it. He really had worked from dawn to dusk, seven days a week. She, stuck in a house that wasn't hers, hadn't even known where to begin tossing out or fixing anything.

Spare as the house was, it held a lot of memories. That pile of magazines, for one. It was a little too easy to imagine the women who'd lived here reading the same damn ones over and over again, just to have something to do. Or keeping busy with crocheting, quilting and cooking when they weren't doing housework.

She went to the bookcases, opening the glass door and looking again at the books Lije said were old friends. He hadn't opened one the whole time she'd been here, not that she'd fault him for that. On a ranch, men and women lived fundamentally different lives, and while she was sure it had changed some since his mother's day, it hadn't changed enough to suit her.

"We're equals."

His words came back to her with startling clarity, almost as if he was in the room and had spoken them.

"I don't want a woman who's meek and mild. I expect you to raise hell when you're not happy."

He hadn't welcomed her criticism or complaints, to say the least. And as for changing his ways, that hadn't even been up for discussion.

Maybe she should take a magazine or two just to remind her of this place, so she wouldn't come back. Lije wouldn't miss them, wouldn't care.

She walked out of the kitchen, twisting the blue flowered scarf around her hand, and went to the pile. From the middle, she pulled one out at random.

It was a *Ranch Romance*. She looked at the cover illustration of a pretty cowgirl from decades ago, looking flirtatiously up at a manly cowboy from under her gigantic straw hat. And he was looking at . . . his horse. Figured.

Women of the West, unite. It really was time to get the hell out of Dodge. Until recently she'd basically been too depressed to understand her feelings of isolation, let alone talk about them.

And now, according to Lije, it was over. She burst into heart-wrenching sobs and threw the magazine across the room. It hit the wall and fell to the floor, fluttering open to some pointless love story.

The morning sun found a tear-drenched pillow and suitcases stacked beside the kitchen door. Diana sat at the table, staring at the cup of black coffee out of eyes that were ringed with dark circles. There weren't any more tears left. She felt drained of all emotion, a hollow shell of a person with nothing left inside to feel pain or anguish.

An hour before she'd seen Lije from the kitchen window, walking across the ranch yard to get into the jeep. He hadn't even glanced toward the house. As he drove out of sight, the last thread of hope for a reconciliation disappeared with him. There wasn't even going to be a last good-bye.

The soft, catlike tread on the porch floor announced the arrival of Jim Two Pony to help her with her things so she could leave the ranch. Diana inhaled deeply as he walked through the door, drawing her protective cloak of pride more securely around her before she raised her head to meet his gaze. She expected to see a superior look on his face, but she was taken aback by the gentle sympathy that showed in his eyes. It almost made her cry.

"My suitcases are there by the door," she said, struggling for composure. "You might as well begin carrying them out to the car. My car," she corrected herself, but she felt no pride in claiming ownership of it today.

"Nope. We have to take the truck," he said dispassionately. "The car has a leak in the radiator. I saw the puddle under it and I checked the fluid level."

"Can it be fixed?"

"I think so. Has to be towed, though. Forget about driving it for now. Maybe we can wangle a rental driveaway in Santa Fe."

So much for that. Remembering what the insurance had cost was a bracing dose of reality. She wasn't sure she could afford to pay for a major repair and the rental and buy enough gas to get to Dallas. At least she still had a place to go back to. She hadn't been that much of a damn fool.

The thought was cold comfort.

"Are you sure you want me to load up?" Jim asked quietly, his black eyes never leaving her face.

"I can't carry everything. Not quickly, anyway," Diana said, deliberately misunderstanding his question. She rose to her feet.

Jim hesitated for a minute before reaching down to pick up one of the biggest bags. After slipping on her jacket, she reached for her purse, then followed him out the door.

"Where are you going?"

"Back where I came from. It doesn't really matter, does it?" Diana answered coldly, absorbed in her own misery. She didn't see any need to chitchat with someone who not too long ago would have been glad to see her go. Besides, what she told him would get back to Lije. "It feels pretty good to be on my way out of this godforsaken piece of country."

"That may have been true once, when you first came." He glanced at her sideways. "But if you are honest with yourself, you don't feel that way about the ranch now."

The truth of his words sent a wave of pain through her heart. A whinny from the stable area intensified it. She would never see her pretty horse again, either. But Diana didn't let go of her seeming indifference. That and her pride were her only defenses against the unbearable agony that was just below the surface.

"Don't, Jim. Just don't. I'm going. End of story."

"I'm not happy about it. You and I were getting along okay lately."

"Maybe so," Diana retorted. "But you made it plain from the beginning that you didn't think I belonged here. Aren't you happy that you were right about that?"

"I said I wasn't happy. And I don't know what you're talking about."

He set the luggage in the back of the pickup and turned to look at her.

"Oh, come on. You remember the conversation we had in the barn shortly after I arrived," she said. "The one about the yucca plant and the rose? I got the point—I was the rose. And roses are too high maintenance to survive out here."

"You misunderstood." Jim shook his head sadly. "I was trying to explain that you had to choose which you were going to be, useful and self-sufficient like the yucca or decorative and pampered like the rose."

"You know," she began, wishing Lije was around to hear her, "a little pampering never hurt anyone. I've been taking mental notes. Lije likes to get loved up and you like home cooking. And no one would call either of you a rose, especially not after you've been working in the hot sun all day."

Jim's face softened just a little, as if he were about to smile, but he didn't and he didn't reply.

"And while you're listening, which is more than I can say for your boss and best friend, I just so happened to learn a little about those roses and the lady who tried to grow them."

"From who?" Jim seemed suddenly wary.

"Herb Bigelow."

"The old cowboy down at the newspaper? I know him."

She gave a curt nod. "He seems to know everybody."

"He kinda does, I guess."

"Once he found out I was Lije's w-wife"—her tongue tripped over the word—"he got to talking. He told me that Lije's mother lugged bathwater out from the house for those roses."

"That's true. She did."

She clenched her fists. "I don't get the comparison you made. All she wanted was something beautiful near her to look at every day. That wasn't stupid or crazy. And what's wrong with a rose?"

"Nothing. I didn't say it right and you took it wrong, Diana." The words he spoke had a gravity that made her calm down and listen. "I wasn't too friendly at first, I admit. It's not like I had time to get used to the idea of you being Lije's wife and living on the ranch. And you had to get accustomed to being here, and the animals. But after a while, when you were ready, you pitched in without a complaint, even helping with the horses."

"I don't understand," Diana whispered. She wanted to doubt his words but the sincerity in his voice was plain. "Then why were you so cold to me? You barely talked to me unless I made you."

"I . . ." He paused in search of the right words. "I don't make friends easily. Partly, I admit, because I am a Navajo and few white people are really interested in being my friend, let alone a white woman. I didn't know at the beginning whether you were just being friendly because of Lije or what. We Navajos have a lot of pride."

"Lije told me that. In so many words," she murmured.

"So you were a little bit uneasy about me before you got here."

"He told me you two were like brothers," she admitted. "And as soon as I saw you my first thought was that you didn't approve."

"Getting married—well, that was Lije's decision. I didn't object, or question him. But I was surprised. I was waiting, maybe, to see if you would stay. If it was real."

Diana's head was bent forward, her hair hiding her face. Then she tossed her head, sending her hair cascading down her back. "I think Lije assumed I didn't like you because you were around so much. He couldn't understand that I thought you didn't like me or want me here—probably because he knew you better than he knew me."

"Then your leaving is my fault."

"No." She reached out and touched his arm. "No, it isn't. Lije and I quarreled because of Ty Spalding. He thought—" Diana couldn't bring herself to voice what her soon-to-be-ex-husband thought, but even if she didn't say it out loud, Jim knew. "But I suppose he told you all about it."

"He didn't speak of it to me. Although he did seem surprised when I told him you had fed the horses. I remember what he said. 'So that's why she was in the barn.'"

"I'd tripped over some baling twine and Ty was helping me up when Lije walked in." There was a poignantly emotional look in her eyes as she glanced at the barn.

"And you didn't explain that?"

"I was so hurt"—a sob crept into her voice—"that he could believe I'd ever do what he thought I was doing. I'm afraid I can be very stubborn," she said with a half laugh. "Later, when he asked me to explain, I . . . I refused. That's when we really started quarreling. And"—Diana looked out over the expansive horizon, shimmering in golden sunlight with a hint of spring green—"and that's when I told him how much I hated living here."

"You seemed like you wanted to be happy," Jim said softly.

She nodded. "I did. But it hadn't been long at all when being out here so alone and cut off from everybody got me feeling sorry for myself. No one to talk to. Nowhere to go. I just couldn't—couldn't connect."

"I think I understand."

"That damn car and the one day of freedom it gave me snapped me back to reality." She took a half breath and went on in a rush of words, afraid she would cry. "The few people I met here are kind and friendly and the land really is beautiful in its own strange way and I'm not even sure I want to leave. But maybe it isn't the land of enchantment for everybody."

"Oh." Jim didn't say anything more than that.

She scrubbed at her welling tears. Another battle lost. "The magic didn't work for me. I wanted it to happen. I still do."

Jim reached into the back of the pickup truck and took out the two suitcases he'd just put in there.

"What are you doing?" Diana asked as he started walking toward the house with them.

"I'm not taking you anywhere," Jim said firmly. A smile took some of the harshness out of his voice. "If Lije wants you to leave, then he's going to have to take you himself. And if I were you, I would tell him exactly what you just told me . . . if you still love him, which I think you do."

She just stared at him, flooded with a sudden rush of hope. The hurtful fight with Lije, the lingering exhaustion of her sleepless night, her overwhelming sense of despair—it all vanished in the face of Jim's plain-spoken advice.

Did she still love him? The answer to that was *yes*. But that didn't mean a reconciliation was going to be easy. There were two sides to this one and she couldn't begin to guess what Lije might do or say now.

"I wouldn't know where to begin."

"Keep it simple. Just say you're sorry for the part that's your fault. And make him say he's sorry for not paying attention in the first place." He set down one of the suitcases and held open the door for Diana. She stepped inside, expecting Jim to follow, but he only placed the bags inside and walked back out.

"Where are you going?" she called after him.

"I thought I would let Lije know there's someone at the house who wants to speak to him," Jim answered with a decided twinkle in his eyes.

It was as if he understood her better than she understood herself at the moment.

"I hope it works out. Oh, do I hope so. Thank you, Jim," Diana said softly. The screen door shaded her face, so Jim didn't see the diamond-bright glitter of tears that intensified the blue of her eyes.

"Don't thank me yet," he said, smiling, "you haven't talked to Lije."

The rumbling roar of an accelerating engine got their attention. Jim and Diana turned toward the sound to see the jeep bouncing over the uneven ground to the ranch yard. Only one person was in the vehicle and both of them knew it was Lije. Diana stood silently inside the screen door unconsciously holding her breath.

"Don't let him see you," Jim said under his breath, heading back the way he'd come.

The jeep stopped beside the pickup truck with Lije hopping out almost before the engine stopped turning over. Diana stepped away from the door as she saw Lije's long strides eating the distance between the jeep and the house.

He stopped when he reached Jim, who kept on walking. "Where's Diana?" Lije demanded harshly.

"Why?" Jim asked.

Not rude, not friendly, she thought. Calm. If only she could be.

"Because I want to see her. Now, damn it, where did you take her? To Ventana? To the Santa Fe bus station?"

Lije made no attempt to conceal his impatience, and Diana wished she could see his face.

"No."

Jim still sounded remarkably unruffled, she thought, considering the anger in Lije's voice.

"Then where?"

"I didn't take her anywhere," Jim said flatly.

It was as if the whole world had come to a halt, so deep was the silence. Slowly Diana stepped in front of the screen door to look at her husband, whose mouth opened in silent surprise while his whole attention became focused on her.

"I'm right here, Lije," she said quietly.

Their gazes met and locked through the mesh of the screen. Jim glanced back at Diana briefly before silently stepping past Lije and walking away. Again Diana experienced that strange communication with Lije's gray eyes that she had felt when they first met. Without being all that aware of it, she opened the screen door for Lije to enter.

"Did you want to see me?" she asked.

"Yes." But he made no move toward the opened door. "I guess this is good-bye."

"Maybe not."

"What?" His eyes narrowed. "Don't play games with me, Diana."

"I'm not trying to, Lije. But you and I had better talk. I might not be leaving," Diana began. He still had that terrible mask of remoteness on his face. There was no indication whether he was pleased or angry with what she'd just said, so she rushed on. "At least, not until I've had a chance to tell you that I didn't mean any of those things I said yesterday. And . . . and I . . . I still love you. I'll always love you, Lije. But we can't keep going on like we have been."

Something flickered across the strong bronzed lines of his face that looked like pain.

"Is that all you have to say?" he asked. But there wasn't a trace of arrogance in his tone.

"It's not that I hate the ranch, because I don't," she began. "At first, I admit, everything was strange and lonely, but that started to change while you were away."

"I had to go. I hope me not being here wasn't the reason why you felt better," he said, a flicker of worry in his dark eyes.

"But it did help snap me out of it," she said honestly. "Stacy's friend brought the car and all of a sudden—oh, hell, it's hard to describe. Whatever had been weighing me down just lifted."

"That heap of junk did the trick? Hey, I'm glad the thing ran for at least twenty-four hours," he said dryly. "But you're out of luck today."

"Jim thinks it can be fixed."

Lije cast a backward glance at his friend. "If not, you got yourself a nice hunk of scrap metal for a souvenir. Or I do. Maybe that would serve me right for saying what I did about Ty."

He still seemed wary to her, as if he didn't believe she wanted to stay. "I can explain—"

"No!" The word exploded in the air as he covered the distance between them in one lithe move. His hands gripped her shoulders as he simultaneously stepped into the house and pulled her against his chest. "Don't say any more, Diana." He spoke softly, his voice muffled in her silken hair. "I can't bear to hear you talk like that when I'm the one who should be begging you to forgive me. I know exactly what happened in the barn yesterday."

"How?" Diana twisted a bit so she could look at him, a mixture of disbelief and happiness on her face.

"I just had a long talk with Spalding at the drilling site. I was too angry yesterday to do more than order him to stay away from you." He smiled down at her in that way that would always steal her breath. She would have spoken, but he covered her mouth gently with his hand for just a second. "I know you tripped, and that he was just trying to help. Which doesn't make him any less of a jerk."

Diana looked at him with some surprise. "So why is he still working for you?"

"We need the water." He gave her a rueful grin. "And I was wrong. Once I calmed down, I realized I could qualify for the title of jerk myself. Nothing justified my failure to trust you. The only reason I can give for acting like I did is that I was jealous. I was outside when I heard you laugh. Girl, do you have any idea how long it's been since I heard that?"

"I don't know." She could barely remember herself. Her depression had blurred a lot of days into indistinct shades of gray.

"Not since the first day I brought you here. When I walked in the barn and saw you with Ty and thought that he'd made you laugh when I failed, I was crazy with jealousy and anger."

She took a deep breath. "Somehow that still isn't an apology." She kissed the tips of the fingers that had begun to caress her face. "Of course, it has to be mutual. If you can forgive me for the way I hurt you—"

"I deserved it," he murmured, gathering her closer in his arms. "But that's why I came looking for you—so you would know that I knew the truth. If I could, I was going to persuade you to come back."

"And I was half-afraid you were going to be angry because I was still here." Her laugh was brittle. "Things have to change."

"Diana." He blew out his breath. "Just tell me what you want."

He walked into the kitchen and sat down at the table. His presence there seemed unreal somehow.

She took a seat across from him. "Lije, if it takes an angry explosion to bring us together— well, that isn't how I want to live my life. We went for weeks without really talking."

His hand on the table twitched and his fingers began to drum softly on it. "Look, Diana, I'm a rodeo cowboy. I don't always think first, but I act fast."

"You *were* a rodeo cowboy. But now you're a rancher. And you're married to me. A lot of things are different. You have to adapt."

He *hemmed* and *hawed* for a minute, then raked both hands through his hair, leaning back so far in his chair she thought he might fall over. "Not sure I know what you're getting at," he said at last.

"You have to slow down some."

He nodded. "Yeah. I can't argue that."

"And you can't just be strong and silent. Or storm in and out. You can't leave me here alone so much."

He groaned. "I'm working for us. Night and day. The ranch has to turn a profit or we can forget the future. Is that so hard to understand?"

"No. It isn't." She held up a hand to get his attention. "I admit I was so wrapped up in my own misery, it took a while for that to sink in."

"Why? You're so smart," he complained.

"You say that like it's a bad thing."

"Damn it, Diana, don't put words in my mouth!"

"Sorry."

Lije began again, leaning forward now, his arms crossed on the table. "I guess I meant that I expected you would figure things out on your own. If I did it all for you, you wouldn't ever learn. And besides, I didn't have the time to babysit you."

She stiffened. "Have you ever been depressed?"

"No."

"It was a first for me. And I hope it never happens to you. But it's not about being a baby. Not at all."

Lije flattened his hand on the table and looked at it. "Then what is it like?"

Diana considered her words for a minute before replying. "Like you're inside a gray box. You can see out, but you can't get out. And nobody can really reach you."

"Mind if I ask a few searching questions?"

"Go ahead. Everything's on the table now."

"What made it happen? Is it going to happen again?"

Diana shrugged, but not in a casual way. "The isolation, I think, was the trigger. But you know about my childhood, Lije—although I'm not going to blame everything on that. And I have to say—"

He sat up tall. "Give it to me straight. Both barrels. C'mon. Ready. Aim. Fire."

"I don't think I was the only one who was depressed. And don't look over your shoulder." His eyes widened but they were more defiant than understanding. "I mean you, and you know it."

"Diana," he began slowly. "I feel blue sometimes, like everyone else. But I never let it get to me. I go riding and outpace it, or head for a bar with the boys and obliterate it, or have a good time with a—a friend and—"

"Be honest. A buckle bunny."

"Okay. Once or twice, I have done that."

She sniffed and he gave her a defensive look.

"They're always around the rodeos and all a man has to do is say howdy and they come running." He looked at her nervously. "Life is different when you look at it from the height of a horse. You just aren't afraid of much. But then you happened along. And I think maybe I was a little afraid of how I felt."

"Now you're talking," she said.

Lije gave an exasperated sigh. "Now, don't turn this discussion into one of those afternoon TV shows where everything you say means the opposite of what you think. I won't have it."

"I don't watch TV. In case you've forgotten, there is no reception at the ranch. No cell phones. No Internet."

"Diana, I got that you had nothing to do that was important to you. And you're right, damn it. I wasn't feeling too happy about suddenly being responsible for nine million and one things when all I used to do was knock around from one rodeo to the next, doing what I just said in the off-hours. Or sleeping. About the only thing left as a way for me to let off steam was riding. I didn't want to do any of the others," he added hastily.

"Exactly. Let me break it down. You got hitched, came home, and your life went from 60 to 0. You're used to doing the exact opposite."

He looked at her levelly. "Never in a million years would I call you a zero. You're the best damn thing that ever happened to me. Ask Jim if I ever brought another woman home to the ranch. Go ahead. Ask him." He waved in the general direction Jim had disappeared to, as if his friend were standing right outside the house and would walk through the wall to vouch for him.

"I'd rather talk to you, if you don't mind."

"Can I ask you another question?" He didn't wait for an answer. "Is talking like this helping?"

"Yeah. Actually, it is. So you're worried I'm going to get depressed again, is that it?" she confirmed.

"Correct."

"And I don't know if you're going to go out roughhousing and drinking and hooking up with buckle bunnies again."

"Never again to all three. I haven't done a one since you and I got married and I promise I never will. You have my solemn word and it is worth something, Diana."

She seized on that. "While we're on that

subject, didn't we both promise to care for each other in sickness and in health?"

"Yes, we did," he said. "I think you're saying I didn't do that for you when you were so sad."

She nodded.

"I am once again ashamed to say that you're right. I don't think I kept that vow. Mostly because I didn't know how to. But if talking helps"—being male to the bone he seemed baffled by the idea—"then let's keep talking. Whatever you need."

"Hey, a loving word now and then does work wonders. And patience too. And understanding that I can't stay at the house or in the house day after day and be expected to keep my sanity."

He raised his hand. "I want to amend my wedding vows. I promise to love, honor and cherish your car also. And change the oil every five hundred miles because that engine will melt if I don't."

Diana began to giggle, not able to help herself. "Lije, don't forget that we fell in love because we were having fun. There's going to be a hole in a fence or two now and then, and an escaped cow and a whole bunch of other stuff, but all that can't always come first. Otherwise we're going to lose—"

"That amazing connection," he said slowly. "The second I looked into those crystal-blue eyes of yours I felt it. Your soul was as beautiful as your face."

She ignored his flattery. "We need to be a couple. Go dancing. Have a dinner out, nothing fancy. Ordinary things."

He stared at the table. "Guess it never occurred to you that I wanted to take my beautiful baby out in something other than that old pickup."

"I don't give a damn what you drive," she said vehemently. "Just let me off this mountain once in a while."

"Yes, ma'am!"

The rumble of a truck sounded outside and Diana glanced that way. "Expecting someone? I hope it's not Ty."

He shook his head and got up. "It's Luis, one of the shepherds. I told him to stop by for some pills for the ewe that's ailing. And he found my hat after it blew off, so I gotta get that too." Lije put his hands on the table and leaned over a little. "Tell me one thing. You sure you don't miss the big city and the bright lights?"

She waited a little bit before replying, trying to compose herself. "I missed you, Lije. Don't you understand that?" Tears welled in her eyes as she looked up at him.

He took that in. "I do now. And thank you for telling it to me that straight."

She only nodded.

Lije studied her for a long moment. "About

that eight seconds you threw in my face—you had a point. About all I ever had to do in my life so far was hang on that long, and the crowds went wild."

"I did too," she said wistfully, remembering the thrill of watching him from the stands. "Once upon a time." It seemed like ages ago.

"Diana . . ." He seemed on the verge of reaching out to her, but he stayed on his side of the table. "I'll trade you that eight seconds for eight months, from now until the end of December. I can change my ways, but I can't promise I'll be perfect."

"I'm not asking for perfection, Lije."

"Well, good." He gave her a rueful grin. "But I know I can do better. And you do whatever you need to do. Talk to someone else besides me, maybe. Like a whatdoyoucallit—"

"A therapist."

He nodded. "If that's what you need, we'll find the damn money somehow. And make some friends around here so you don't have to rely on me so much."

"Okay."

"Eight months. We can do it. If things don't get better, then we can part. But at least we'll know we did our damnedest. Do we have a deal?"

Her lower lip trembled and she bit it to keep from crying. "Yes."

Lije straightened as the truck outside sounded

its horn. They had forgotten all about Luis. But Lije didn't turn to go just yet.

"Hell, I'm afraid if I leave you alone, you'll bolt. So . . . you staying or going?"

She thought hard, really hard, for a few more seconds before she answered. "Staying," she said.

"You sure?"

"Ninety-nine percent sure, yes."

He nodded and went to the high metal cabinet where he kept the animal medicines and took out a vial. Then he headed for the door. "Be right back. This won't take but a minute, I promise. Luis is a man of few words."

There seems to be a lot of them around here, she thought, absentmindedly admiring his broad shoulders and the long length of him from the back as she watched him charge out the door to the waiting truck.

She sat there, lost in thought, until suddenly he was back, hat in his hand, but holding it by the crown and not the brim. He came in, closing the door quietly. "Got something I wanted to show you."

"What is it?"

He walked to the table and lowered the hat. In it were two tiny puppies, sandy colored with white noses and paws and stubby tails.

"Aww. Look at them." She gazed into the hat and watched them squirm, then settle down again, curled against each other. "Their eyes aren't even open."

"No, not yet. The momma dog is in the car."

"Does she belong to Luis?"

Lije nodded, stroking one with a finger. An acknowledging but very faint yap issued from its tiny pink mouth. "His best sheepdog. But she surprised him with a litter. There were three."

"They're not even a week old, are they?"

"About that. Luis is going to keep the biggest—he already named it Ace. And he has takers for these two, but we have first choice. If we want them, that is."

"They're so sweet, Lije."

One puppy yawned and plopped its round head right back down on top of the other's. Diana laughed tenderly at the sight of his blissful little sleeping face. "What are their names?"

"They're brothers. I thought we could call them Deuce and Trey."

"We. You mean I."

"Well, yes," he said casually, stroking both puppies now. "You're home more'n me."

One puppy lifted its head and bumped it against the band on the inside of the hat, tasting the material and trying to suck on it.

"Now, now," Lije crooned. "No milk in that. They want their momma," he said to Diana. "I have to bring them back. She'll jump out the truck window to get them if I don't. So what do you say? Want to raise these babies?"

She looked into the Stetson again, touched by the innocence of its precious cargo. "They really are cute." The hungry pup turned its head blindly toward her and yapped. "All right. Sure. I could do with the company, and they'll always have each other to play with if we take both."

"They'll be weaned in another couple of months and ready to go." Looking very pleased with himself, he dropped a kiss on the top of her head.

"You really don't play fair, Lije," she murmured. She could feel him grin against her hair.

"You wanted something to do, now you have it. They'll keep you laughing and they'll guard the house. Say adios to the lady, boys," he said into the hat.

The tiny puppies vibrated with small snores as she gave them one last look. "Bye, Deuce and Trey. Sweet dreams. They really are adorable." She petted their soft fur with her fingertips, then Lije went through the door to return them to their momma in the truck.

When she heard it drive off, he was coming back in. "You won't be sorry. But they're going to grow up so smart you'll wonder who's training who sometimes."

She groaned. "What have I done?"

"You just said *yes*. Where's the harm in that?"

Diana gave him a bemused look. "I expect I'll find out. Now, why do you think I should raise puppies?"

Lije took a chair again and leaned back, rocking a little on the back legs. "You said you were ninety-nine percent sure you were staying. Those cute little critters make up the one percent difference."

"I don't know whether to kiss you or slap you."

"Option one," he said eagerly.

She said *yes* to the unspoken longing in his eyes and came around the table to sit in his lap and give him a kiss that would shut him up for a little while. She was hungry for it too.

"I love you, Diana." He looked deep in her eyes when she finally quit and sat up a little. His hand was on her waist, sliding around it inside her T-shirt. His other hand rested on her shoulders, massaging them gently.

She closed her eyes, feeling as happy as the puppies in the hat. "Don't stop," she murmured. "Mmm. Oh. Yes."

"I won't." He kept it up, doing some very skillful moves right about where her neck began. "You sure about those pups, now? I don't want you saying I manipulated you into taking them."

"Mmm. You did, though. Ah. Yes."

He increased his pleasurable rubbing. If he'd had her by the scruff of the neck, she couldn't have been more limp with bliss.

"It was that last little bit of not-sure. I could never let you go, even if I knew I was making your life miserable. That's how selfish I am."

"Don't give yourself any blue ribbons for that, pal," she teased him.

"I deserve one, though," he teased back.

"No. Not really."

He wouldn't give up and he was starting to tickle her. "Not even a tin-plated buckle with FIRST PRIZE FOR OBNOXIOUS MALE BEHAVIOR engraved on it?"

She finally had to pummel him. "Come Christmas, maybe. If I'm still around. Now, if you don't hurry up and kiss me again, you're going to make my life very miserable. So get started."

"You're rarin' to go, aren't you?" Lije laughed. Then he proceeded to kiss her thoroughly, making up for those empty days and sad nights when he'd been gone, sweeping her into a vortex of ever-rising passion until neither of them was satisfied with the physical restrictions of their embrace.

"We have some lost time to make up for, Diana," he whispered against the hollow of her neck.

"Yes," she agreed fervently, her mouth tender from the fierceness of his kisses. She craved more. She wanted all of him.

"Shall we do something about it now?" He lifted his head from hers to gaze down into her eyes, rarin' to go himself. "How am I doing on the interpersonal communication?"

"Better," she breathed.

"Sometimes it's best not to talk at all, Diana."

She straightened, pulling her hair off her neck and arching her back in a stretch that pretty much put her T-shirt-clad breasts into his face.

"Hello," he growled, cupping his hands to caress them. She got him by the wrists and wouldn't let him.

"On that subject—"

"What?" He laughed softly, amused by her sensually low voice.

"There's something else I want to do first," she murmured.

"What's that?" A frown creased his forehead.

Diana got up and took his hand, then led him outside over his protests. There she walked over and grabbed the thick rope that hung from the metal bell.

"Where did that come from?" Lije asked as Diana began pulling the clapper so that the bell rang loudly in the quiet countryside.

"Jim hung it for me while you were gone," she said with a beaming smile. Down at one of the small sheds, she saw Jim Two Pony step into the open, his hand waving in recognition of the bell. She waved back before walking over to her husband and putting her arms around his waist. "You do know that Jim refused to take me away from here, don't you?"

"I got that impression." Lije smiled.

"I thought it was only fair to let him know that all is well between us."

"I'm glad," he said softly, his eyes shining with pride and love. Then he was sweeping her off her feet and cradling her in his arms. "Ready to get behind a closed door with me, Mrs. Masters?"

"I think I am, Mr. Masters." Her arms went around his neck as he once again carried her over the threshold.

Chapter Fourteen

A few months later . . .

The summer came on strong, and, as Jim had promised, it was scorching nearly every day. Waves of heat rose from the baked earth of the New Mexico landscape, rising in a constant, shimmering dance to the infinite blue of the sky. Diana rarely went outside in the middle of the day, and even the house was filled with brilliant light.

Even when she closed her eyes, it sounded like summer. There was a constant, pleasant hum of insects she couldn't see and that didn't bother her. They were pursued by swift little lizards, moving over hot stones like the flick of a whip.

Deuce and Trey went from their well-shaded pen—built by Lije and Jim when the pups were small so they would be safe from marauding coyotes—through a door into the house whenever they wanted. It was hard to believe they had ever fit inside of Lije's Stetson. They were at the gangly stage, with paws too large for their legs and an avidly curious look on their nearly identical faces.

Once inside, they were blocked by a system of ridiculous gates inside the house, created from old pieces of fence that Jim found for her. There wasn't any other way to paint the interior with dogs roaming inside that were halfway between puppy craziness and adult behavior. Left to their own devices, they would stick their noses in the gallon cans of white latex, she was sure of it.

But they were good dogs, and going to be great dogs when they grew up.

They watched her kneel and pour more thick, creamy paint into the roller pan, listening to the faint squishing sound as she filled her roller as if it were the most amazing noise on the planet.

"Can't beat you two for paying attention," she murmured to them. Lije had been shrewd about offering them to her. She never felt lonely now during the days, and Lije put a lot more loving into the nights. She hummed contentedly. Deuce put a paw on the gate.

"Stay there," she told him. Diana straightened and laid on the first fat stripe of fresh paint. It seemed darker. "What do you think, boys? Does that color look the same as the chip from the store?"

They panted eagerly.

"I think so too." The room would be transformed when the job was done.

But summer was over when she finally finished it. That and other renovations had to be completed on the cheap, and they scraped together every penny so as not to take out a loan. She'd done most of the work including taking down the old gingham curtains in the kitchen, which turned out to be so stiff with dust and grease that they stood up by themselves on the floor. The new ones weren't expensive and her idea for painting the metal cabinets with simple flowers added just the right touch of handmade charm.

When she wasn't tackling projects like that, she was writing articles for Herb Bigelow at the *Bee-Gazette*. Just short ones because she didn't have the time for more and the paper didn't have the space, anyway—funny, fish-out-of-water themes that proved popular with his Northern New Mexico readers. Of course, she still had to drive down the mountain to deliver them, even though they were written on Lije's laptop. She'd been afraid that it would get jolted to death on the rutted road, and she was thankful for flash drives. Diana saved each article to the one she kept on her key chain and downloaded them from it to Herb's computer a couple of times a month.

She'd gotten to know him and his wife, Dottie, and Lije seemed very happy about that. And Lisa Griswold and her friend Raynetta, the plump redhead with the ringlets who was not named Destiny after all, had become good friends to her. The eight months were halfway over and she couldn't have been happier.

Right now she and Lije were in the living room, shoving the furniture back into position.

"I can't believe it took so long to finish this room."

"How many coats was it again?"

"Five. Those walls just drank paint," she said.

"Looks great." He stood up with a hand on his back. "Ow. I think I hurt something."

"Really? Lije, are you okay?"

The two dogs were right behind her, her concern mirrored in their worried expressions. They sat on either side of her when she came to a stop in front of Lije and wagged their tails, looking as if they were laughing at him.

He laughed when he looked down at all three of them. "Well, at least Deuce and Trey know when I'm lying."

He swept her up in his arms and carried her off to the bedroom, kicking the door closed behind them.

"Are you sure you're okay?" she asked one last time.

"Yes. Moving furniture always puts me in the mood."

He whirled her around until she was laughing and dizzy. "Lije! Stop! Put me down!"

"Mmm-kay." He pressed kisses to her neck and collarbone as she arched and wriggled in his arms, managing to push up her T-shirt as he did. They fell on the bed in a sensual tangle of legs and arms, his hands caressing her while she kissed him avidly.

"Is this my reward for fixing up the house?"

"No," he groaned into her neck, "this is because watching you do it makes me crazy with lust. You are so hot, do you know that?"

She laughed in a low voice, turning her head to let him trace his teeth along the outside of her ear and nip the lobe.

"I can't stand it. But I can't look away, either." He nibbled the cord of her neck. "The way you reach to dust something . . . then bend over in those ripped jeans." He moved lower, a lot lower. "Stretching up so I can see your belly button."

His nuzzling there made her scream with excited laughter.

He had most of her clothes off in another minute and he was down to just jeans himself, his boots kicked off. When the boots hit the wall one by one, the dogs barked in the next room, then they went outside through their door and settled down in their pen.

He was over her, looking down at her with so much love, she felt a little misty-eyed.

"Want me, girl?" His voice was husky and strong but filled with emotion.

"Yes, I do," she whispered.

They made love all that afternoon, and she went to shower while he lay sleeping. Diana came back into the bedroom wrapped in a big white towel and rubbing another one against her wet ear.

"Come here," he said drowsily, raising an arm that was heavy with flexed muscle.

Naked under the sheets, he was a gorgeous sight himself. She crawled back next to him, towel and all, and was encircled in a hug that lasted a while longer.

"That was my idea of how to spend a September afternoon," he said, buttoning his shirt while he watched her put on makeup, standing behind her as she looked into the mirror at her vanity table.

He had on jeans and cowboy boots, and it seemed to him like a crying shame to add anything else to her. But they did have plans to go out.

"Mmm," she said, pursing her lips and slicking on a light-colored natural gloss.

"Look at you, all pink and pearly. And not a bit surly."

She grinned at him, which was as good a way as any to check her teeth for lipstick. "Thanks to you."

"Happy to help a lady." He tipped an imaginary hat to her. "Hey, have you seen my Stetson?"

"Look on the hat rack." She was applying eye pencil and it was a painstaking task.

"I can't take you out to dinner without it. The Western code of honor forbids the escortation of a lady to a steakery without the proper hattitude."

She laughed and heard one of the dogs give a happy bark from outside. "Would you see if they have water, honey? We've been in here a while."

"Sure."

Diana heard him run water into a pitcher from the kitchen sink, then walk outside to the pen. "Deuce, Trey, you boys thirsty?" he called as he went around the side of the house. "Hey—give that back!"

There was a splash as if the pitcher had been dropped. And a tussling sound, as if one of the dogs was playing tug-of-war with him.

In no hurry, Diana got up and went outside herself to see. With a scowl on his face, Lije was dusting off his favorite Stetson, the weathered one that he'd had for years, creased just right, now with a slight nick in the brim.

"Oh, no," she said, coming closer. "That's your favorite hat."

"Tell me about it. Those damn dogs—"

Inside their pen, they looked at him with lolling tongues and lazy, who-me grins.

"How'd they get it? Deuce, Trey—you should be ashamed of yourselves."

They considered that and went back to grinning.

Lije brushed the last speck of dust off his hat and put it on his head. "We weren't paying attention, now, were we?"

"No, but—are you going to scold them? It's not that damaged, is it? They chew your stuff because they like you."

He shook his head. "Those damn dogs get to plea-bargain every time with you as their defense lawyer," he joked.

Deuce and Trey followed the conversation with doggy interest, heads swiveling from him to her.

"They look innocent, but it's safe to say they're guilty. Let me see that hat."

He took it off his head. "Send it to forensics. See if the tooth marks match either of the perpetrators."

Diana pretended to examine it herself, but she was just checking the tag for the size. There weren't any holes or tears in the crown, just chew marks on the brim. He needed a new hat, anyway. And since they were going to be in

Taos for dinner, she might just stop in at the Western-wear store in the central square.

She flicked the tag up with a fingernail and memorized the size.

"It'll do for now. Only the brim is a little bit damaged. If they'd chewed the crown, you'd have cross-ventilation. But they didn't."

He laughed and put it back on his head at a rakish angle, slapping her on the butt. Deuce and Trey barked in her defense, and she let the dogs out so she and Lije could play with them for a while before leaving for the evening.

He wore the same old hat all through October and into the cold of November. They hadn't had his size in Taos on the night they went, and Lije had balked at the cost of the style he wanted.

Diana hadn't pushed it.

"You can't separate a cowboy from his hat," he'd growled, and she'd let it go.

That night, when he'd come home late, dead-tired and dirty, she entered the living room to find him warming his backside in front of the fire, his sheepskin jacket on and his hands holding the slightly squashed roast beef sandwich he'd taken with him for lunch. Deuce and Trey watched him closely as he devoured it, but they behaved themselves. He was shivering mightily.

"Thanks for keeping the fire going," he said. "Whew. I can't seem to get warm."

"Look at you, Lije. At least let me make you something hot to eat."

The last bite of cold roast beef and bread disappeared into his mouth. "No thanks," he mumbled. "This'm do. Not ver' hungry." He brushed the crumbs from his hands and they were Hoovered up by the dogs.

"You have to take a hot shower and change, right now. Those jeans are covered with wet mud."

He relinquished his sheepskin jacket, which she put over a chair away from the fireplace. The jacket had somehow escaped the mud, but it was damp and would dry best if it wasn't right next to the fire. He handed her the hat next, and she took it, enjoying the warm, comfortable feel of the battered felt in her hand, brushing off the light snow on it into the fire. The tiny, crystalline flakes fell into the flames and sizzled.

"What were you doing out there?" She held the hat a moment longer, wishing she hadn't listened to him and had just gone ahead and purchased a new one in thicker felt. At least his hair was dry. Then she set the old Stetson to one side. The dogs were past the chewing-everything stage, thank goodness, and ignored it.

"A cow got stuck in the gulley. Jim found her late this afternoon when he was out riding just as the light was dying. Took both of us and Luis to get her loose. And she wasn't in a mood to cooperate." He circled his hands into a single fist and blew into it. "If there's a critter on earth stupider and more stubborn than a cow, I hope I never meet it. Can you turn the heat in the house up higher? I don't think this fire is enough."

She gave him a worried look as she went to the thermostat and did as he asked. "Come on. You have to change."

He rubbed his hands together and followed her, smelling like cold mud and warm man and New Mexico in November all rolled together.

Diana had the pleasure of stripping him herself.

"You sneak. You got me into this bathroom just so I'd help you with the steel buttons on your jeans," she said and laughed.

"I couldn't do it myself. My hands really are that cold," he insisted. He put his cupped palms on her cheeks and she shrank back.

"Ow. That almost hurts. All right, in you go. No more arguing with me." She turned on the hot water full blast, and guided him in all his brawny, naked glory into the shower.

He sang some old cowboy song while he let the hot spray pound him. Deuce and Trey listened anxiously from the hall as the loud song concluded with several extended yodels and *yippee-yi-yays*, looking to Diana for reassurance.

She patted each shaggy head in turn. "You're

scaring the dogs," she called into the bathroom as the shower was forcibly turned off.

"Tough," he said. "Got a towel for me?"

"I warmed up the giant one by the fire."

His dripping head poked out from the side of the curtain. "Seriously?"

"Yeah. And you're going under the down comforter in our bedroom with a hot water bottle after you have a shot of whiskey."

"Make that two. One for me and one for you. And come to bed."

"It's too early," she protested. "And I don't feel like drinking."

"Aww," he grumbled as she handed him the warmed towel. "You're no fun."

"You need to warm up," she said firmly.

She could still feel a faint trembling when she touched him and there was a high color in his face that she didn't think was from the hot shower.

Diana normally would have begged for a kiss from him, but she was pretty sure he was coming down with something and she didn't want to catch it. But he was easy enough to distract with a little pampering. He tossed down the whiskey when she brought him a double shot in a thick-bottomed glass, rolled himself up in the comforter and was fast asleep the next time she looked in on him.

* * *

He woke up in the middle of the night with a fever so high she felt scorched. Lije was sitting straight up in bed, gasping, as she struggled to open her eyes.

"Can't breathe," he said, flinging off the covers.

Diana sat up and looked at him, then put a hand to his forehead. "You're going to the hospital," she said, wide-awake now.

"N-no. Not that sick."

He fell backward into the pillows as if holding himself up was a huge effort. She hovered anxiously over him. His eyes glittered and the high color she'd seen in his face earlier in the evening was still there, deeper, as if it had stained his skin. He couldn't seem to breathe very well lying down and he rose halfway.

Acting on instinct, she thrust all the pillows under his upper back.

"Stay up—just like that. Don't move too much. You're really sick, Lije, and this is an emergency. I'm going out to warm up the car and we're going."

"G-get Jim." His teeth were chattering and his whole body was shaking now.

The next few minutes were a blur. She threw on a robe and, in the living room, a coat over that, sticking her bare feet into boots. Then, running wildly to the cabin, she banged on the door. Jim came out in long johns, and, once he heard what was wrong, grabbed clothes as fast as she had.

She ran back home and called the hospital in the next big town, fifty miles from Ventana, to let them know they were coming in. It wasn't a trauma case, but Lije's fever was dangerously high. She refused ambulance transport, afraid that the EMT vehicle could go off the side of the mountain dirt road, especially in the dark.

"We'll get him there," Diana told the intake person. "Just be ready." She hung up and grabbed her purse and his wallet, mentally thanking the PRCA for footing a large part of the bill for his expensive health insurance. She hoped the insurance card was in Lije's wallet, but that was the least of her worries.

Between her and Jim, they half-dragged, half-carried Lije, too feverish and weak to stand, to the back of the car, where they propped him on firm sofa pillows she'd hurried back inside to get, and buckled him up as best they could.

Lije felt every rut in the road, moaning when the car jolted and slid. Jim remained calm, gripping the wheel to stay in control. The cold night had turned frosty and there was ice to contend with too.

The highway, when they got to that, had been empty. Diana twisted under her seat belt and reached back to touch Lije's hand. "We're on our way. You're going to be all right." She saw with horror that he was unconscious.

* * *

But they made it. The cold, sterile corridors of the hospital echoed as Lije was moved on a gurney from the emergency room, Diana and Jim by his side as long as they could stay. At the ICU, a nurse with a clipboard admitted the accompanying medical team and their patient, but she shook her head at Diana and Jim.

"Sorry. You have to go back to Admitting." She pointed her pencil and closed the door behind the gurney and the last member of the team.

Diana turned to Jim and burst into tears.

For several minutes they just stood there in an embrace that comforted them both. Then they made their way, making a few wrong turns, but ending up in the ER eventually.

Her mind sharpened by worry, Diana saw to the paperwork, assisted by an efficient clerk, who also managed to be kind. There was nothing to do but wait.

So they waited.

At dawn, a doctor appeared and gestured them over to a small room near the ER with a plain table and blue vinyl chairs. He held charts and things like that, which he put on the table, gesturing to them to sit down.

"Mrs. Masters and—?" He looked at Jim.

"I'm Jim Two Pony," he introduced himself.

"I grew up with Lije. I still live on the Masterses' ranch."

The doctor nodded. "Okay. I'm Dr. Rollins and I just want to give you an update."

Update, Diana thought numbly. That meant her husband was still alive. They didn't give updates on patients who didn't make it.

Dr. Rollins glanced at his papers. "Mr. Masters—Elijah—seems to have a particularly virulent pneumonia. We don't have the cultures back, but because of the swift onset and rapid negative impact on some organ functions, we suspect it's bacterial, relatively rare, and multiple-drug-resistant. What that means in plain English is that he's extremely ill and has to stay in the ICU."

"For how long?" Diana whispered.

"Until he can breathe on his own."

Jim asked a question after a little while. "Can we see him?"

"Not until we know exactly what bacteria is causing it. And even then, visits have to be short and limited to talking."

"Is he conscious?" Diana asked.

"No. He's been sedated, which helps with the breathing tube that was inserted, and the intravenous antibiotics."

The hideous vision of Lije, alone and hooked up to machines, struggling for his life when only hours ago he'd been walking and talking, was appalling. But there was nothing they could do, it seemed, for now.

"It was a good thing that you two got him here so quickly," the doctor said. "Sometimes people wait—in certain cases, you shouldn't. So he has a good shot at recovery."

"Is that all?" Jim asked, a faint crack in his voice.

"Maybe more. We think he's going to make it. But for the next few days he will remain in the ICU and intubated. After that, he can be moved but we'll see. Bringing him in as fast as you did was crucial. I'd be happy to give you updates for the rest of today, and the doctor on the shift after mine will do the same. Or you can call the nurse's station in the ICU. I assume you both have cell phones?"

"Actually, we don't," Diana said.

The doctor looked a little surprised. "Where can we reach you, then? At the ranch? That's the number on the admitting paperwork, isn't it?"

Diana and Jim looked at each other and at that moment became a team of two.

"I'll stay at the ranch house," he said, "where I can be reached. That way I can take care of the horses and the dogs."

"I'll stay with Herb and Dottie Bigelow," she told him. She reached into her purse and took out her wallet, looking for the old cowboy's business card. His home phone was on the back. She found it. "Ready?" she asked the doctor.

Dr. Rollins didn't look up, pen in hand. She read the Bigelows' number aloud, then wrote it down for Jim on another business card. Hers.

"I'm grateful you called us. We want to help and it's no trouble at all. You come right in." Dottie seemed shaken by the news, but she took Diana inside immediately, settling her on the couch with a cup of tea before she turned to go upstairs. "Let me wake Herb. He didn't hear the phone ring and it's right by his head."

"No. Let him sleep," Diana whispered.

"I can't do that," Dottie said. "He'd give me hell. Back in a minute." She lifted the hem of her quilted bathrobe and ascended the stairs.

Diana held on to the steaming cup, grateful for its warmth, but not wanting to drink it. Her throat was nearly closed by an agonizing lump.

In another minute, Herb rode down on the stair elevator. Dottie went ahead and had the walker waiting for him.

He rose and took it, going over to Diana as swiftly as if he could walk on his own. But he stayed standing.

"Dottie told me everything, so you don't have to say a word. Just sit here and recover for a bit. When you're ready, we can have breakfast. Or not. Whatever you want."

The thought of food made her queasy, but she nodded. Jim had told her in his laconic way

to eat something and keep up her strength.
There was more than one reason to follow his
good advice now, she thought dully.

The Bigelows were a team of two as well,
and they'd been at it for more than fifty years.
By noon, they'd sent Lisa up to the ranch for
clothes for Diana, and found a couple of volun-
teers to help Jim with the ranch chores and
responsibilities.

That left her with nothing to do but wait
some more. She remembered that Dr. Rollins
was going off shift later in the day, and she
wanted to talk to him before he left. She found
the number in her purse and turned to Dottie,
who was just coming out of the kitchen.

"Dottie—can I make a call to the hospital
somewhere private?"

"Yes, of course." Dottie bustled by her,
wiping her hands on her apron and heading
for the living room, where she picked up an
old, rotary dial phone from a small table.
Diana watched the phone's long, thin cord
unkink itself as she followed Dottie to a pretty
little parlor that didn't seem to ever be used.

The older woman plunked down the heavy
phone on another small table and pulled out
a chair for Diana next to it. "There you go. I'll
close the door behind me."

"Thanks."

Dottie exited, kicking the cord to one side so she wouldn't trip on it, and then carefully shut the door over it with a polite click.

Diana just stared at the phone and then at the number on the card in her hand, not quite sure how to use the old-fashioned phone. She picked up the receiver, heard a dial tone, and then channeled some old movie scene. It wasn't hard to dial, just a bit tougher on her manicure and a little slower to respond. It gave her a minute to compose herself. Dr. Rollins picked up on the third ring and identified himself.

"Hi, Dr. Rollins. It's Diana Masters. How is Lije?"

"Hello. Good to hear from you. His condition has stabilized."

Her voice faltered. "But he's not better?"

"He's not out of the woods yet, Mrs. Masters. But the best news is that there is no decline in vital organ functioning. So far the infection is confined to his lungs and we're fighting that with a cocktail of very strong antibiotics, which he seems to be tolerating. Adverse drug reactions can also be a problem in cases like this . . ."

He said more, meticulous in his attention to the details of Lije's treatment. Diana listened but she hadn't brought pen and paper with her. "Thank you for the good news," she said softly when he paused. "I think it is good news, anyway."

"It is. But stay in touch."

Something had been left unsaid, she knew that. *Just in case things change for the worse. Just in case Lije slips away without ever waking up.*

All she wanted to do was be with him, see his face again, love him up and kiss him for all she was worth. But she couldn't.

"Thank you, Dr. Rollins."

He told her the name of the physician who was on the next shift and gave Diana his number. She nodded, not thinking that he couldn't see her, then said thank you. She could remember the new name and get the number from the hospital, and there was always the nurse's station as a backup.

"Talk to you tomorrow, then," she said to Dr. Rollins before she said a final thank-you and hung up. She sat in the little parlor for several minutes in silence, her hands folded in her lap, staring out the window. Without her noticing it, snow had begun to fall in thick flakes that drifted down like feathers, slowly, as if they wanted to stay in the air and not touch the earth before they had to.

When she did notice them, she got up and touched her hand to the windowpane, letting the coldness of it bring her back to reality.

She said a silent prayer for her husband, willing him to live. He had to.

Dottie took the phone from her when she walked down the hall from the parlor, waiting unobtrusively at the end of it. "Don't trip on that cord, now. Herb insists that we keep that old thing. I use a cordless myself. Or my cell."

Diana smiled wanly. "I can see why he likes it. I do too. It lets you think. No one-touch, no nothing. Anyway"—she hesitated—"I called Dr. Rollins and he said that Lije is—that his condition has stabilized and that he's tolerating the drugs, which are strong."

"That's good to hear!" Dottie said warmly.

Herb appeared in the kitchen doorway, his still-strong arms holding him up on the bars of his rolling walker. "Rollins knows his stuff. He treated me when I had pneumonia, Diana."

"Really?"

"Got taken to the same hospital as Lije too. And I'm about a thousand years older than your young feller." He raised one hand and thumped his chest. "And here I am. Still going strong."

Dottie beamed at him and then at Diana. "You ready to eat yet, honey?"

"I think so, yes."

She went into the kitchen, which had a comfortably cluttered, lived-in-for-fifty-years look and still managed to be immaculate. Dottie had been baking and a light smell of cinnamon filled the room.

"I made a tea cake. And I can soft-boil an egg for you, if you like."

Diana felt her stomach flip at the word "egg."

"I'd love some cake. But no thanks on the egg."

"That's the idea," the older woman said in a motherly way. "Just eat lightly, little meals, several times a day."

Herb Bigelow winked at her. "You're in good hands, Diana."

Later, after she had checked in with the nurse's station and heard a more encouraging report on Lije, she called Jim at the ranch.

"He's doing better," she said excitedly. "I just talked to the head ICU nurse. Vitals, lung function, everything."

"Can he talk yet?" Jim asked.

"Not too well, but he asked for me. Jim, she said I could come in tomorrow!"

"That's great, Diana. You say hello for me."

"I will." She knew his terse message was all that needed to be said between those two.

They chatted for a little while longer.

"Well, it's freezing up here," Jim said. "The horses are fine. The dogs are crazy, but what else is new. Those guys the Bigelows sent up are really helping. Might keep them on as temporary hands next year. And it's snowing. Not sticking, though. Too much wind."

"We got some here too. It's pretty."

"Yeah."

She valued Jim's calm reticence more than ever, but she knew he had been under the same strain and suffering the same uncertainty as she over Lije's condition.

"I'll call you later," she promised him. "After I talk to Dr. Rollins. They still don't know exactly what kind of pneumonia he has."

"Thanks, Diana. You take care now."

"I will, Jim," she said softly. "You too."

Diana heard the shuffling sound of Herb coming down the hall, singing under his breath. "Jingle" this and "jingle" that. With a start, she realized he was singing a Christmas carol.

Of course. Thanksgiving had come and gone—they'd had a quiet celebration at the ranch, just she and Lije and Jim and his girl, Tina—and it was now the beginning of December.

The eighth month of their agreement to stay together and work things out. Life had a way of radically changing everything overnight, she thought. So much for plans and agreements and the stupid arguments that had come between them. She wasn't giving up on Lije, not for a minute, or on the marriage, not ever. No matter what.

Together, they were strong. And there was love enough between them for a lifetime and then some.

He was going to *live*. And he was going to go back to the ranch he loved, as soon as the doctors gave him the go-ahead. She and Jim could run it between them, with some help, until Lije had completely regained his strength.

She got up and went to Herb. "I heard everything you just said," he told her, "so no need to repeat it. Eavesdropping saves a lot of time."

"You're terrible." She planted a light kiss on his cheek as he stopped to let her go by.

"What was that for?" he asked, his eyes twinkling.

"Because you and Dottie are my inspiration," she said.

"Dottie!" he called. "Dottie! Are you listening?"

"The whole street is, Herb," she said from the side room, where she was engrossed in an online chat with her Grandmas' group. Dottie and Herb had no children, but the grandmas made up the rules as they went along, anyway.

"Diana says we're her inspiration."

Dottie got up and poked her head out. "Why?" She laughed.

"Because," Diana said, smiling. "You just are."

The Bigelows exchanged a fond look before Dottie went back to what she was doing.

"Say, Diana, you didn't happen to bring that flash drive with you in all the confusion, did you?"

"It's on my key chain," she replied. "So, yes, I did."

"I was thinking we could go over your article before it goes into the paper. The one about your first trip to the mercantile—you only gave me a first draft."

"Oh, right. Yeah, I saved the final version on the flash drive, so, sure. I'd love to hear what you think."

She knew he'd waited to provide a little distraction like that until he was sure Lije had gained some ground and she wasn't sick with worry over him. Herb led the way to his home office, which Dottie had done up in Old West style, with a wonderful old lamp that had a cowboy on a wild bronco hand-painted on the parchment shade. The lamp's finial was a tiny Stetson, as if the painted cowboy had thrown it high in the air.

Herb reached down to switch it on and went over to his computer, while she left him for a minute to retrieve the flash drive. Returning, she handed it to him and he stuck it in the USB port. Diana leaned over his shoulder and found the file, clicking on the mouse to the right of the computer and opening it.

"Want me to save this to your Documents folder?" she asked.

"Sure."

She did, and opened it in wide format so they both could read it easily. Herb laughed after he finished. "Bacon in a can, that's a funny bit. That stuff comes in handy, though."

"If I'd gotten this in before Thanksgiving, I

would have added something about wondering whether you could get turkey in a can too."

"Oh, sure. That's not a problem."

"Really?" she asked. "I mean, I know they put turkey chunks in soup and gravy and stuff, but what I was thinking of was a whole turkey."

"Well, that's different," Herb said. "What you would need is a really big can and a very cooperative turkey."

They shared a good laugh over that notion and then companionably settled down to work together. The house was cozy, and neither Diana nor the Bigelows noticed the steady fall of the snow outside.

When she clicked a final SAVE for the article, she looked up and saw the way the snow was coming down. Diana went to the window, delighted. Then another thought made her turn to Herb with a sad expression.

"Wish Lije could see it. They don't have windows in the ICU."

"Hell, snow is snow," Herb said gruffly. "There's always more, sooner or later. This being December, it will be sooner."

"Think it'll be a white Christmas?" she asked.

"Hard to tell. Sometimes we get one, sometimes we don't. The young'uns love it, of course. But at my age, I'd rather look at snow than get stuck in it."

She thought about Lije and what he would

do in the snow out at the ranch when he wasn't working.

He'd be invigorated. Happy. Diana just bet he was deadly accurate with a snowball too.

Again she sent up a silent prayer that he would get better and get home in time for Christmas.

"Hey there," Herb said. "You're a million miles away."

"Just thinking."

He got up awkwardly. "Want to check your e-mail and whatnot? I know you said that that laptop on the ranch isn't too good at sniffing out a wireless signal."

"Oh—okay." She had used his office computer for just that reason when she'd come into Ventana now and again during the fall. "Thanks, Herb. That would be great."

"Think I'll go help Dottie. Unless she shoos me away, of course."

Diana sat down in the chair where he'd been, signing into her e-mail account and catching up with a few messages. There was one from Stella. Now, that was a surprise. She hadn't connected with her friend and fellow model since the day she'd quit to marry Lije.

She sent a tentative hello, just to see how Stella was doing before she told her what had happened to Lije.

Diana! Long time no e. How ARE u . . . and the Cowboy God?????????

Okay . . . That was an invitation to talk. Diana took a deep breath and filled up the screen with the short version of everything that had happened in the past ten months, concluding with Lije's sudden serious illness and ending on a hopeful note. She sat back and waited for a reply, meanwhile deleting the spam that had gotten through and the usual improbable offers. Then . . .

OMG!

The talkative Stella went on for a lot longer than that, of course. By the time the exchange had finished, Diana had asked her friend to drive up to Ventana by the third week of December, just to hang out and see the area. She'd learned that Vanessa was now in New York, making serious money; that Connie had taken a job at a department store; and that Rick the photographer had married some skinny chick who was too decadent herself to care about his philandering. The whole world of modeling seemed awfully far away as if Diana had never been paid for just standing there and looking pretty day after day. Diana was surprised to find that she honestly didn't miss it. She'd made a living, nothing more.

She sent one last e-mail to Stella, and then one to Lisa Griswold, updating her on the latest health bulletin, knowing that Lisa would do the rest of the work of telling the entire county including people who'd never heard of Lije.

Lisa also got back to her right away:

Me and Raynetta and some other people are taking you Christmas shopping in Taos next Tuesday. Pick you up at Casa Bigelows at 10 AM. Sorry about stupid, freakin' car—called the ranch and Jim said the radiator was shot and it was too icy to drag it down the mountain. If we could, we'd buy you a new radiator, but not yet. Buy whatever you want or need, we're paying, so hah. Raynetta says we need the good karma, so you can't say no. We won't listen. See ya.

Lisa's breezy tone was intended to help chase away Diana's blues. Diana held back a gallon of tears and typed in a reply.

You're the best. Yes.

Diana got back a huge smiley face.

Then, with a sigh, she typed in the e-mail address for her online banking account. One username plus a password later, she was scrolling through bad news. She had a negative balance and their mortgage payment check had bounced. She swore under her breath so neither of the Bigelows would hear, even though

she knew Herb could outcuss her any day of
the week.

It might be a merry Christmas if Lije got out
of the hospital and got home, but it wasn't
going to be a solvent one. In a daze, trying to
keep this new worry in some kind of perspective, Diana got up from the computer without
signing out. She went into the room where the
Bigelows had her all set up with her clothes
and things, looking for the checkbook just to
make sure the mortgage payment had been
properly deducted.

She couldn't find it. Diana plopped down
on the bed, neatly made for her by Dottie, and
allowed herself a luxury that was actually free:
tears.

When she was done, she rose and steeled
herself to call the bank manager who handled
local mortgages for ranchers and townspeople
alike. It was possible, she'd heard, to negotiate
lower payments. And that was what she was
going to. First, though, she'd look up the ins
and outs online, and then she'd call.

When she got back to Herb's computer,
the chair was still empty but her session had
timed out.

She pulled up the information again, getting
exact numbers and dates, and did the research
she needed. Apparently such things were handled on a case-by-case basis. She wasn't asking
for charity. The ranch was at stake and losing

it would break Lije's heart. Diana looked at the numbers she'd jotted down in neat rows. So much in actual income. So much in projected income. Fixed expenses. Fluctuating expenses— there were a lot of those in a ranching operation. The well Ty Spalding had drilled had been the most recent and the biggest.

Diana straightened up and reached for the phone, dialing the number on the bank manager's card. She had her facts lined up and ready. The bank manager was male—she'd met him and he seemed very nice. Kinda flirty but respectful. So, if she couldn't convince him with her figures, she'd head over to his office and flutter her eyelashes at him until he fell over backward in his solid-oak chair. Whatever it took.

The phone discussion was brief. He was really nice about it all, but asked her for more documentation, which was at the ranch. Diana told him she would ask Jim to find it and bring it down when he could. In the meantime, the manager stopped the clock on the loan schedule. So far, so good.

The phone on the desk rang, and she assumed it was someone for the Bigelows. Diana didn't answer it.

In another minute, Dottie ventured in and spoke to her. "Honey, it's Dr. Rollins. I'm sure you want to talk to him."

"Huh?—oh. Of course. Thanks, Dottie."

She picked up the receiver and took a deep breath, letting it out once the doctor said hello.

"How is he today, Dr. Rollins?"

"Better than yesterday." His tone was encouraging and warm. "His progress is remarkable. Your husband is a strong man, Mrs. Masters."

"I know," she said softly. "I know."

He cleared his throat. "We got most of the tests back. There's good news there too."

"Thank God," she breathed.

"It's a nasty bug, and not a very common one." He named it, something long and scientific-sounding. "Not something you'd sign up to get, but not the worst thing you could catch, either. And Elijah—I mean Lije," he corrected himself, having figured out that by now.

Or had Lije set him straight? The thought made her smile.

"Lije is responding well to the array of antibiotics. He's scheduled to get up and walk today, with assistance, of course, and he's also scheduled for pulmonary therapy to keep his lungs clear during the recovery period."

She wanted to jump for joy, swing from the curtains, run down the hall whooping and hollering, but instead she quietly asked a single question.

"When can he come home?"

"Sooner than we thought. But I can't give you an exact date. You can visit now, though. There are certain restrictions for visitors in the ICU, but the nurse will go over those with you. I think that about covers it."

Tears were streaming down her face.

"Mrs. Masters? You there?"

"Sort of," she said. "Actually, I'm on cloud nine. Thank you, Dr. Rollins. Thank you so incredibly much for everything you've done."

"You're welcome. We medical mavens love a happy ending, believe me."

"Can I visit him today?"

"Sure."

Chapter Fifteen

A nurse opened the door to one part of the ICU and with a clipboard waved in Diana. "He's awake," she said quietly. "But please keep your voice low. I mean, it's noisy in here, but there are other patients."

Diana nodded, feeling her heart race when she saw Lije in the bed. He was still—so still—and there was a thin clear tube in his nose and a monitoring cuff on his left upper arm. He wasn't looking her way and he didn't seem to hear her, but the *whooshes* and beeps and assorted other sounds of medical equipment made the nurse's footsteps and hers inaudible.

The nurse moved into his line of vision and again gestured with her clipboard. Lije looked up at her and then his gaze moved to Diana. He lay still but his eyes seemed to embrace her, moving rapidly all over her, drinking her in.

"Diana," he whispered. "I love you. I love you so much. And the inside of my nose hurts. But I love you."

"Lije," she said softly, wishing she could kiss his stubbly cheek. "That has to be the most romantic thing you ever said to me."

"He's still experiencing some of the effects of the sedation," the nurse explained, trying to keep a straight face. "And he hates that tube. Not to worry, Mr. Masters. It's coming out as soon as Doc Rollins gives the okay."

Diana wiped away some big, fat tears and went to his side, leaning over him to carefully put her arms around what she could hold, mindful of the things attached to him. The nurse looked a little misty-eyed as she glanced at the two of them, and then at the monitor screens. Diana turned her head that way too, afraid she'd done something.

"Just look at those readings," the nurse said, chuckling softly. "He's definitely responding. Go easy on him, Mrs. Masters. We want him out of here as much as you do."

Diana let go and straightened up, feeling desperately guilty until she saw the shaky grin on Lije's face.

"You heard the lady," he said to his wife. "But don't listen. Come back here and hold me some more. That's about the best hug I ever had in my life. You smell so good. You smell like life. Stay by me. Until they make you go."

The smiling nurse nodded to her. Diana didn't have words for what she felt, but it didn't matter. They were together again.

The next day, when he was stronger, they moved him to a regular room and took out the tube in his nose. An orderly brought her a cot and blankets, and Diana moved in. When he was awake, she caught him up on the news of the ranch, conveying Jim's messages and reports on the horses and their herds, and how Deuce and Trey rode everywhere with Jim, since they hated being alone at the house, and how their friends had all pitched in to help. He seemed disbelieving at first, but he took it all in. Mostly they were quiet. He listened to music on headphones—Raynetta had downloaded practically every country-western hit of the past forty years onto a new iPod that someone from her church had donated anonymously for him.

Sometimes he sang along softly and sometimes he just slept. The days went by and his progress was steady, with never a setback.

She didn't tell him about the mortgage. The banker hadn't called back at the Bigelows', and they would just cross that bridge when they got to it.

He endured his pulmonary therapy, submitting to *thumps* and tests and breathing exercises. And he walked down the corridors like it was his new religion, assisted by a brawny ex-Marine nurse at first, then with a cane in one hand and the other clasping Diana's.

Dr. Rollins had explained that his unsteadiness would disappear, and gave a very hopeful prognosis otherwise. The last thing he'd said, to her joy, was that Lije would be home for Christmas.

Not at the Bigelows' little house in Ventana, although they'd been kind enough to offer it, but at their own home on the ranch, where Jim had a tree cut and waiting in the living room for them to decorate.

Lisa and Raynetta had taken Diana shopping in Taos just as they'd promised, and bought her as many useful gifts as there were wonderful ones, wrapping everything in gaudy, shiny paper just for the hell of it. They had pooled their money and a whole lot of donations Herb Bigelow had hustled up. Contacted by them, Stella had chipped in too, and also forwarded a healthy check from Vanessa.

But there was one gift that was from her alone. That one was going to be opened on Christmas Eve before any of the others.

Diana sighed, thinking about it, and looked over at him. He'd fallen asleep suddenly, the way he often did, and so she didn't have to tell him why she was leaving or where she was going.

She left the room but didn't take her coat, heading for a different wing of the hospital. A friendly technician welcomed her into an office and helped her up onto the examining table in the inner office, then helped her lie back. As Diana made herself comfortable, the woman chatted, preparing her for a sonogram.

Diana shivered when cold jelly was spread over her belly, and then the technician moved the device that was linked to a monitor screen faced so that they both could see it. Several times the technician stopped the device in a certain position and pressed a button to get a still image.

For her part, Diana wasn't exactly sure what she was seeing until a tiny arm waved in the grayness of the image. And then there was the head—and, was she seeing double?

"Hey," said the technician. "I think I see twins. Let's get Dr. Kumar and see what she thinks, okay?"

Chapter Sixteen

The day of Lije's homeward-bound journey dawned clear but freezing cold. Diana had gone back to the Bigelows to collect her belongings, and Lisa was waiting outside in a four-wheel drive SUV that would bring them both back to the ranch in relative comfort.

She heard the phone ring and let Dottie pick it up, half-listening to the older woman's side of the conversation.

"Yes, she's still here," Dottie said. "Diana! Call for you!" She held her hand over the receiver. "He said he's with the bank."

Uh-oh. Today of all days—she prayed it was good news. Dottie tactfully disappeared and Diana took the call alone.

"Hey there, Mrs. Masters," said the bank manager. "Turns out there's no problem with that mortgage payment."

"You mean"—she faltered—"was the statement in error?"

"Nope. The overdraft has been covered. The original check has been cleared and the January payment has been made in advance."

"What—who?"

"I wish I could give you a name. But I can't."

"I understand," she whispered, turning to look at Dottie and Herb.

"Well, maybe not," the bank manager said. "The reason I can't give you a name is that the money came from the whole damn town. So there you go."

"Thank you." Her lips had formed the words but no sound had come out. She hung up and stared at the Bigelows.

"We put in some," Herb said. "You didn't sign out of your online banking account. Hell, yes, I snooped. Life is short and I'm not a patient man. And you wouldn't have told me if I'd asked. Anyway, we passed the hat."

She rushed into their arms and that was that.

It was late in the day by the time they finally finished the claims forms and all the other paperwork and everything else that was needed to get Lije out of the hospital. He made his way over the snow-packed sidewalk to the cleared parking lot, still using a cane but not relying on her as much. She and Lisa helped him get settled, then put in all the bags, driving out and down toward Ventana, fifty miles away. She hoped the ride wouldn't tire him—they still had to get up the mountain. He looked out the window, studying the long, blue-purple shadows stretching over the snow.

When they turned off the highway, they saw tiny, twinkling lights up ahead. And when they drove down the main street of Ventana, they saw why. Every house was decorated with rows of luminarias, blinking through the darkness. And the street was lined with well-wishers, bearing signs, which they held up, hollering happily.

WELCOME HOME, LIJE AND DIANA!
MERRY CHRISTMAS TO MR. AND MRS. MASTERS!
GET WELL SOON OR ELSE.
GOD BLESS ALL Y'ALL.

And Lije's personal favorite:

YOU OWE ME A VACATION.

Jim and Tina were holding that one.
"Will you look at that," Lije said softly.
Lisa slowed down and she and Diana waved and shouted. It was one hell of a homecoming. But there was more.

Diana got him settled by the tree, which they would decorate tomorrow. But the huge stack of gifts under it made it look festive all the same. "Okay," she said, once the ecstatic dogs had settled down too. "I have a gift for you, but I didn't wrap it."

"That's okay, angel. I don't want anything other than what I have right here, right now."

She shook her head and reached behind the chair, bringing up the new Stetson she'd stashed there.

"Aw, now, Diana. I don't need a new one," he began.

"There's something inside."

"It's not more puppies, is it?" he asked with a look of alarm. "These two maniacs are enough right now, don't you think?"

"Just look."

"Well, give it to me, then."

She laughed, not realizing that she still was holding the hat. Lije took it and turned it around, admiring it.

"That's a fine hat. And, yes, I see there's a piece of paper tucked in the brim and I hope it's a winning lottery ticket, because I don't know how the hell else we're ever going to pay the bills in January—"

"Open it!"

He finally did and he read with wonder what she'd written. "Twins? Really?" He spread his arms wide and she went into them, sitting on his lap. "If that don't beat all—oh, Diana— how I love you—you don't know how much, you just don't—" He covered her face with kisses, hugging her and laughing.

"I love you too. And we're going to be all right. The whole damn town pitched in to pay our bills through January, including the mortgage. After that—" she whispered.

Lije stood up with her as if he'd never been ill at all. The strength she felt in him flowed through his arms to her. "I can carry all three of you. Not a problem. Everything's gonna work out fine."

Did you enjoy this Janet Dailey book?
Then try her Calder Family series. . . .

CALDER STORM

With his rugged-cowboy looks, Trey Calder could have his pick of women. But he's been holding out for someone special, and the minute he lays eyes on photographer Sloan Davis, he knows he's found her, and within weeks the two are married. It's a dream come true for the orphaned Sloan . . . until Trey makes a startling discovery about just who Sloan is and what she's really after.

Passion turns into suspicion and a dangerous game is set in motion, putting everything the Calders have worked for over the generations on the line. A formidable enemy has been lying in wait. Someone who will use whatever means necessary to control their land, their lives, and their legacy forever. Trey Calder has been trained to take over his family's ranch, to protect what is theirs. Now the time has come for a Calder son to make a stand and hope that his way is the right way.

LONE CALDER STAR

Quint Echohawk is a lawman, not a rancher, but he's a Calder through and through. And when someone sets out to undermine the Calders' Texas outfit, it's time for him to step in and investigate.

From the moment Quint's boots touch Texas dirt, it's clear that everyone in town is running scared from Max Rutledge, the ruthless owner of a competing ranch. Posing as a cowboy looking for work, Quint has no one to trust but "Empty" Garner and his granddaughter, Dallas. In Empty, Quint finds a steadfast ally; in Dallas, Quint finds something more—the promise of a future.

In a town where betrayal lies around every corner, where every unlocked door, thrown punch, or suspicious fire is just a hint of deadlier things to come, the Calders will be tested as never before. And this time, it could cost them more than their land . . . it could cost them everything.

CALDER PROMISE

All Laura Calder wants is everything. . . . Young and beautiful, she isn't content to live on a Montana ranch. Touring Europe with her "Aunt" Tara brings her into contact with the sophisticated world she's craved . . . and with the two men—and ultimate rivals—who will lay claim to her heart. Boone Rutledge is the son of a Texas billionaire and used to getting what he wants. He wants Laura . . . and so does Sebastian Dunshill, Earl of Crawford, a handsome, sexy Londoner with a few secrets he can't share.

Caught up in a whirlwind courtship with both men that will take her from the nightclubs of Rome to the manor houses of England, across the dusty flatlands of Texas and finally home to the Triple C Ranch, Laura is determined to make her choice on her own terms. But Calder pride will lead Laura into a danger for which her sheltered background has never prepared her . . . and to a man who is a threat to the family she loves more than she knows. . . .

SHIFTING CALDER WIND

Chase Calder has no recollection of who he is, why he came to Fort Worth . . . or who tried to put a bullet in his head the night that a cowboy named Laredo Smith saved his life. Laredo recognizes him as the owner of Montana's Triple C Ranch—but according to the local papers, Chase has just been declared dead, the victim of a fiery car crash.

The only place Chase can find answers is at the Triple C . . . and the only person he can trust is his level-headed daughter-in-law, Jessy Calder. Helping Chase brings Jessy into conflict with headstrong Cat Calder, and into an uneasy alliance with the mysterious and seductive Laredo. And when another family member is found murdered on Calder soil, Chase resolves to come out of hiding and track down a ruthless killer . . . before the killer finds him first. . . .

GREEN CALDER GRASS

Their land . . . their family . . . their pride. When the Calders fight for the things they love, they fight to win.

Jessy Niles Calder grew up on the Triple C ranch, six hundred square miles of grassland that can be bountiful or harsh, that bends to no man's will—just like a Calder. As Ty Calder's wife, Jessy finally has all she's ever wanted. But even in the midst of this new happiness there are hidden enemies, greedy for the rich Montana land, and willing to shed blood to get it. Not to mention Ty's ex-wife Tara, causing trouble wherever she goes. And soon Jessy will be faced with the fight of her life—one that will change the Triple C forever. . . .